1954

IN THE MIDST OF LIFE

IN THE
MIDST
OF LIFE

Tales of
Soldiers and Civilians

BY

AMBROSE BIERCE

Introduction by

GEORGE STERLING

**THE
MODERN LIBRARY
NEW YORK**

Random House IS THE PUBLISHER OF

THE MODERN LIBRARY

BENNETT A. CERF · DONALD S. KLOPFER · ROBERT K. HAAS

Manufactured in the United States of America

Printed by Parkway Printing Company   Bound by H. Wolff

PREFACE
TO THE FIRST EDITION

DENIED existence by the chief publishing houses of the country, this book owes itself to Mr. E. L. G. Steele, merchant, of this city. In attesting Mr. Steele's faith in his judgment and his friend, it will serve its author's main and best ambition.

A. B.

SAN FRANCISCO, Sept. 4, 1891.

CONTENTS

SOLDIERS

CIVILIANS

CONTENTS

INTRODUCTION

I REGRET that I may not use the forbidden metaphor, "a star rising in the West." None other would so well express the gathering light and slow inevitability of ascension of Ambrose Bierce's fame. The Wise Men of the East first saw it as a feeble spark, scarcely to be detected through the haze and murk of the western horizon. "A little," they might have said, "and it will have set." But a little, and it had crept a degree farther up the literary heavens, and was finally visible even from Europe.

It had a strange quality, that star, a "cold inclemency of light" such as we find in Vega on a clear midnight of spring, an austerity in its blue crystal, the bleak brilliance that lances from the larger diamonds. There was a ray that touched man only in his hour of pain, of terror, of death—a ray that revealed what we hesitate to behold and which leaves the weaker beholders ungrateful for the vision accorded. The clairvoyance of the Greek dramatist was here, revealing man as an august yet helpless figure in the clutch of the main tide of destiny. These tales were not cheerful ones; rather they held the reader as the serpent's eyes are fabled to fascinate the bird. Here was no comfort, no flattering exposition of man's vaunted triumph over his fates. He sat among Shadows, some of them akin to the shadows in his own soul. There was no care for him in the universe, no justice as he dreamed justice should be rendered to his race. But while he indignantly rejected the testimony, he could not forget it, nor put the witness from his mind. He began to ask: "Who is Ambrose Bierce?" And the fame of "the Shadow-Maker" began at the inevitable question.

More than one biography of Bierce is contemplated. Till one appear, the best account of his life may be found in Bertha Clark Pope's preface to his "Letters," published by the Book Club of California in 1922. In that volume is also contained a brief memoir by myself, and other such reminiscences may be found in my article in the October, 1925, number of the *American Mercury*. A summary of the records would relate that Am-

brose Gwinett Bierce was born in Meiggs
County, Ohio, on June 24, 1842, was given
such education as the country school of that
day afforded (he was an inveterate reader as
a boy), and volunteered as a private at the
outbreak of the Civil War, in 1861. He served
for the entire duration of the strife, and during its latter years was an officer on the staff of
General Hazen. He twice rescued wounded
companions, at grave risk, and was himself
twice wounded, once in the heel, and once, far
more severely, in the head, this casualty during
the battle of Kenesaw Mountain.

The war ended, he was brevetted Major for
distinguished services, by especial act of Con-
gress. He then joined his elder brother, Albert, in San Francisco, and took a position
in the United States Mint there. But our
Lady of the Inkwell was soon to call him, and
not long afterwards he gave up that occupation for creative work, holding editorial positions consecutively on several San Francisco
weeklies, the *News Letter,* the *Argonaut* and
The Wasp.

In 1872, however, he went to London, where
for four years he was on the staff of *Fun,* and
an intimate friend of George Augustus Sala

and the younger Tom Hood. It was during this period that he published those three little volumes, now rare, called "The Fiend's Delight," "Nuggets and Dust," and "Cobwebs from an Empty Skull." They were original in their often ghastly humor, but, though Gladstone himself had a good word for them, remain almost unknown, nor would Bierce himself acknowledge his authorship to the extent of autographing copies.

He returned to San Francisco in 1876, and lived in that city and such small towns as Auburn, Angwin and Wright for the next twenty-one years, his only absence from California being a brief period of employment as general manager of a mining company near Deadwood, Dakota. He was at first editor of *The Wasp,* whose caustic qualities lost nothing for his connection with that weekly. From this position he was allured by William Randolph Hearst, who had just begun the career that was to prove so ominously successful, and till the final years of his life was to conduct a department on the editorial page of Hearst's Sunday *Examiner* and, after his removal to Washington, D. C., on the New York *Amer-*

ican and finally in the pages of the *Cosmopolitan Magazine.*

By far the greater part of this work was polemical in its nature. Journalism in the West had not yet become entirely tame, had not yet resorted to the amenities and timidities of the more cultured regions of the planet. Bierce's pen was dipped in wormwood and acid, and he being, as H. L. Mencken has justly asserted, then and to this day the keenest wit of America, his assaults were more dreaded than the bowie knife and revolver, since relegated to the eastern centers of civilization. He spared no one whom he thought deserving of his castigations. From millionaire to labor-leader, all were to know the "strength and terror" of his verbal onsets. Nor did he take refuge in words only: to my own knowledge he always carried, at least when in California, a large revolver, and was quite ready "to go farther into the matter" with such as cared to meet him on that plane! I have no memory that he was ever so challenged, though he once broke a cane over the head of a friend who had become a friend no longer.

It was during these twenty-one years in California, spent mostly in the country hamlets and towns that I have mentioned, that Bierce wrote practically all the work on which his fame is to rest. After his hegira to Washington, in 1896, his literary toils were perceptibly lighter, his satiric verse milder and his short-stories (though he did not believe this) much less fascinating. But his work had been done, and further efforts were to awaken but echoes in the dim caverns of the ghostly domains where he had wandered so far. Some of his contributions to the *American* never found publication, and are lost to this day. The short-stories that appeared in the *Cosmopolitan* seem alone of any especial value.

Bierce, himself, thought that he would be remembered, if at all, as a satirist. In these days of universal tolerance and courtesy, the breed is almost extinct, but had he lived in the time of Pope he would have made that writer's work seem, by comparison, mild stuff indeed. There is little invective so terrible as that poured forth by him on California's fools and rascals—instances, in most cases, of breaking the butterfly on the wheel. But no English satirist has equaled the blistering intensity of wit that ran so easily from his pen.

Bierce had married, early in his western career, the beautiful Molly Day. The couple took separate ways after the birth of two sons and a daughter, nor were they ever to meet again. Day Bierce, the brighter of the boys, was murdered in northern California, as the result of a love affair. Leigh, the younger, died when an assistant editor of a newspaper in New York City. Helen, the daughter, lives with her husband, Francis Isgrigg, Esq., in Los Angeles. As for Bierce himself, he entered Mexico, in November, 1913, and was for a while on the staff of the insurgent Villa, but by January all letters from him ceased, and though, at the close of the war, diligent inquiry was made for him by both our State and War Departments, no trace of his actions nor fate was forthcoming until five years had passed.

It was then that an account of his death appeared, written by George F. Weeks, a correspondent in the field during the revolutionary period. It relates Mr. Weeks' friendship with Dr. Edmund Melero, a young man of Durango, who said that he was "the best of friends" with Bierce while the two were still connected with Villa's forces. He readily

identified Bierce's photograph, and promised
to make inquiry as to his fate.

That promise was fulfilled when, a few
months later, he came to Mr. Weeks' office,
in Mexico City, and related his meeting with
a friend who had been a sergeant in General
Tomas Urbina's forces under Villa. This man
recognized Bierce in memory, from Don
Urbina's description, and indeed Bierce was
an unforgetable personality, what with his
six feet of height, his ruddy face, snow-white
hair and mustache, and piercing blue eyes.
Bierce, said the sergeant, had been shot by
command of Urbina.

According to the circumstances alleged,
Bierce must have deserted Villa's army and
joined that of the Constitutionalists, for the
man's story went that Urbina, during a forced
march, captured near the village of Icamole
a pack-train of ammunition, all its guards escaping with the exception of a Mexican and
an America. Brought before Urbina, they
were questioned, but the American merely
shook his head in reply, when interrogated.
As none of Urbina's men could speak English,
communication was impossible, and Urbina,
being in extreme haste, promptly ordered both

men to be shot. The order was executed at once, and both bodies buried in the same shallow grave. So, to quote Mr. Weeks: "This was undoubtedly the fate of Ambrose Bierce —exactly the fate he had expressed a desire to meet." And as this is the only account of the affair that diligent search has revealed, it may safely be taken as an accurate statement of the end of the author. Melero afterward brought his sergeant friend to see me, and he repeated his story as already given, also identifying a photograph which was shown him as that of the American whom he saw so summarily executed. Urbina fell out with Villa not long after this execution, and was himself killed by "Butcher" Fierro, the more or less private executioner for Villa.

Now appears, in a late issue of one of our quarterlies, a more circumstantial account of Bierce's end, in an article by one Adolph Danziger ("Adolphe de Castro"). Danziger flatly states that Bierce, after Villa's capture of Chihuahua and the inaction following, proposed to a peon acquaintance that they desert to the Carranza side. Villa, somehow hearing of this, obtained by torture a confession from the peon, and ordered him, sardonically, to lead Bierce to the Carranzista forces. This attempted, they were shot down by night, before they had gone more than a quarter of a mile, by a squad of soldiers, and their bodies left to the dogs and vultures.

Danziger goes on to relate that, ten years afterward, he obtained an interview with Villa, who scowled at the mention of Bierce, but who would go no further than to state that he had turned traitor and hence had been "driven away."

So the reader may take his choice between the two versions of the tragedy. Among those who knew Bierce, the Danziger account is laid open to grave doubts by his deliberate mendacity in asserting that Bierce once worked for M. H. de Young, and had also endeavored to find a position with the Southern Pacific Railway, both acts for which he would cheerfully have suffered crucifixion rather than commit. Danziger was the person over whose head Bierce broke his cane to fragments, as hereinbefore stated, and his article, patently malicious, bears more than the above evidence of being a postponed revenge. One is left to wonder that he did not repair to Chihuahua and feast on the bones of Bierce.

I have gone to this length in writing of Bierce's possible fate, because its mystery has become one of profound interest to all readers of his work. It is significant that Bierce (if it was indeed he) refused to reply to Urbina. And yet Bierce had at least a slight acquaintance with the Spanish tongue. Again provided that it was he, the refusal is entirely in line with his evident wish to be slain in war. For he had definitely indicated that he was entering Mexico with that hope. "I am so old," he wrote (he was but seventy-one, with the vitality of a lion), "that I'm ashamed to be alive." And again: "To be a Gringo in Mexico—that is indeed euthanasia!" Icamole or Chihuahua—the Peace was the same.

I have said that Bierce's first appearance between book covers was with the publication in London of three small volumes whose paternity he was slow to acknowledge and whose literary worth he was wont to disavow. His next book was not to appear until 1891, with the publication, under the unimaginative title of "Tales of Soldiers and Civilians," of the stories in this volume. It failed, what with obtuse critics and the benighted public, to create the sensation that he expected. One purblind creature, reviewing the book in the New York *Sun,* went even so far as to suggest that it was written to scare children and timid old ladies—that, of these tremendous and impeccable tales! Bierce replied that the stories were published because he thought them good and true art, which is a modest estimate.

"The Monk and the Hangman's Daughter," Bierce's only romance, written at the suggestion of Dr. Danziger, the plot being the creation of Professor Richard Voss, appeared the next year, and was followed by his first book of satiric verse, entitled "Black Beetles in Amber." No further stories appeared, for all his prolific pen, for the following twenty years; but in 1898, G. P. Putnam's Sons republished "Tales of Soldiers and Civilians" under the present title. In 1899, appeared "Fantastic Fables"; in 1903, the second volume of satiric verse, "Shapes of Clay"; in 1906, "The Cynic's Word Book," a collection of epigrams, diabolically astute, for which he had hoped to be permitted the title, "The Devil's Dictionary"; in 1909, "Write It Right," a blacklist of literary faults, and "The Shadow on the Dial," a collection of essays recording some of his dislikes, and finally, during the years from 1909 to 1912, "The Collected Works of Ambrose Bierce."

With the publication in these last volumes of such of his work as he felt best fitted to represent him in the annals of literature, Bierce laid by his pen. In the dust-thatched numbers of the weeklies, including the Sunday *Examiner,* to which he contributed his thousands of columns, lie, however, almost inexhaustible treasures of wit and wisdom, which, with the continuous growth of his fame and interest in his vivid personality, are sure to be brought back to the light of future years. A laborious task, indeed, and one whose outcome yet awaits a discerning public of numbers sufficient to make publication profitable. And yet the thing will be accomplished, some day, and the time to come will marvel at the mind that found so chary a welcome during its own existence.

It is hardly to be wondered at. Bierce, the first of the "columnists," never troubled to conceal his justifiable contempt for humanity at its present stage of development, a contempt truly Caligulan in its scope and intensity. Man leaped naked under that furious scourging, for Bierce was a "perfectionist," a quality that in his case led to an intolerance involving merciless cruelty. He demanded in all others, men or women, the same ethical virtues that he found essential to his own manner of life and mentation, and to deviate from his point of view, indeed, to disagree with him even in slight particulars, was the unpardonable sin. One was to have none other god beside him, and though he might, at the time, evince no anger at any *lèse majesté,* the offense was nevertheless recorded in his unerring memory, to be used as a weapon of wrath when the final break came, as come it did with practically all of his friends. His brother Albert attributed this failing to the wound in the head that Ambrose received in the Civil War, asserting that after that casualty his entire nature underwent a change of which a certain assumption of infallibility, combined with implacable severity, was the most disconcerting element. Be that as it may, his pessimism was darker than even Swift's, though, like his, of the same sophomoric quality that concerned itself with the immediate condition of the race, and was innocent of the far more terrible implications of infinity.

But whatever his opinion of mankind, he

left it richer by his tremendous short stories, the richest trophies he was to wrest from oblivion, and the most notable of which are between the covers of this volume. Their highest claim to distinction is, I think, their style, of a clarity and simplicity unequaled in English letters. It is as crystal clear, yet as disquieting, as the waters of a haunted well. His heroes, or rather victims, are lonely men, passing to unpredictable dooms, and hearing, from inaccessible crypts of space, the voices of unseen malevolencies. No easy optimism is here, but one is made aware of the possible horrors of life, like cobras hidden in heaped orchids. Dislike the stories one may; forget them one cannot. Perhaps the greatest "terror tale" in our literature is Poe's "The Fall of the House of Usher." But close behind it, that granted, come a dozen of Bierce's stories, prominent among them "The Death of Halpin Fraser." While in "An Occurrence at Owl Bridge"—Bierce was not fortunate in his choice of titles—we have one of the very greatest stories in the world's literature. It is absurd to claim that he derived from Poe, and indeed he wrote his tales with the intention in mind to have them differ from them as much as possible, so that we have in them a steely reserve that makes Poe's, usually, seem almost boyish by comparison. Of course, the "terror tale" was neither Poe's discovery nor sole property. It was Bierce's fortune to make it less fantastic, yet no less remarkable. But his tales do not depend, for their strange and dreadful impact, on the cerements and putridities that make those of Poe indelible. Bierce's tragedies are not of the tomb.

The stories are, naturally, in the "old style," the manner superseded not, as many imagine, by O. Henry, but by Kipling. As for the former, read any of his tales but "The Lost Leaf," and you have read it forever: the plot once known, the flippant manner is negligible. While in the case of Bierce's stories the reverse is in evidence, and one finds, in proof of their supreme artistry, that they can be read over and over, with continually increasing pleasure, what with their perfection of style, a style at once inimitable and unforgetable.

GEORGE STERLING.

San Francisco, October, 1926.

SOLDIERS

A HORSEMAN IN THE SKY

I

ONE sunny afternoon in the autumn of the year 1861 a soldier lay in a clump of laurel by the side of a road in western Virginia. He lay at full length upon his stomach, his feet resting upon the toes, his head upon the left forearm. His extended right hand loosely grasped his rifle. But for the somewhat methodical disposition of his limbs and a slight rhythmic movement of the cartridge-box at the back of his belt he might have been thought to be dead. He was asleep at his post of duty. But if detected he would be dead shortly afterward, death being the just and legal penalty of his crime.

The clump of laurel in which the criminal lay was in the angle of a road which after ascending southward a steep acclivity to that point turned sharply to the west, running along the summit for perhaps one hundred yards. There it turned southward again and went zigzagging downward through the forest. At the salient of that second angle was a

large flat rock, jutting out northward, overlooking the deep valley from which the road
ascended. The rock capped a high cliff; a
stone dropped from its outer edge would have
fallen sheer downward one thousand feet to
the tops of the pines. The angle where the
soldier lay was on another spur of the same
cliff. Had he been awake he would have commanded a view, not only of the short arm of
the road and the jutting rock, but of the entire
profile of the cliff below it. It might well
have made him giddy to look.

The country was wooded everywhere except at the bottom of the valley to the northward, where there was a small natural
meadow, through which flowed a stream
scarcely visible from the valley's rim. This
open ground looked hardly larger than an
ordinary door-yard, but was really several
acres in extent. Its green was more vivid than
that of the inclosing forest. Away beyond it
rose a line of giant cliffs similar to those upon
which we are supposed to stand in our survey
of the savage scene, and through which the
road had somehow made its climb to the
summit. The configuration of the valley, indeed, was such that from this point of observation it seemed entirely shut in, and one could

but have wondered how the road which found a way out of it had found a way into it, and whence came and whither went the waters of the stream that parted the meadow more than a thousand feet below.

No country is so wild and difficult but men will make it a theatre of war; concealed in the forest at the bottom of that military rat-trap, in which half a hundred men in possession of the exits might have starved an army to submission, lay five regiments of Federal infantry. They had marched all the previous day and night and were resting. At nightfall they would take to the road again, climb to the place where their unfaithful sentinel now slept, and descending the other slope of the ridge fall upon a camp of the enemy at about midnight. Their hope was to surprise it, for the road led to the rear of it. In case of failure, their position would be perilous in the extreme; and fail they surely would should accident or vigilance apprise the enemy of the movement.

II

The sleeping sentinel in the clump of laurel was a young Virginian named Carter Druse. He was the son of wealthy parents, an only child, and had known such ease and cultivation and high living as wealth and taste were able to command in the mountain country of western Virginia. His home was but a few miles from where he now lay. One morning he had risen from the breakfast-table and said, quietly but gravely: " Father, a Union regiment has arrived at Grafton. I am going to join it."

The father lifted his leonine head, looked at the son a moment in silence, and replied: "Well, go, sir, and whatever may occur do what you conceive to be your duty. Virginia, to which you are a traitor, must get on without you. Should we both live to the end of the war, we will speak further of the matter. Your mother, as the physician has informed you, is in a most critical condition; at the best she cannot be with us longer than a few weeks, but that time is precious. It would be better not to disturb her."

So Carter Druse, bowing reverently to his father, who returned the salute with a stately courtesy that masked a breaking heart, left the home of his childhood to go soldiering. By conscience and courage, by deeds of devotion and daring, he soon commended himself to his fellows and his officers; and it was to these qualities and to some knowledge of the coun-

try that he owed his selection for his present
perilous duty at the extreme outpost. Nevertheless, fatigue had been stronger than resolution and he had fallen asleep. What good or
bad angel came in a dream to rouse him from
his state of crime, who shall say? Without a
movement, without a sound, in the profound
silence and the languor of the late afternoon,
some invisible messenger of fate touched with
unsealing finger the eyes of his consciousness
—whispered into the ear of his spirit the mysterious awakening word which no human lips
ever have spoken, no human memory ever has
recalled. He quietly raised his forehead from
his arm and looked between the masking stems
of the laurels, instinctively closing his right
hand about the stock of his rifle.

His first feeling was a keen artistic delight.
On a colossal pedestal, the cliff,—motionless
at the extreme edge of the capping rock and
sharply outlined against the sky,—was an
equestrian statue of impressive dignity. The
figure of the man sat the figure of the horse,
straight and soldierly, but with the repose of a
Grecian god carved in the marble which lim-
its the suggestion of activity. The gray cos-
tume harmonized with its aërial background;
the metal of accoutrement and caparison was

softened and subdued by the shadow; the animal's skin had no points of high light. A carbine strikingly foreshortened lay across the pommel of the saddle, kept in place by the right hand grasping it at the "grip"; the left hand, holding the bridle rein, was invisible. In silhouette against the sky the profile of the horse was cut with the sharpness of a cameo; it looked across the heights of air to the confronting cliffs beyond. The face of the rider, turned slightly away, showed only an outline of temple and beard; he was looking downward to the bottom of the valley. Magnified by its lift against the sky and by the soldier's testifying sense of the formidableness of a near enemy the group appeared of heroic, almost colossal, size.

For an instant Druse had a strange, half-defined feeling that he had slept to the end of the war and was looking upon a noble work of art reared upon that eminence to commemorate the deeds of an heroic past of which he had been an inglorious part. The feeling was dispelled by a slight movement of the group: the horse, without moving its feet, had drawn its body slightly backward from the verge; the man remained immobile as before. Broad awake and keenly alive to the significance of the situation, Druse now brought the butt of his rifle against his cheek by cautiously pushing the barrel forward through the bushes, cocked the piece, and glancing through the sights covered a vital spot of the horseman's breast. A touch upon the trigger and all would have been well with Carter Druse. At that instant the horseman turned his head and looked in the direction of his concealed foeman—seemed to look into his very face, into his eyes, into his brave, compassionate heart.

Is it then so terrible to kill an enemy in war—an enemy who has surprised a secret vital to the safety of one's self and comrades —an enemy more formidable for his knowledge than all his army for its numbers? Carter Druse grew pale; he shook in every limb, turned faint, and saw the statuesque group before him as black figures, rising, falling, moving unsteadily in arcs of circles in a fiery sky. His hand fell away from his weapon, his head slowly dropped until his face rested on the leaves in which he lay. This courageous gentleman and hardy soldier was near swooning from intensity of emotion.

It was not for long; in another moment his face was raised from earth, his hands resumed their places on the rifle, his forefinger sought the trigger; mind, heart, and eyes were clear, conscience and reason sound. He could not hope to capture that enemy; to alarm him would but send him dashing to his camp with his fatal news. The duty of the soldier was plain: the man must be shot dead from ambush—without warning, without a moment's spiritual preparation, with never so much as an unspoken prayer, he must be sent to his account. But no—there is a hope; he may have discovered nothing—perhaps he is but admiring the sublimity of the landscape. If permitted, he may turn and ride carelessly away in the direction whence he came. Surely it will be possible to judge at the instant of his withdrawing whether he knows. It may well be that his fixity of attention— Druse turned his head and looked through the deeps of air downward, as from the surface to the bottom of a translucent sea. He saw creeping across the green meadow a sinuous line of figures of men and horses—some foolish commander was permitting the soldiers of his escort to water their beasts in the open, in plain view from a dozen summits!

Druse withdrew his eyes from the valley and fixed them again upon the group of men

and horse in the sky, and again it was through the sights of his rifle. But this time his aim was at the horse. In his memory, as if they were a divine mandate, rang the words of his father at their parting: "Whatever may occur, do what you conceive to be your duty." He was calm now. His teeth were firmly but not rigidly closed; his nerves were as tranquil as a sleeping babe's—not a tremor affected any muscle of his body; his breathing, until suspended in the act of taking aim, was regular and slow. Duty had conquered; the spirit had said to the body: "Peace, be still." He fired.

III

An officer of the Federal force, who in a spirit of adventure or in quest of knowledge had left the hidden *bivouac* in the valley, and with aimless feet had made his way to the lower edge of a small open space near the foot of the cliff, was considering what he had to gain by pushing his exploration further. At a distance of a quarter-mile before him, but apparently at a stone's throw, rose from its fringe of pines the gigantic face of rock, towering to so great a height above him that it made him giddy to look up to where its edge cut a sharp, rugged line against the sky. It

presented a clean, vertical profile against a background of blue sky to a point half the way down, and of distant hills, hardly less blue, thence to the tops of the trees at its base. Lifting his eyes to the dizzy altitude of its summit the officer saw an astonishing sight—a man on horseback riding down into the valley through the air!

Straight upright sat the rider, in military fashion, with a firm seat in the saddle, a strong clutch upon the rein to hold his charger from too impetuous a plunge. From his bare head his long hair streamed upward, waving like a plume. His hands were concealed in the cloud of the horse's lifted mane. The animal's body was as level as if every hoofstroke encountered the resistant earth. Its motions were those of a wild gallop, but even as the officer looked they ceased, with all the legs thrown sharply forward as in the act of alighting from a leap. But this was a flight!

Filled with amazement and terror by this apparition of a horseman in the sky—half believing himself the chosen scribe of some new Apocalypse, the officer was overcome by the intensity of his emotions; his legs failed him and he fell. Almost at the same instant he

heard a crashing sound in the trees—a sound that died without an echo—and all was still.

The officer rose to his feet, trembling. The familiar sensation of an abraded shin recalled his dazed faculties. Pulling himself together he ran rapidly obliquely away from the cliff to a point distant from its foot; thereabout he expected to find his man; and thereabout he naturally failed. In the fleeting instant of his vision his imagination had been so wrought upon by the apparent grace and ease and intention of the marvelous performance that it did not occur to him that the line of march of aërial cavalry is directly downward, and that he could find the objects of his search at the very foot of the cliff. A half-hour later he returned to camp.

This officer was a wise man; he knew better than to tell an incredible truth. He said nothing of what he had seen. But when the commander asked him if in his scout he had learned anything of advantage to the expedition he answered:

"Yes, sir; there is no road leading down into this valley from the southward."

The commander, knowing better, smiled.

IV

After firing his shot, Private Carter Druse reloaded his rifle and resumed his watch. Ten minutes had hardly passed when a Federal sergeant crept cautiously to him on hands and knees. Druse neither turned his head nor looked at him, but lay without motion or sign of recognition.

"Did you fire?" the sergeant whispered.

"Yes."

"At what?"

"A horse. It was standing on yonder rock —pretty far out. You see it is no longer there. It went over the cliff."

The man's face was white, but he showed no other sign of emotion. Having answered, he turned away his eyes and said no more. The sergeant did not understand.

"See here, Druse," he said, after a moment's silence, "it's no use making a mystery. I order you to report. Was there anybody on the horse?"

"Yes."

"Well?"

"My father."

The sergeant rose to his feet and walked away. "Good God!" he said.

AN OCCURRENCE AT OWL CREEK BRIDGE

I

A MAN stood upon a railroad bridge in northern Alabama, looking down into the swift water twenty feet below. The man's hands were behind his back, the wrists bound with a cord. A rope closely encircled his neck. It was attached to a stout cross-timber above his head and the slack fell to the level of his knees. Some loose boards laid upon the sleepers supporting the metals of the railway supplied a footing for him and his executioners—two private soldiers of the Federal army, directed by a sergeant who in civil life may have been a deputy sheriff. At a short remove upon the same temporary platform was an officer in the uniform of his rank, armed. He was a captain. A sentinel at each end of the bridge stood with his rifle in the position known as "support," that is to say, vertical in front of the left shoulder, the hammer resting on the forearm thrown straight across the chest—a

formal and unnatural position, enforcing an
erect carriage of the body.   It did not appear
to be the duty of these two men to know what
was occurring at the centre of the bridge;
they merely blockaded the two ends of the
foot planking that traversed it.

Beyond one of the sentinels nobody was in
sight; the railroad ran straight away into a
forest for a hundred yards, then, curving, was
lost to view.   Doubtless there was an outpost
farther along.   The other bank of the stream
was open ground—a gentle acclivity topped
with a stockade of vertical tree trunks, loop-
holed for rifles, with a single embrasure
through which protruded the muzzle of a
brass cannon commanding the bridge.   Mid-
way of the slope between bridge and fort were
the spectators—a single company of infantry
in line, at " parade rest," the butts of the rifles
on the ground, the barrels inclining slightly
backward against the right shoulder, the
hands crossed upon the stock.   A lieutenant
stood at the right of the line, the point of his
sword upon the ground, his left hand resting
upon his right.   Excepting the group of four
at the centre of the bridge, not a man moved.
The company faced the bridge, staring ston-
ily, motionless.   The sentinels, facing the

banks of the stream, might have been statues to adorn the bridge. The captain stood with folded arms, silent, observing the work of his subordinates, but making no sign. Death is a dignitary who when he comes announced is to be received with formal manifestations of respect, even by those most familiar with him. In the code of military etiquette silence and fixity are forms of deference.

The man who was engaged in being hanged was apparently about thirty-five years of age. He was a civilian, if one might judge from his habit, which was that of a planter. His features were good—a straight nose, firm mouth, broad forehead, from which his long, dark hair was combed straight back, falling behind his ears to the collar of his well-fitting frock-coat. He wore a mustache and pointed beard, but no whiskers; his eyes were large and dark gray, and had a kindly expression which one would hardly have expected in one whose neck was in the hemp. Evidently this was no vulgar assassin. The liberal military code makes provision for hanging many kinds of persons, and gentlemen are not excluded.

The preparations being complete, the two private soldiers stepped aside and each drew away the plank upon which he had been

standing. The sergeant turned to the captain, saluted and placed himself immediately behind that officer, who in turn moved apart one pace. These movements left the condemned man and the sergeant standing on the two ends of the same plank, which spanned three of the cross-ties of the bridge. The end upon which the civilian stood almost, but not quite, reached a fourth. This plank had been held in place by the weight of the captain; it was now held by that of the sergeant. At a signal from the former the latter would step aside, the plank would tilt and the condemned man go down between two ties. The arrangement commended itself to his judgment as simple and effective. His face had not been covered nor his eyes bandaged. He looked a moment at his "unsteadfast footing," then let his gaze wander to the swirling water of the stream racing madly beneath his feet. A piece of dancing driftwood caught his attention and his eyes followed it down the current. How slowly it appeared to move! What a sluggish stream!

He closed his eyes in order to fix his last thoughts upon his wife and children. The water, touched to gold by the early sun, the brooding mists under the banks at some dist-

ance down the stream, the fort, the soldiers, the piece of drift—all had distracted him. And now he became conscious of a new disturbance. Striking through the thought of his dear ones was a sound which he could neither ignore nor understand, a sharp, distinct, metallic percussion like the stroke of a blacksmith's hammer upon the anvil; it had the same ringing quality. He wondered what it was, and whether immeasurably distant or near by—it seemed both. Its recurrence was regular, but as slow as the tolling of a death knell. He awaited each stroke with impatience and—he knew not why—apprehension. The intervals of silence grew progressively longer; the delays became maddening. With their greater infrequency the sounds increased in strength and sharpness. They hurt his ear like the thrust of a knife; he feared he would shriek. What he heard was the ticking of his watch.

He unclosed his eyes and saw again the water below him. "If I could free my hands," he thought, " I might throw off the noose and spring into the stream. By diving I could evade the bullets and, swimming vigorously, reach the bank, take to the woods and get away home. My home, thank God,

is as yet outside their lines; my wife and little ones are still beyond the invader's farthest advance."

As these thoughts, which have here to be set down in words, were flashed into the doomed man's brain rather than evolved from it the captain nodded to the sergeant.   The sergeant stepped aside.

II

Peyton Farquhar was a well-to-do planter, of an old and highly respected Alabama family.   Being a slave owner and like other slave owners a politician he was naturally an original secessionist and ardently devoted to the Southern cause.   Circumstances of an imperious nature, which it is unnecessary to relate here, had prevented him from taking service with the gallant army that had fought the disastrous campaigns ending with the fall of Corinth, and he chafed under the inglorious restraint, longing for the release of his energies, the larger life of the soldier, the opportunity for distinction.   That opportunity, he felt, would come, as it comes to all in war time.   Meanwhile he did what he could. No service was too humble for him to perform in aid of the South, no adventure too perilous for him to undertake if consistent

with the character of a civilian who was at heart a soldier, and who in good faith and without too much qualification assented to at least a part of the frankly villainous dictum that all is fair in love and war.

One evening while Farquhar and his wife were sitting on a rustic bench near the entrance to his grounds, a gray-clad soldier rode up to the gate and asked for a drink of water. Mrs. Farquhar was only too happy to serve him with her own white hands. While she was fetching the water her husband approached the dusty horseman and inquired eagerly for news from the front.

"The Yanks are repairing the railroads," said the man, "and are getting ready for another advance. They have reached the Owl Creek bridge, put it in order and built a stockade on the north bank. The commandant has issued an order, which is posted everywhere, declaring that any civilian caught interfering with the railroad, its bridges, tunnels or trains will be summarily hanged. I saw the order."

"How far is it to the Owl Creek bridge?" Farquhar asked.

"About thirty miles."

"Is there no force on this side the creek?"

"Only a picket post half a mile out, on the

railroad, and a single sentinel at this end of the bridge."

"Suppose a man—a civilian and student of hanging—should elude the picket post and perhaps get the better of the sentinel," said Farquhar, smiling, "what could he accomplish?"

The soldier reflected. "I was there a month ago," he replied. "I observed that the flood of last winter had lodged a great quantity of driftwood against the wooden pier at this end of the bridge. It is now dry and would burn like tow."

The lady had now brought the water, which the soldier drank. He thanked her ceremoniously, bowed to her husband and rode away. An hour later, after nightfall, he repassed the plantation, going northward in the direction from which he had come. He was a Federal scout.

III

As Peyton Farquhar fell straight downward through the bridge he lost consciousness and was as one already dead. From this state he was awakened—ages later, it seemed to him —by the pain of a sharp pressure upon his throat, followed by a sense of suffocation. Keen, poignant agonies seemed to shoot from

his neck downward through every fibre of his body and limbs. These pains appeared to flash along well-defined lines of ramification and to beat with an inconceivably rapid periodicity. They seemed like streams of pulsating fire heating him to an intolerable temperature. As to his head, he was conscious of nothing but a feeling of fulness—of congestion. These sensations were unaccompanied by thought. The intellectual part of his nature was already effaced; he had power only to feel, and feeling was torment. He was conscious of motion. Encompassed in a luminous cloud, of which he was now merely the fiery heart, without material substance, he swung through unthinkable arcs of oscillation, like a vast pendulum. Then all at once, with terrible suddenness, the light about him shot upward with the noise of a loud plash; a frightful roaring was in his ears, and all was cold and dark. The power of thought was restored; he knew that the rope had broken and he had fallen into the stream. There was no additional strangulation; the noose about his neck was already suffocating him and kept the water from his lungs. To die of hanging at the bottom of a river!—the idea seemed to him ludicrous. He opened his eyes in the darkness and saw above him a gleam of light, but how distant, how inaccessible! He was still sinking, for the light became fainter and fainter until it was a mere glimmer. Then it began to grow and brighten, and he knew that he was rising toward the surface—knew it with reluctance, for he was now very comfortable. "To be hanged and drowned," he thought, "that is not so bad; but I do not wish to be shot. No; I will not be shot; that is not fair."

He was not conscious of an effort, but a sharp pain in his wrist apprised him that he was trying to free his hands. He gave the struggle his attention, as an idler might observe the feat of a juggler, without interest in the outcome. What splendid effort!—what magnificent, what superhuman strength! Ah, that was a fine endeavor! Bravo! The cord fell away; his arms parted and floated upward, the hands dimly seen on each side in the growing light. He watched them with a new interest as first one and then the other pounced upon the noose at his neck. They tore it away and thrust it fiercely aside, its undulations resembling those of a water-snake. "Put it back, put it back!" He thought he shouted these words to his hands, for the undoing of the noose had been succeeded by the direst pang that he had yet experienced. His neck ached horribly; his brain was on fire; his heart, which had been fluttering faintly, gave a great leap, trying to force itself out at his mouth. His whole body was racked and wrenched with an insupportable anguish! But his disobedient hands gave no heed to the command. They beat the water vigorously with quick, downward strokes, forcing him to the surface. He felt his head emerge; his eyes were blinded by the sunlight; his chest expanded convulsively, and with a supreme and crowning agony his lungs engulfed a great draught of air, which instantly he expelled in a shriek!

He was now in full possession of his physical senses. They were, indeed, preternaturally keen and alert. Something in the awful disturbance of his organic system had so exalted and refined them that they made record of things never before perceived. He felt the ripples upon his face and heard their separate sounds as they struck. He looked at the forest on the bank of the stream, saw the individual trees, the leaves and the veining of each leaf—saw the very insects upon them: the locusts, the brilliant-bodied flies, the gray spiders stretching their webs from twig to twig. He noted the prismatic colors in all the dewdrops upon a million blades of grass. The humming of the gnats that danced above the eddies of the stream, the beating of the dragon-flies' wings, the strokes of the water-spiders' legs, like oars which had lifted their boat—all these made audible music. A fish slid along beneath his eyes and he heard the rush of its body parting the water.

He had come to the surface facing down the stream; in a moment the visible world seemed to wheel slowly round, himself the pivotal point, and he saw the bridge, the fort, the soldiers upon the bridge, the captain, the sergeant, the two privates, his executioners. They were in silhouette against the blue sky. They shouted and gesticulated, pointing at him. The captain had drawn his pistol, but did not fire; the others were unarmed. Their movements were grotesque and horrible, their forms gigantic.

Suddenly he heard a sharp report and something struck the water smartly within a few inches of his head, spattering his face with spray. He heard a second report, and saw one of the sentinels with his rifle at his shoulder, a light cloud of blue smoke rising from the muzzle. The man in the water saw the eye of the man on the bridge gazing into his own through the sights of the rifle. He observed that it was a gray eye and remembered having read that gray eyes were keenest, and that all famous markmen had them. Nevertheless, this one had missed.

A counter-swirl had caught Farquhar and turned him half round; he was again looking into the forest on the bank opposite the fort. The sound of a clear, high voice in a monotonous singsong now rang out behind him and came across the water with a distinctness that pierced and subdued all other sounds, even the beating of the ripples in his ears. Although no soldier, he had frequented camps enough to know the dread significance of that deliberate, drawling, aspirated chant; the lieutenant on shore was taking a part in the morning's work. How coldly and pitilessly—with what an even, calm intonation, presaging, and enforcing tranquillity in the men—with what accurately measured intervals fell those cruel words:

"Attention, company! . . . Shoulder arms! . . . Ready! . . . Aim! . . . Fire!"

Farquhar dived—dived as deeply as he could. The water roared in his ears like the voice of Niagara, yet he heard the dulled thunder of the volley and, rising again toward the surface, met shining bits of metal, singularly flattened, oscillating slowly downward. Some of them touched him on the face and hands, then fell away, continuing their descent. One lodged between his collar and neck; it was uncomfortably warm and he snatched it out.

As he rose to the surface, gasping for breath, he saw that he had been a long time under water; he was perceptibly farther down stream—nearer to safety. The soldiers had almost finished reloading; the metal ramrods flashed all at once in the sunshine as they were drawn from the barrels, turned in the air, and thrust into their sockets. The two sentinels fired again, independently and ineffectually.

The hunted man saw all this over his shoulder; he was now swimming vigorously with the current. His brain was as energetic as his arms and legs; he thought with the rapidity of lightning.

"The officer," he reasoned, "will not make that martinet's error a second time. It is as easy to dodge a volley as a single shot. He has probably already given the command to fire at will.   God help me, I cannot dodge them all!"

An appalling plash within two yards of him was followed by a loud, rushing sound, *diminuendo,* which seemed to travel back through the air to the fort and died in an explosion which stirred the very river to its deeps! A rising sheet of water curved over him, fell down upon him, blinded him, strangled him! The cannon had taken a hand in the game.   As he shook his head free from the commotion of the smitten water he heard the deflected shot humming through the air ahead, and in an instant it was cracking and smashing the branches in the forest beyond.

"They will not do that again," he thought; "the next time they will use a charge of grape.   I must keep my eye upon the gun; the smoke will apprise me—the report arrives too late; it lags behind the missile.   That is a good gun."

Suddenly he felt himself whirled round and round—spinning like a top.   The water, the banks, the forests, the now distant bridge, fort and men—all were commingled and blurred. Objects were represented by their colors only; circular horizontal streaks of color—that was all he saw. He had been caught in a vortex and was being whirled on with a velocity of advance and gyration that made him giddy and sick. In a few moments he was flung upon the gravel at the foot of the left bank of the stream—the southern bank—and behind a projecting point which concealed him from his enemies. The sudden arrest of his motion, the abrasion of one of his hands on the gravel, restored him, and he wept with delight. He dug his fingers into the sand, threw it over himself in handfuls and audibly blessed it. It looked like diamonds, rubies, emeralds; he could think of nothing beautiful which it did not resemble. The trees upon the bank were giant garden plants; he noted a definite order in their arrangement, inhaled the fragrance of their blooms. A strange, roseate light shone through the spaces among their trunks and the wind made in their branches the music of æolian harps. He had no wish to perfect his escape—was content to remain in that enchanting spot until retaken.

A whiz and rattle of grapeshot among the branches high above his head roused him from his dream. The baffled cannoneer had fired him a random farewell. He sprang to his feet, rushed up the sloping bank, and plunged into the forest.

All that day he traveled, laying his course by the rounding sun. The forest seemed interminable; nowhere did he discover a break in it, not even a woodman's road. He had not known that he lived in so wild a region. There was something uncanny in the revelation.

By nightfall he was fatigued, footsore, famishing. The thought of his wife and children urged him on. At last he found a road which led him in what he knew to be the right direction. It was as wide and straight as a city street, yet it seemed untraveled. No fields bordered it, no dwelling anywhere. Not so much as the barking of a dog suggested human habitation. The black bodies of the trees formed a straight wall on both sides, terminating on the horizon in a point, like a diagram in a lesson in perspective. Overhead, as he looked up through this rift in the wood, shone great golden stars looking unfamiliar and grouped in strange constellations. He was sure they were arranged in some order which had a secret and malign significance. The wood on either side was full of singular noises, among which—once, twice,

and again—he distinctly heard whispers in an
unknown tongue.

His neck was in pain and lifting his hand
to it he found it horribly swollen. He knew
that it had a circle of black where the rope
had bruised it. His eyes felt congested; he
could no longer close them. His tongue was
swollen with thirst; he relieved its fever by
thrusting it forward from between his teeth
into the cold air. How softly the turf had
carpeted the untraveled avenue—he could no
longer feel the roadway beneath his feet!

Doubtless, despite his suffering, he had
fallen asleep while walking, for now he sees
another scene—perhaps he has merely recovered from a delirium. He stands at the gate
of his own home. All is as he left it, and all
bright and beautiful in the morning sunshine.
He must have traveled the entire night. As
he pushes open the gate and passes up the
wide white walk, he sees a flutter of female
garments; his wife, looking fresh and cool and
sweet, steps down from the veranda to meet
him. At the bottom of the steps she stands
waiting, with a smile of ineffable joy, an attitude of matchless grace and dignity. Ah,
how beautiful she is! He springs forward
with extended arms. As he is about to clasp

her he feels a stunning blow upon the back of the neck; a blinding white light blazes all about him with a sound like the shock of a cannon—then all is darkness and silence!

Peyton Farquhar was dead; his body, with a broken neck, swung gently from side to side beneath the timbers of the Owl Creek bridge.

CHICKAMAUGA

ONE sunny autumn afternoon a child strayed away from its rude home in a small field and entered a forest unobserved. It was happy in a new sense of freedom from control, happy in the opportunity of exploration and adventure; for this child's spirit, in bodies of its ancestors, had for thousands of years been trained to memorable feats of discovery and conquest—victories in battles whose critical moments were centuries, whose victors' camps were cities of hewn stone. From the cradle of its race it had conquered its way through two continents and passing a great sea had penetrated a third, there to be born to war and dominion as a heritage.

The child was a boy aged about six years, the son of a poor planter. In his younger manhood the father had been a soldier, had fought against naked savages and followed the flag of his country into the capital of a civilized race to the far South. In the peaceful life of a planter the warrior-fire survived; once kindled, it is never extinguished. The man loved military books and pictures and the

boy had understood enough to make himself
a wooden sword, though even the eye of his
father would hardly have known it for what it
was. This weapon he now bore bravely, as
became the son of an heroic race, and pausing
now and again in the sunny space of the forest
assumed, with some exaggeration, the postures
of aggression and defense that he had been
taught by the engraver's art. Made reckless
by the ease with which he overcame invisible
foes attempting to stay his advance, he committed the common enough military error of
pushing the pursuit to a dangerous extreme,
until he found himself upon the margin of a
wide but shallow brook, whose rapid waters
barred his direct advance against the flying
foe that had crossed with illogical ease. But
the intrepid victor was not to be baffled; the
spirit of the race which had passed the great
sea burned unconquerable in that small breast
and would not be denied. Finding a place
where some bowlders in the bed of the stream
lay but a step or a leap apart, he made his way
across and fell again upon the rear-guard of
his imaginary foe, putting all to the sword.

Now that the battle had been won, prudence required that he withdraw to his base
of operations. Alas; like many a mightier

conqueror, and like one, the mightiest, he could not
                curb the lust for war,
Nor learn that tempted Fate will leave the loftiest star.

Advancing from the bank of the creek he suddenly found himself confronted with a new and more formidable enemy: in the path that he was following, sat, bolt upright, with ears erect and paws suspended before' it, a rabbit! With a startled cry the child turned and fled, he knew not in what direction, calling with inarticulate cries for his mother, weeping, stumbling, his tender skin cruelly torn by brambles, his little heart beating hard with terror—breathless, blind with tears—lost in the forest! Then, for more than an hour, he wandered with erring feet through the tangled undergrowth, till at last, overcome by fatigue, he lay down in a narrow space between two rocks, within a few yards of the stream and still grasping his toy sword, no longer a weapon but a companion, sobbed himself to sleep. The wood birds sang merrily above his head; the squirrels, whisking their bravery of tail, ran barking from tree to tree, unconscious of the pity of it, and somewhere far away was a strange, muffled thunder. as if the partridges were drumming

in celebration of nature's victory over the son
of her immemorial enslavers. And back at
the little plantation, where white men and
black were hastily searching the fields and
hedges in alarm, a mother's heart was breaking for her missing child.

Hours passed, and then the little sleeper
rose to his feet. The chill of the evening was
in his limbs, the fear of the gloom in his heart.
But he had rested, and he no longer wept.
With some blind instinct which impelled to
action he struggled through the undergrowth
about him and came to a more open ground—
on his right the brook, to the left a gentle acclivity studded with infrequent trees; over all,
the gathering gloom of twilight. A thin,
ghostly mist rose along the water. It frightened and repelled him; instead of recrossing,
in the direction whence he had come, he
turned his back upon it, and went forward
toward the dark inclosing wood. Suddenly
he saw before him a strange moving object
which he took to be some large animal—a
dog, a pig—he could not name it; perhaps it
was a bear. He had seen pictures of bears,
but knew of nothing to their discredit and had
vaguely wished to meet one. But something
in form or movement of this object—some-

thing in the awkwardness of its approach—
told him that it was not a bear, and curiosity
was stayed by fear. He stood still and as it
came slowly on gained courage every moment,
for he saw that at least it had not the long,
menacing ears of the rabbit. Possibly his im-
pressionable mind was half conscious of something familiar in its shambling, awkward gait.
Before it had approached near enough to re-
solve his doubts he saw that it was followed
by another and another. To right and to left
were many more; the whole open space about
him was alive with them—all moving toward
the brook.

They were men. They crept upon their
hands and knees. They used their hands
only, dragging their legs. They used their
knees only, their arms hanging idle at
their sides. They strove to rise to their
feet, but fell prone in the attempt. They
did nothing naturally, and nothing alike,
save only to advance foot by foot in the
same direction. Singly, in pairs and in little
groups, they came on through the gloom, some
halting now and again while others crept
slowly past them, then resuming their movement. They came by dozens and by hundreds; as far on either hand as one could see

in the deepening gloom they extended and the black wood behind them appeared to be inexhaustible. The very ground seemed in motion toward the creek. Occasionally one who had paused did not again go on, but lay motionless. He was dead. Some, pausing, made strange gestures with their hands, erected their arms and lowered them again, clasped their heads; spread their palms upward, as men are sometimes seen to do in public prayer.

Not all of this did the child note; it is what would have been noted by an elder observer; he saw little but that these were men, yet crept like babes. Being men, they were not terrible, though unfamiliarly clad. He moved among them freely, going from one to another and peering into their faces with childish curiosity. All their faces were singularly white and many were streaked and gouted with red. Something in this—something too, perhaps, in their grotesque attitudes and movements—reminded him of the painted clown whom he had seen last summer in the circus, and he laughed as he watched them. But on and ever on they crept, these maimed and bleeding men, as heedless as he of the dramatic contrast between his laughter and their own ghastly gravity. To him it was a merry spectacle. He had seen his father's negroes creep upon their hands and knees for his amusement—had ridden them so, "making believe" they were his horses. He now approached one of these crawling figures from behind and with an agile movement mounted it astride. The man sank upon his breast, recovered, flung the small boy fiercely to the ground as an unbroken colt might have done, then turned upon him a face that lacked a lower jaw—from the upper teeth to the throat was a great red gap fringed with hanging shreds of flesh and splinters of bone. The unnatural prominence of nose, the absence of chin, the fierce eyes, gave this man the appearance of a great bird of prey crimsoned in throat and breast by the blood of its quarry. The man rose to his knees, the child to his feet. The man shook his fist at the child; the child, terrified at last, ran to a tree near by, got upon the farther side of it and took a more serious view of the situation. And so the clumsy multitude dragged itself slowly and painfully along in hideous pantomime—moved forward down the slope like a swarm of great black beetles, with never a sound of going—in silence profound, absolute.

with his martial environment, but as heedless
of the grandeur of the struggle as the dead
who had died to make the glory.

The fire beyond the belt of woods on the
farther side of the creek, reflected to earth
from the canopy of its own smoke, was now
suffusing the whole landscape. It transformed the sinuous line of mist to the vapor
of gold. The water gleamed with dashes of
red, and red, too, were many of the stones
protruding above the surface. But that was
blood; the less desperately wounded had
stained them in crossing. On them, too, the
child now crossed with eager steps; he was
going to the fire. As he stood upon the farther bank he turned about to look at the companions of his march. The advance was arriving at the creek. The stronger had already drawn themselves to the brink and
plunged their faces into the flood. Three or
four who lay without motion appeared to have
no heads. At this the child's eyes expanded
with wonder; even his hospitable understanding could not accept a phenomenon implying
such vitality as that. After slaking their
thirst these men had not had the strength to
back away from the water, nor to keep their
heads above it. They were drowned. In

rear of these, the open spaces of the forest showed the leader as many formless figures of his grim command as at first; but not nearly so many were in motion. He waved his cap for their encouragement and smilingly pointed with his weapon in the direction of the guiding light—a pillar of fire to this strange exodus.

Confident of the fidelity of his forces, he now entered the belt of woods, passed through it easily in the red illumination, climbed a fence, ran across a field, turning now and again to coquet with his responsive shadow, and so approached the blazing ruin of a dwelling. Desolation everywhere! In all the wide glare not a living thing was visible. He cared nothing for that; the spectacle pleased, and he danced with glee in imitation of the wavering flames. He ran about, collecting fuel, but every object that he found was too heavy for him to cast in from the distance to which the heat limited his approach. In despair he flung in his sword—a surrender to the superior forces of nature. His military career was at an end.

Shifting his position, his eyes fell upon some outbuildings which had an oddly familiar appearance, as if he had dreamed of them. He stood considering them with won-

'der, when suddenly the entire plantation, with its inclosing forest, seemed to turn as if upon a pivot. His little world swung half around; the points of the compass were reversed. He recognized the blazing building as his own home!

For a moment he stood stupefied by the power of the revelation, then ran with stumbling feet, making a half-circuit of the ruin. There, conspicuous in the light of the conflagration, lay the dead body of a woman— the white face turned upward, the hands thrown out and clutched full of grass, the clothing deranged, the long dark hair in tangles and full of clotted blood. The greater part of the forehead was torn away, and from the jagged hole the brain protruded, overflowing the temple, a frothy mass of gray, crowned with clusters of crimson bubbles—the work of a shell.

The child moved his little hands, making wild, uncertain gestures. He uttered a series of inarticulate and indescribable cries—something between the chattering of an ape and the gobbling of a turkey—a startling, soulless, unholy sound, the language of a devil. The child was a deaf mute.

Then he stood motionless, with quivering lips, looking down upon the wreck.

A SON OF THE GODS

A STUDY IN THE PRESENT TENSE

A BREEZY day and a sunny land-scape. An open country to right and left and forward; behind, a wood. In the edge of this wood, facing the open but not venturing into it, long lines of troops, halted. The wood is alive with them, and full of confused noises—the occasional rattle of wheels as a battery of artillery goes into position to cover the advance; the hum and murmur of the soldiers talking; a sound of innumerable feet in the dry leaves that strew the interspaces among the trees; hoarse commands of officers. Detached groups of horsemen are well in front—not altogether exposed —many of them intently regarding the crest of a hill a mile away in the direction of the interrupted advance. For this powerful army, moving in battle order through a forest, has met with a formidable obstacle—the open country. The crest of that gentle hill a mile away has a sinister look; it says, Beware! Along it runs a stone wall extending to left

and right a great distance.   Behind the wall
is a hedge; behind the hedge are seen the tops
of trees in rather straggling order.   Among
the trees—what?   It is necessary to know.

Yesterday, and for many days and nights
previously, we were fighting somewhere; always there was cannonading, with occasional
keen rattlings of musketry, mingled with
cheers, our own or the enemy's, we seldom
knew, attesting some temporary advantage.
This morning at daybreak the enemy was
gone. We have moved forward across his
earthworks, across which we have so often
vainly attempted to move before, through the
débris of his abandoned camps, among the
graves of his fallen, into the woods beyond.

How curiously we had regarded everything! how odd it all had seemed! Nothing
had appeared quite familiar; the most com-
monplace objects—an old saddle, a splintered
wheel, a forgotten canteen—everything had
related something of the mysterious personality of those strange men who had been killing us. The soldier never becomes wholly
familiar with the conception of his foes as
men like himself; he cannot divest himself of
the feeling that they are another order of beings, differently conditioned, in an environ-

ment not altogether of the earth. The smallest
vestiges of them rivet his attention and engage
his interest. He thinks of them as inaccessible; and, catching an unexpected glimpse of
them, they appear farther away, and therefore
larger, than they really are—like objects in a
fog. He is somewhat in awe of them.

From the edge of the wood leading up the
acclivity are the tracks of horses and wheels—
the wheels of cannon. The yellow grass is
beaten down by the feet of infantry. Clearly
they have passed this way in thousands; they
have not withdrawn by the country roads.
This is significant—it is the difference between retiring and retreating.

That group of horsemen is our commander,
his staff and escort. He is facing the distant
crest, holding his field-glass against his eyes
with both hands, his elbows needlessly elevated. It is a fashion; it seems to dignify the
act; we are all addicted to it. Suddenly he
lowers the glass and says a few words to those
about him. Two or three aides detach themselves from the group and canter away into
the woods, along the lines in each direction.
We did not hear his words, but we know
them: "Tell General X. to send forward the
skirmish line." Those of us who have been

out of place resume our positions; the men resting at ease straighten themselves and the ranks are re-formed without a command. Some of us staff officers dismount and look at our saddle girths; those already on the ground remount.

Galloping rapidly along in the edge of the open ground comes a young officer on a snow-white horse. His saddle blanket is scarlet. What a fool! No one who has ever been in action but remembers how naturally every rifle turns toward the man on a white horse; no one but has observed how a bit of red enrages the bull of battle. That such colors are fashionable in military life must be accepted as the most astonishing of all the phenomena of human vanity. They would seem to have been devised to increase the death-rate.

This young officer is in full uniform, as if on parade. He is all agleam with bullion—a blue-and-gold edition of the Poetry of War. A wave of derisive laughter runs abreast of him all along the line. But how handsome he is!—with what careless grace he sits his horse!

He reins up within a respectful distance of the corps commander and salutes. The old soldier nods familiarly; he evidently knows him. A brief colloquy between them is going

on; the young man seems to be preferring
some request which the elder one is indisposed
to grant. Let us ride a little nearer. Ah! too
late—it is ended. The young officer salutes
again, wheels his horse, and rides straight toward the crest of the hill!

A thin line of skirmishers, the men deployed at six paces or so apart, now pushes
from the wood into the open. The commander speaks to his bugler, who claps his
instrument to his lips. *Tra-la-la! Tra-la-la!*
The skirmishers halt in their tracks.

Meantime the young horseman has advanced a hundred yards. He is riding at a
walk, straight up the long slope, with never
a turn of the head. How glorious! Gods!
what would we not give to be in his place—
with his soul! He does not draw his sabre;
his right hand hangs easily at his side. The
breeze catches the plume in his hat and flut-
ters it smartly. The sunshine rests upon his
shoulder-straps, lovingly, like a visible benediction. Straight on he rides. Ten thousand
pairs of eyes are fixed upon him with an intensity that he can hardly fail to feel; ten
thousand hearts keep quick time to the inaudible hoof-beats of his snowy steed. He is
not alone—he draws all souls after him. But

we remember that we laughed! On and on, straight for the hedge-lined wall, he rides. Not a look backward. O, if he would but turn—if he could but see the love, the adoration, the atonement!

Not a word is spoken; the populous depths of the forest still murmur with their unseen and unseeing swarm, but all along the fringe is silence. The burly commander is an equestrian statue of himself. The mounted staff officers, their field glasses up, are motionless all. The line of battle in the edge of the wood stands at a new kind of " attention," each man in the attitude in which he was caught by the consciousness of what is going on. All these hardened and impenitent man-killers, to whom death in its awfulest forms is a fact familiar to their every-day observation; who sleep on hills trembling with the thunder of great guns, dine in the midst of streaming missiles, and play at cards among the dead faces of their dearest friends—all are watching with suspended breath and beating hearts the outcome of an act involving the life of one man. Such is the magnetism of courage and devotion.

If now you should turn your head you would see a simultaneous movement among the spectators—a start, as if they had received an electric shock—and looking forward again to the now distant horseman you would see that he has in that instant altered his direction and is riding at an angle to his former course. The spectators suppose the sudden deflection to be caused by a shot, perhaps a wound; but take this field-glass and you will observe that he is riding toward a break in the wall and hedge. He means, if not killed, to ride through and overlook the country beyond.

You are not to forget the nature of this man's act; it is not permitted to you to think of it as an instance of bravado, nor, on the other hand, a needless sacrifice of self. If the enemy has not retreated he is in force on that ridge. The investigator will encounter nothing less than a line-of-battle; there is no need of pickets, videttes, skirmishers, to give warning of our approach; our attacking lines will be visible, conspicuous, exposed to an artillery fire that will shave the ground the moment they break from cover, and for half the distance to a sheet of rifle bullets in which nothing can live. In short, if the enemy is there, it would be madness to attack him in front; he must be manœuvred out by the immemorial plan of threatening his line of communication, as necessary to his existence as to the diver at the bottom of the sea his air tube. But how ascertain if the enemy is there? There is but one way,—somebody must go and see. The natural and customary thing to do is to send forward a line of skirmishers. But in this case they will answer in the affirmative with all their lives; the enemy, crouching in double ranks behind the stone wall and in cover of the hedge, will wait until it is possible to count each assailant's teeth. At the first volley a half of the questioning line will fall, the other half before it can accomplish the predestined retreat. What a price to pay for gratified curiosity! At what a dear rate an army must sometimes purchase knowledge! "Let me pay all," says this gallant man—this military Christ!

There is no hope except the hope against hope that the crest is clear. True, he might prefer capture to death. So long as he advances, the line will not fire—why should it? He can safely ride into the hostile ranks and become a prisoner of war. But this would defeat his object. It would not answer our question; it is necessary either that he return unharmed or be shot to death before our eyes. Only so shall we know how to act. If captured—why, that might have been done by a half-dozen stragglers.

Now begins an extraordinary contest of intellect between a man and an army. Our horseman, now within a quarter of a mile of the crest, suddenly wheels to the left and gallops in a direction parallel to it. He has caught sight of his antagonist; he knows all. Some slight advantage of ground has enabled him to overlook a part of the line. If he were here he could tell us in words. But that is now hopeless; he must make the best use of the few minutes of life remaining to him, by compelling the enemy himself to tell us as much and as plainly as possible—which, naturally, that discreet power is reluctant to do. Not a rifleman in those crouching ranks, not a cannoneer at those masked and shotted guns, but knows the needs of the situation, the imperative duty of forbearance. Besides, there has been time enough to forbid them all to fire. True, a single rifle-shot might drop him and be no great disclosure. But firing is infectious—and see how rapidly he moves, with never a pause except as he whirls his horse about to take a new direction, never directly backward toward us, never directly forward toward his executioners. All this is visible through the glass; it seems occurring within pistol-shot; we see all but the enemy, whose presence, whose thoughts, whose motives we infer. To the unaided eye there is nothing but a black figure on a white horse, tracing slow zigzags against the slope of a distant hill —so slowly they seem almost to creep.

Now—the glass again—he has tired of his failure, or sees his error, or has gone mad; he is dashing directly forward at the wall, as if to take it at a leap, hedge and all! One moment only and he wheels right about and is speeding like the wind straight down the slope—toward his friends, toward his death! Instantly the wall is topped with a fierce roll of smoke for a distance of hundreds of yards to right and left. This is as instantly dissipated by the wind, and before the rattle of the rifles reaches us he is down. No, he recovers his seat; he has but pulled his horse upon its haunches. They are up and away! A tremendous cheer bursts from our ranks, relieving the insupportable tension of our feelings. And the horse and its rider? Yes, they are up and away. Away, indeed—they are making directly to our left, parallel to the now steadily blazing and smoking wall. The rattle of the musketry is continuous, and every bullet's target is that courageous heart.

Suddenly a great bank of white smoke pushes upward from behind the wall. Another and another—a dozen roll up before the thunder of the explosions and the humming of the missiles reach our ears and the missiles themselves come bounding through clouds of dust into our covert, knocking over here and there a man and causing a temporary distraction, a passing thought of self.

The dust drifts away. Incredible!—that enchanted horse and rider have passed a ravine and are climbing another slope to unveil another conspiracy of silence, to thwart the will of another armed host. Another moment and that crest too is in eruption. The horse rears and strikes the air with its forefeet. They are down at last. But look again —the man has detached himself from the dead animal. He stands erect, motionless, holding his sabre in his right hand straight above his head. His face is toward us. Now he lowers his hand to a level with his face and moves it outward, the blade of the sabre describing a downward curve. It is a sign to us, to the world, to posterity. It is a hero's salute to death and history.

Again the spell is broken; our men attempt to cheer; they are choking with emotion; they utter hoarse, discordant cries; they clutch their weapons and press tumultuously forward into the open. The skirmishers, without orders, against orders, are going forward at a keen run, like hounds unleashed. Our cannon speak and the enemy's now open in full chorus; to right and left as far as we can see, the distant crest, seeming now so near, erects its towers of cloud and the great shot pitch roaring down among our moving masses. Flag after flag of ours emerges from the wood, line after line sweeps forth, catching the sunlight on its burnished arms. The rear battalions alone are in obedience; they preserve their proper distance from the insurgent front.

The commander has not moved. He now removes his field-glass from his eyes and glances to the right and left. He sees the human current flowing on either side of him and his huddled escort, like tide waves parted by a rock. Not a sign of feeling in his face; he is thinking. Again he directs his eyes forward; they slowly traverse that malign and awful crest. He addresses a calm word to his bugler. *Tra-la-la! Tra-la-la!* The injunction has an imperiousness which enforces it. It is repeated by all the bugles of all the subordinate commanders; the sharp metallic notes assert themselves above the hum of the advance and penetrate the sound of the cannon. To halt is to withdraw. The colors move slowly back; the lines face about and sullenly follow, bearing their wounded; the skirmishers return, gathering up the dead.

Ah, those many, many needless dead! That great soul whose beautiful body is lying over yonder, so conspicuous against the sere hillside—could it not have been spared the bitter consciousness of a vain devotion? Would one exception have marred too much the pitiless perfection of the divine, eternal plan?

ONE OF THE MISSING

JEROME SEARING, a private soldier of General Sherman's army, then confronting the enemy at and about Kennesaw Mountain, Georgia, turned his back upon a small group of officers with whom he had been talking in low tones, stepped across a light line of earthworks, and disappeared in a forest.   None of the men in line behind the works had said a word to him, nor had he so much as nodded to them in passing, but all who saw understood that this brave man had been intrusted with some perilous duty. Jerome Searing, though a private, did not serve in the ranks; he was detailed for service at division headquarters, being borne upon the rolls as an orderly.   "Orderly" is a word covering a multitude of duties.   An orderly may be a messenger, a clerk, an officer's servant—anything.   He may perform services for which no provision is made in orders and army regulations.   Their nature may depend upon his aptitude, upon favor, upon accident. Private Searing, an incomparable marksman, young, hardy, intelligent and insensible to fear, was a scout. The general commanding his division was not content to obey orders blindly without knowing what was in his front, even when his command was not on detached service, but formed a fraction of the line of the army; nor was he satisfied to receive his knowledge of his *vis-à-vis* through the customary channels; he wanted to know more than he was apprised of by the corps commander and the collisions of pickets and skirmishers. Hence Jerome Searing, with his extraordinary daring, his woodcraft, his sharp eyes, and truthful tongue. On this occasion his instructions were simple: to get as near the enemy's lines as possible and learn all that he could.

In a few moments he had arrived at the picket-line, the men on duty there lying in groups of two and four behind little banks of earth scooped out of the slight depression in which they lay, their rifles protruding from the green boughs with which they had masked their small defenses. The forest extended without a break toward the front, so solemn and silent that only by an effort of the imagination could it be conceived as populous with armed men, alert and vigilant—a forest formidable with possibilities of battle. Pausing a moment in one of these rifle-pits to apprise the men of his intention Searing crept stealthily forward on his hands and knees and was soon lost to view in a dense thicket of underbrush.

"That is the last of him," said one of the men; "I wish I had his rifle; those fellows will hurt some of us with it."

Searing crept on, taking advantage of every accident of ground and growth to give himself better cover. His eyes penetrated everywhere, his ears took note of every sound. He stilled his breathing, and at the cracking of a twig beneath his knee stopped his progress and hugged the earth. It was slow work, but not tedious; the danger made it exciting, but by no physical signs was the excitement manifest. His pulse was as regular, his nerves were as steady as if he were trying to trap a sparrow.

"It seems a long time," he thought, "but I cannot have come very far; I am still alive."

He smiled at his own method of estimating distance, and crept forward. A moment later he suddenly flattened himself upon the earth and lay motionless, minute after minute. Through a narrow opening in the bushes he had caught sight of a small mound of yellow clay—one of the enemy's rifle-pits. After some little time he cautiously raised his head, inch by inch, then his body upon his hands, spread out on each side of him, all the while intently regarding the hillock of clay. In another moment he was upon his feet, rifle in hand, striding rapidly forward with little attempt at concealment. He had rightly interpreted the signs, whatever they were; the enemy was gone.

To assure himself beyond a doubt before going back to report upon so important a matter, Searing pushed forward across the line of abandoned pits, running from cover to cover in the more open forest, his eyes vigilant to discover possible stragglers. He came to the edge of a plantation—one of those forlorn, deserted homesteads of the last years of the war, upgrown with brambles, ugly with broken fences and desolate with vacant buildings having blank apertures in place of doors and windows. After a keen reconnoissance from the safe seclusion of a clump of young pines Searing ran lightly across a field and through an orchard to a small structure which stood apart from the other farm buildings, on a slight elevation. This he thought would enable him to overlook a large scope of

country in the direction that he supposed the
enemy to have taken in withdrawing. This
building, which had originally consisted of a
single room elevated upon four posts about
ten feet high, was now little more than a roof;
the floor had fallen away, the joists and planks
loosely piled on the ground below or resting
on end at various angles, not wholly torn from
their fastenings above. The supporting posts
were themselves no longer vertical. It looked
as if the whole edifice would go down at the
touch of a finger.

Concealing himself in the débris of joists
and flooring Searing looked across the open
ground between his point of view and a spur
of Kennesaw Mountain, a half-mile away. A
road leading up and across this spur was
crowded with troops—the rear-guard of the
retiring enemy, their gun-barrels gleaming in
the morning sunlight.

Searing had now learned all that he could
hope to know. It was his duty to return to
his own command with all possible speed and
report his discovery. But the gray column of
Confederates toiling up the mountain road
was singularly tempting. His rifle—an ordinary " Springfield," but fitted with a globe
sight and hair-trigger—would easily send its

ounce and a quarter of lead hissing into their midst. That would probably not affect the duration and result of the war, but it is the business of a soldier to kill. It is also his habit if he is a good soldier. Searing cocked his rifle and " set " the trigger.

But it was decreed from the beginning of time that Private Searing was not to murder anybody that bright summer morning, nor was the Confederate retreat to be announced by him. For countless ages events had been so matching themselves together in that wondrous mosaic to some parts of which, dimly discernible, we give the name of history, that the acts which he had in will would have marred the harmony of the pattern. Some twenty-five years previously the Power charged with the execution of the work according to the design had provided against that mischance by causing the birth of a certain male child in a little village at the foot of the Carpathian Mountains, had carefully reared it, supervised its education, directed its desires into a military channel, and in due time made it an officer of artillery. By the concurrence of an infinite number of favoring influences and their preponderance over an infinite number of opposing ones, this officer

of artillery had been made to commit a breach
of discipline and flee from his native country
to avoid punishment. He had been directed
to New Orleans (instead of New York),
where a recruiting officer awaited him on the
wharf. He was enlisted and promoted, and
things were so ordered that he now commanded a Confederate battery some two miles
along the line from where Jerome Searing, the
Federal scout, stood cocking his rifle. Nothing had been neglected—at every step in the
progress of both these men's lives, and in the
lives of their contemporaries and ancestors,
and in the lives of the contemporaries of their
ancestors, the right thing had been done to
bring about the desired result. Had anything
in all this vast concatenation been overlooked
Private Searing might have fired on the
retreating Confederates that morning, and
would perhaps have missed. As it fell out, a
Confederate captain of artillery, having nothing better to do while awaiting his turn to
pull out and be off, amused himself by sight-
ing a field-piece obliquely to his right at what
he mistook for some Federal officers on the
crest of a hill, and discharged it. The shot
flew high of its mark.

As Jerome Searing drew back the hammer

of his rifle and with his eyes upon the distant Confederates considered where he could plant his shot with the best hope of making a widow or an orphan or a childless mother,—perhaps all three, for Private Searing, although he had repeatedly refused promotion, was not without a certain kind of ambition,—he heard a rushing sound in the air, like that made by the wings of a great bird swooping down upon its prey.   More quickly than he could apprehend the gradation, it increased to a hoarse and horrible roar, as the missile that made it sprang at him out of the sky, striking with a deafening impact one of the posts supporting the confusion of timbers above him, smashing it into matchwood, and bringing down the crazy edifice with a loud clatter, in clouds of blinding dust!

When Jerome Searing recovered consciousness he did not at once understand what had occurred.   It was, indeed, some time before he opened his eyes.   For a while he believed that he had died and been buried, and he tried to recall some portions of the burial service. He thought that his wife was kneeling upon his grave, adding her weight to that of the earth upon his breast.   The two of them, widow and earth, had crushed his coffin.   Unless the children should persuade her to go home he would not much longer be able to breathe. He felt a sense of wrong. " I cannot speak to her," he thought; " the dead have no voice; and if I open my eyes I shall get them full of earth."

He opened his eyes. A great expanse of blue sky, rising from a fringe of the tops of trees. In the foreground, shutting out some of the trees, a high, dun mound, angular in outline and crossed by an intricate, pattern-less system of straight lines; the whole an immeasurable distance away—a distance so inconceivably great that it fatigued him, and he closed his eyes. The moment that he did so he was conscious of an insufferable light. A sound was in his ears like the low, rhythmic thunder of a distant sea breaking in successive waves upon the beach, and out of this noise, seeming a part of it, or possibly coming from beyond it, and intermingled with its cease-less undertone, came the articulate words: " Jerome Searing, you are caught like a rat in a trap—in a trap, trap, trap."

Suddenly there fell a great silence, a black darkness, an infinite tranquillity, and Jerome Searing, perfectly conscious of his rathood, and well assured of the trap that he was in, remembering all and nowise alarmed, again opened his eyes to reconnoitre, to note the strength of his enemy, to plan his defense.

He was caught in a reclining posture, his back firmly supported by a solid beam. Another lay across his breast, but he had been able to shrink a little away from it so that it no longer oppressed him, though it was immovable. A brace joining it at an angle had wedged him against a pile of boards on his left, fastening the arm on that side. His legs, slightly parted and straight along the ground, were covered upward to the knees with a mass of débris which towered above his narrow horizon. His head was as rigidly fixed as in a vise; he could move his eyes, his chin—no more. Only his right arm was partly free. "You must help us out of this," he said to it. But he could not get it from under the heavy timber athwart his chest, nor move it outward more than six inches at the elbow.

Searing was not seriously injured, nor did he suffer pain. A smart rap on the head from a flying fragment of the splintered post, incurred simultaneously with the frightfully sudden shock to the nervous system, had momentarily dazed him. His term of unconsciousness, including the period of recov-

ery, during which he had had the strange
fancies, had probably not exceeded a few seconds, for the dust of the wreck had not wholly
cleared away as he began an intelligent survey
of the situation.

With his partly free right hand he now
tried to get hold of the beam that lay across,
but not quite against, his breast. In no way
could he do so. He was unable to depress the
shoulder so as to push the elbow beyond that
edge of the timber which was nearest his
knees; failing in that, he could not raise the
forearm and hand to grasp the beam. The
brace that made an angle with it downward
and backward prevented him from doing anything in that direction, and between it and his
body the space was not half so wide as the
length of his forearm. Obviously he could
not get his hand under the beam nor over it;
the hand could not, in fact, touch it at all.
Having demonstrated his inability, he de-
sisted, and began to think whether he could
reach any of the débris piled upon his legs.

In surveying the mass with a view to determining that point, his attention was arrested by what seemed to be a ring of shining
metal immediately in front of his eyes. It
appeared to him at first to surround some

perfectly black substance, and it was somewhat more than a half-inch in diameter. It
suddenly occurred to his mind that the black-
ness was simply shadow and that the ring was
in fact the muzzle of his rifle protruding from
the pile of débris.   He was not long in satisfy-
ing himself that this was so—if it was a satisfaction.   By closing either eye he could look
a little way along the barrel—to the point
where it was hidden by the rubbish that held
it.   He could see the one side, with the corresponding eye, at apparently the same angle as
the other side with the other eye.   Looking
with the right eye, the weapon seemed to be
directed at a point to the left of his head, and
vice versa.   He was unable to see the upper
surface of the barrel, but could see the under
surface of the stock at a slight angle.   The
piece was, in fact, aimed at the exact centre of
his forehead.

In the perception of this circumstance, in
the recollection that just previously to the
mischance of which this uncomfortable situation was the result he had cocked the rifle
and set the trigger so that a touch would discharge it, Private Searing was affected with a
feeling of uneasiness.   But that was as far as
possible from fear; he was a brave man, some-

what familiar with the aspect of rifles from
that point of view, and of cannon too. And
now he recalled, with something like amusement, an incident of his experience at the
storming of Missionary Ridge, where, walking up to one of the enemy's embrasures from
which he had seen a heavy gun throw charge
after charge of grape among the assailants he
had thought for a moment that the piece had
been withdrawn; he could see nothing in the
opening but a brazen circle. What that was
he had understood just in time to step aside as
it pitched another peck of iron down that
swarming slope. To face firearms is one of
the commonest incidents in a soldier's life—
firearms, too, with malevolent eyes blazing behind them. That is what a soldier is for.
Still, Private Searing did not altogether relish
the situation, and turned away his eyes.

After groping, aimless, with his right hand
for a time he made an ineffectual attempt to
release his left. Then he tried to disengage
his head, the fixity of which was the more an-
noying from his ignorance of what held it.
Next he tried to free his feet, but while exert-
ing the powerful muscles of his legs for that
purpose it occurred to him that a disturbance
of the rubbish which held them might dis-

charge the rifle; how it could have endured
what had already befallen it he could not
understand, although memory assisted him
with several instances in point. One in particular he recalled, in which in a moment of mental
abstraction he had clubbed his rifle and beaten
out another gentleman's brains, observing
afterward that the weapon which he had been
diligently swinging by the muzzle was loaded,
capped, and at full cock—knowledge of
which circumstance would doubtless have
cheered his antagonist to longer endurance.
He had always smiled in recalling that
blunder of his "green and salad days" as a
soldier, but now he did not smile. He turned
his eyes again to the muzzle of the rifle and
for a moment fancied that it had moved; it
seemed somewhat nearer.

Again he looked away. The tops of the
distant trees beyond the bounds of the plantation interested him: he had not before observed how light and feathery they were, nor
how darkly blue the sky was, even among
their branches, where they somewhat paled it
with their green; above him it appeared almost black. "It will be uncomfortably hot
here," he thought, "as the day advances. I
wonder which way I am looking."

Judging by such shadows as he could see, he decided that his face was due north; he would at least not have the sun in his eyes, and north—well, that was toward his wife and children.

" Bah! " he exclaimed aloud, " what have they to do with it? "

He closed his eyes. " As I can't get out I may as well go to sleep. The rebels are gone and some of our fellows are sure to stray out here foraging. They'll find me."

But he did not sleep. Gradually he became sensible of a pain in his forehead—a dull ache, hardly perceptible at first, but growing more and more uncomfortable. He opened his eyes and it was gone—closed them and it returned. " The devil! " he said, irrelevantly, and stared again at the sky. He heard the singing of birds, the strange metallic note of the meadow lark, suggesting the clash of vibrant blades. He fell into pleasant memories of his childhood, played again with his brother and sister, raced across the fields, shouting to alarm the sedentary larks, entered the sombre forest beyond and with timid steps followed the faint path to Ghost Rock, standing at last with audible heart-throbs before the Dead Man's Cave and seeking to penetrate its awful mystery. For the first time he observed that the opening of the haunted cavern was encircled by a ring of metal. Then all else vanished and left him gazing into the barrel of his rifle as before. But whereas before it had seemed nearer, it now seemed an inconceivable distance away, and all the more sinister for that. He cried out and, startled by something in his own voice—the note of fear —lied to himself in denial: " If I don't sing out I may stay here till I die."

He now made no further attempt to evade the menacing stare of the gun barrel. If he turned away his eyes an instant it was to look for assistance (although he could not see the ground on either side the ruin), and he permitted them to return, obedient to the imperative fascination. If he closed them it was from weariness, and instantly the poignant pain in his forehead—the prophecy and menace of the bullet—forced him to reopen them.

The tension of nerve and brain was too severe; nature came to his relief with intervals of unconsciousness. Reviving from one of these he became sensible of a sharp, smarting pain in his right hand, and when he worked his fingers together, or rubbed his palm with them, he could feel that they were wet and slippery. He could not see the hand, but he knew the sensation; it was running blood. In his delirium he had beaten it against the jagged fragments of the wreck, had clutched it full of splinters. He resolved that he would meet his fate more manly. He was a plain, common soldier, had no religion and not much philosophy; he could not die like a hero, with great and wise last words, even if there had been some one to hear them, but he could die " game," and he would. But if he could only know when to expect the shot!

Some rats which had probably inhabited the shed came sneaking and scampering about. One of them mounted the pile of débris that held the rifle; another followed and another. Searing regarded them at first with indifference, then with friendly interest; then, as the thought flashed into his bewildered mind that they might touch the trigger of his rifle, he cursed them and ordered them to go away. " It is no business of yours," he cried.

The creatures went away; they would return later, attack his face, gnaw away his nose, cut his throat—he knew that, but he hoped by that time to be dead.

Nothing could now unfix his gaze from the

little ring of metal with its black interior. The pain in his forehead was fierce and incessant. He felt it gradually penetrating the brain more and more deeply, until at last its progress was arrested by the wood at the back of his head.   It grew momentarily more insufferable: he began wantonly beating his lacerated hand against the splinters again to counteract that horrible ache. It seemed to throb with a slow, regular recurrence, each pulsation sharper than the preceding, and sometimes he cried out, thinking he felt the fatal bullet. No thoughts of home, of wife and children, of country, of glory. The whole record of memory was effaced. The world had passed away—not a vestige remained. Here in this confusion of timbers and boards is the sole universe. Here is immortality in time—each pain an everlasting life. The throbs tick off eternities.

Jerome Searing, the man of courage, the formidable enemy, the strong, resolute warrior, was as pale as a ghost. His jaw was fallen; his eyes protruded; he trembled in every fibre; a cold sweat bathed his entire body; he screamed with fear. He was not insane—he was terrified.

In groping about with his torn and bleeding

hand he seized at last a strip of board, and, pulling, felt it give way. It lay parallel with his body, and by bending his elbow as much as the contracted space would permit, he could draw it a few inches at a time. Finally it was altogether loosened from the wreckage covering his legs; he could lift it clear of the ground its whole length. A great hope came into his mind: perhaps he could work it upward, that is to say backward, far enough to lift the end and push aside the rifle; or, if that were too tightly wedged, so place the strip of board as to deflect the bullet. With this object he passed it backward inch by inch, hardly daring to breathe lest that act somehow defeat his intent, and more than ever unable to remove his eyes from the rifle, which might perhaps now hasten to improve its waning opportunity. Something at least had been gained: in the occupation of his mind in this attempt at self-defense he was less sensible of the pain in his head and had ceased to wince. But he was still dreadfully frightened and his teeth rattled like castanets.

The strip of board ceased to move to the suasion of his hand. He tugged at it with all his strength, changed the direction of its length all he could, but it had met some extended obstruction behind him and the end in front was still too far away to clear the pile of débris and reach the muzzle of the gun. It extended, indeed, nearly as far as the trigger guard, which, uncovered by the rubbish, he could imperfectly see with his right eye. He tried to break the strip with his hand, but had no leverage. In his defeat, all his terror returned, augmented tenfold. The black aperture of the rifle appeared to threaten a sharper and more imminent death in punishment of his rebellion. The track of the bullet through his head ached with an intenser anguish. He began to tremble again.

Suddenly he became composed. His tremor subsided. He clenched his teeth and drew down his eyebrows. He had not exhausted his means of defense; a new design had shaped itself in his mind—another plan of battle. Raising the front end of the strip of board, he carefully pushed it forward through the wreckage at the side of the rifle until it pressed against the trigger guard. Then he moved the end slowly outward until he could feel that it had cleared it, then, closing his eyes, thrust it against the trigger with all his strength! There was no explosion; the rifle had been discharged as it dropped from his hand when the building fell. But it did its work.

Lieutenant Adrian Searing, in command of the picket-guard on that part of the line through which his brother Jerome had passed on his mission, sat with attentive ears in his breastwork behind the line. Not the faintest sound escaped him; the cry of a bird, the barking of a squirrel, the noise of the wind among the pines—all were anxiously noted by his overstrained sense. Suddenly, directly in front of his line, he heard a faint, confused rumble, like the clatter of a falling building translated by distance. The lieutenant mechanically looked at his watch. Six o'clock and eighteen minutes. At the same moment an officer approached him on foot from the rear and saluted.

" Lieutenant," said the officer, " the colonel directs you to move forward your line and feel the enemy if you find him. If not, continue the advance until directed to halt. There is reason to think that the enemy has retreated."

The lieutenant nodded and said nothing; the other officer retired. In a moment the men, apprised of their duty by the non-com-

missioned officers in low tones, had deployed
from their rifle-pits and were moving forward
in skirmishing order, with set teeth and beating hearts.

This line of skirmishers sweeps across the
plantation toward the mountain. They pass
on both sides of the wrecked building, observing nothing. At a short distance in their rear
their commander comes. He casts his eyes
curiously upon the ruin and sees a dead body
half buried in boards and timbers. It is so
covered with dust that its clothing is Confederate gray. Its face is yellowish white;
the cheeks are fallen in, the temples sunken,
too, with sharp ridges about them, making the
forehead forbiddingly narrow; the upper lip,
slightly lifted, shows the white teeth, rigidly
clenched. The hair is heavy with moisture,
the face as wet as the dewy grass all about.
From his point of view the officer does not
observe the rifle; the man was apparently
killed by the fall of the building.

"Dead a week," said the officer curtly,
moving on and absently pulling out his watch
as if to verify his estimate of time. Six o'clock
and forty minutes.

KILLED AT RESACA

THE best soldier of our staff was Lieutenant Herman Brayle, one of the two aides-de-camp. I don't remember where the general picked him up; from some Ohio regiment, I think; none of us had previously known him, and it would have been strange if we had, for no two of us came from the same State, nor even from adjoining States. The general seemed to think that a position on his staff was a distinction that should be so judiciously conferred as not to beget any sectional jealousies and imperil the integrity of that part of the country which was still an integer. He would not even choose officers from his own command, but by some jugglery at department headquarters obtained them from other brigades. Under such circumstances, a man's services had to be very distinguished indeed to be heard of by his family and the friends of his youth; and "the speaking trump of fame" was a trifle hoarse from loquacity, anyhow.

Lieutenant Brayle was more than six feet in height and of splendid proportions, with the light hair and gray-blue eyes which men so gifted usually find associated with a high order of courage. As he was commonly in full uniform, especially in action, when most officers are content to be less flamboyantly attired, he was a very striking and conspicuous figure. As to the rest, he had a gentleman's manners, a scholar's head, and a lion's heart. His age was about thirty.

We all soon came to like Brayle as much as we admired him, and it was with sincere concern that in the engagement at Stone's River—our first action after he joined us— we observed that he had one most objectionable and unsoldierly quality: he was vain of his courage. During all the vicissitudes and mutations of that hideous encounter, whether our troops were fighting in the open cotton fields, in the cedar thickets, or behind the railway embankment, he did not once take cover, except when sternly commanded to do so by the general, who usually had other things to think of than the lives of his staff officers—or those of his men, for that matter.

In every later engagement while Brayle was with us it was the same way. He would sit his horse like an equestrian statue, in a storm of bullets and grape, in the most exposed places—wherever, in fact, duty, requiring him to go, permitted him to remain—when, without trouble and with distinct advantage to his reputation for common sense, he might have been in such security as is possible on a battlefield in the brief intervals of personal inaction.

On foot, from necessity or in deference to his dismounted commander or associates, his conduct was the same. He would stand like a rock in the open when officers and men alike had taken to cover; while men older in service and years, higher in rank and of unquestionable intrepidity, were loyally preserving behind the crest of a hill lives infinitely precious to their country, this fellow would stand, equally idle, on the ridge, facing in the direction of the sharpest fire.

When battles are going on in open ground it frequently occurs that the opposing lines, confronting each other within a stone's throw for hours, hug the earth as closely as if they loved it. The line officers in their proper places flatten themselves no less, and the field officers, their horses all killed or sent to the rear, crouch beneath the infernal canopy of hissing lead and screaming iron without a thought of personal dignity.

In such circumstances the life of a staff officer of a brigade is distinctly " not a happy one," mainly because of its precarious tenure and the unnerving alternations of emotion to which he is exposed. From a position of that comparative security from which a civilian would ascribe his escape to a " miracle," he may be despatched with an order to some commander of a prone regiment in the front line —a person for the moment inconspicuous and not always easy to find without a deal of search among men somewhat preoccupied, and in a din in which question and answer alike must be imparted in the sign language. It is customary in such cases to duck the head and scuttle away on a keen run, an object of lively interest to some thousands of admiring marksmen. In returning—well, it is not customary to return.

Brayle's practice was different. He would consign his horse to the care of an orderly,— he loved his horse,—and walk quietly away on his perilous errand with never a stoop of the back, his splendid figure, accentuated by his uniform, holding the eye with a strange fascination. We watched him with suspended breath, our hearts in our mouths. On one occasion of this kind, indeed, one of our num-

ber, an impetuous stammerer, was so possessed
by his emotion that he shouted at me:

"I'll b-b-bet you t-two d-d-dollars they
d-drop him b-b-before he g-gets to that d-d-
ditch!"

I did not accept the brutal wager; I
thought they would.

Let me do justice to a brave man's memory;
in all these needless exposures of life there was
no visible bravado nor subsequent narration.
In the few instances when some of us had
ventured to remonstrate, Brayle had smiled
pleasantly and made some light reply, which,
however, had not encouraged a further pursuit of the subject.   Once he said:

"Captain, if ever I come to grief by forgetting your advice, I hope my last moments
will be cheered by the sound of your beloved
voice breathing into my ear the blessed words,
'I told you so.'"

We laughed at the captain—just why we
could probably not have explained—and that
afternoon when he was shot to rags from an
ambuscade Brayle remained by the body for
some time, adjusting the limbs with needless
care—there in the middle of a road swept by
gusts of grape and canister!   It is easy to condemn this kind of thing, and not very difficult

to refrain from imitation, but it is impossible not to respect, and Brayle was liked none the less for the weakness which had so heroic an expression. We wished he were not a fool, but he went on that way to the end, sometimes hard hit, but always returning to duty about as good as new.

Of course, it came at last; he who ignores the law of probabilities challenges an adversary that is seldom beaten. It was at Resaca, in Georgia, during the movement that resulted in the taking of Atlanta. In front of our brigade the enemy's line of earthworks ran through open fields along a slight crest. At each end of this open ground we were close up to him in the woods, but the clear ground we could not hope to occupy until night, when darkness would enable us to burrow like moles and throw up earth. At this point our line was a quarter-mile away in the edge of a wood. Roughly, we formed a semicircle, the enemy's fortified line being the chord of the arc.

" Lieutenant, go tell Colonel Ward to work up as close as he can get cover, and not to waste much ammunition in unnecessary firing. You may leave your horse."

When the general gave this direction we

were in the fringe of the forest, near the right
extremity of the arc. Colonel Ward was at
the left. The suggestion to leave the horse
obviously enough meant that Brayle was to
take the longer line, through the woods and
among the men. Indeed, the suggestion was
needless; to go by the short route meant absolutely certain failure to deliver the message.
Before anybody could interpose, Brayle had
cantered lightly into the field and the enemy's
works were in crackling conflagration.

"Stop that damned fool!" shouted the
general.

A private of the escort, with more ambition
than brains, spurred forward to obey, and
within ten yards left himself and his horse
dead on the field of honor.

Brayle was beyond recall, galloping easily
along, parallel to the enemy and less than two
hundred yards distant. He was a picture to
see! His hat had been blown or shot from
his head, and his long, blond hair rose and fell
with the motion of his horse. He sat erect in
the saddle, holding the reins lightly in his left
hand, his right hanging carelessly at his side.
An occasional glimpse of his handsome profile
as he turned his head one way or the other
proved that the interest which he took in what

was going on was natural and without affectation.

The picture was intensely dramatic, but in
no degree theatrical. Successive scores of
rifles spat at him viciously as he came within
range, and our own line in the edge of the
timber broke out in visible and audible defense. No longer regardful of themselves or
their orders, our fellows sprang to their feet,
and swarming into the open sent broad sheets
of bullets against the blazing crest of the
offending works, which poured an answering
fire into their unprotected groups with deadly
effect. The artillery on both sides joined the
battle, punctuating the rattle and roar with
deep, earth-shaking explosions and tearing the
air with storms of screaming grape, which
from the enemy's side splintered the trees and
spattered them with blood, and from ours
defiled the smoke of his arms with banks and
clouds of dust from his parapet.

My attention had been for a moment drawn
to the general combat, but now, glancing
down the unobscured avenue between these
two thunderclouds, I saw Brayle, the cause
of the carnage. Invisible now from either
side, and equally doomed by friend and foe,
he stood in the shot-swept space, motionless,

his face toward the enemy. At some little distance lay his horse. I instantly saw what had stopped him.

As topographical engineer I had, early in the day, made a hasty examination of the ground, and now remembered that at that point was a deep and sinuous gully, crossing half the field from the enemy's line, its general course at right angles to it. From where we now were it was invisible, and Brayle had evidently not known about it. Clearly, it was impassable. Its salient angles would have afforded him absolute security if he had chosen to be satisfied with the miracle already wrought in his favor and leapt into it. He could not go forward, he would not turn back; he stood awaiting death. It did not keep him long waiting.

By some mysterious coincidence, almost instantaneously as he fell, the firing ceased, a few desultory shots at long intervals serving rather to accentuate than break the silence. It was as if both sides had suddenly repented of their profitless crime. Four stretcher-bearers of ours, following a sergeant with a white flag, soon afterward moved unmolested into the field, and made straight for Brayle's body. Several Confederate officers and men came out to meet them, and with uncovered heads assisted them to take up their sacred burden. As it was borne toward us we heard beyond the hostile works fifes and a muffled drum—a dirge. A generous enemy honored the fallen brave.

Amongst the dead man's effects was a soiled Russia-leather pocketbook. In the distribution of mementoes of our friend, which the general, as administrator, decreed, this fell to me.

A year after the close of the war, on my way to California, I opened and idly inspected it. Out of an overlooked compartment fell a letter without envelope or address. It was in a woman's handwriting, and began with words of endearment, but no name.

It had the following date line: " San Francisco, Cal., July 9, 1862." The signature was " Darling," in marks of quotation. Incidentally, in the body of the text, the writer's full name was given—Marian Mendenhall.

The letter showed evidence of cultivation and good breeding, but it was an ordinary love letter, if a love letter can be ordinary. There was not much in it, but there was something. It was this:

" Mr. Winters, whom I shall always hate

for it, has been telling that at some battle in Virginia, where he got his hurt, you were seen crouching behind a tree. I think he wants to injure you in my regard, which he knows the story would do if I believed it. I could bear to hear of my soldier lover's death, but not of his cowardice."

These were the words which on that sunny afternoon, in a distant region, had slain a hundred men. Is woman weak?

One evening I called on Miss Mendenhall to return the letter to her. I intended, also, to tell her what she had done—but not that she did it. I found her in a handsome dwelling on Rincon Hill. She was beautiful, well bred—in a word, charming.

"You knew Lieutenant Herman Brayle," I said, rather abruptly. "You know, doubtless, that he fell in battle. Among his effects was found this letter from you. My errand here is to place it in your hands."

She mechanically took the letter, glanced through it with deepening color, and then, looking at me with a smile, said:

"It is very good of you, though I am sure it was hardly worth while." She started suddenly and changed color. "This stain," she said, "is it—surely it is not——"

" Madam," I said, " pardon me, but that is the blood of the truest and bravest heart that ever beat."

She hastily flung the letter on the blazing coals. " Uh! I cannot bear the sight of blood!" she said. " How did he die?"

I had involuntarily risen to rescue that scrap of paper, sacred even to me, and now stood partly behind her. As she asked the question she turned her face about and slightly upward. The light of the burning letter was reflected in her eyes and touched her cheek with a tinge of crimson like the stain upon its page. I had never seen anything so beautiful as this detestable creature.

" He was bitten by a snake," I replied.

THE AFFAIR AT COULTER'S NOTCH

DO you think, Colonel, that your brave Coulter would like to put one of his guns in here? " the general asked.

He was apparently not altogether serious; it certainly did not seem a place where any artillerist, however brave, would like to put a gun. The colonel thought that possibly his division commander meant good-humoredly to intimate that in a recent conversation between them Captain Coulter's courage had been too highly extolled.

" General," he replied warmly, " Coulter would like to put a gun anywhere within reach of those people," with a motion of his hand in the direction of the enemy.

" It is the only place," said the general. He was serious, then.

The place was a depression, a " notch," in the sharp crest of a hill. It was a pass, and through it ran a turnpike, which reaching this highest point in its course by a sinuous ascent through a thin forest made a similar, though less steep, descent toward the enemy. For a mile to the left and a mile to the right, the ridge, though occupied by Federal infantry lying close behind the sharp crest and appearing as if held in place by atmospheric pressure, was inaccessible to artillery. There was no place but the bottom of the notch, and that was barely wide enough for the roadbed. From the Confederate side this point was commanded by two batteries posted on a slightly lower elevation beyond a creek, and a half-mile away. All the guns but one were masked by the trees of an orchard; that one— it seemed a bit of impudence—was on an open lawn directly in front of a rather grandiose building, the planter's dwelling. The gun was safe enough in its exposure—but only because the Federal infantry had been forbidden to fire. Coulter's Notch—it came to be called so—was not, that pleasant summer afternoon, a place where one would " like to put a gun."

Three or four dead horses lay there sprawling in the road, three or four dead men in a trim row at one side of it, and a little back, down the hill. All but one were cavalrymen belonging to the Federal advance. One was a quartermaster. The general commanding the division and the colonel commanding the brigade, with their staffs and escorts, had ridden into the notch to have a look at the enemy's guns—which had straightway obscured themselves in towering clouds of smoke. It was hardly profitable to be curious about guns which had the trick of the cuttle-fish, and the season of observation had been brief. At its conclusion—a short remove backward from where it began—occurred the conversation already partly reported. "It is the only place," the general repeated thought-fully, " to get at them."

The colonel looked at him gravely. "There is room for only one gun, General—one against twelve."

" That is true—for only one at a time," said the commander with something like, yet not altogether like, a smile. " But then, your brave Coulter—a whole battery in himself."

The tone of irony was now unmistakable. It angered the colonel, but he did not know what to say. The spirit of military subordina-tion is not favorable to retort, nor even to deprecation.

At this moment a young officer of artillery came riding slowly up the road attended by his bugler. It was Captain Coulter. He could not have been more than twenty-three years of age. He was of medium height, but very slender and lithe, and sat his horse with something of the air of a civilian. In face he was of a type singularly unlike the men about him; thin, high-nosed, gray-eyed, with a slight blond mustache, and long, rather straggling hair of the same color. There was an apparent negligence in his attire. His cap was worn with the visor a trifle askew; his coat was buttoned only at the sword-belt, showing a considerable expanse of white shirt, tolerably clean for that stage of the campaign. But the negligence was all in his dress and bearing; in his face was a look of intense interest in his surroundings. His gray eyes, which seemed occasionally to strike right and left across the landscape, like search-lights, were for the most part fixed upon the sky beyond the Notch; until he should arrive at the summit of the road there was nothing else in that direction to see. As he came opposite his division and brigade commanders at the roadside he saluted mechanically and was about to pass on. The colonel signed to him to halt.

" Captain Coulter," he said, " the enemy has twelve pieces over there on the next ridge. If I rightly understand the general, he directs that you bring up a gun and engage them."

There was a blank silence; the general

looked stolidly at a distant regiment swarming slowly up the hill through rough undergrowth, like a torn and draggled cloud of blue smoke; the captain appeared not to have observed him. Presently the captain spoke, slowly and with apparent effort:

"On the next ridge, did you say, sir? Are the guns near the house?"

"Ah, you have been over this road before. Directly at the house."

"And it is—necessary—to engage them? The order is imperative?"

His voice was husky and broken. He was visibly paler. The colonel was astonished and mortified. He stole a glance at the commander. In that set, immobile face was no sign; it was as hard as bronze. A moment later the general rode away, followed by his staff and escort. The colonel, humiliated and indignant, was about to order Captain Coulter in arrest, when the latter spoke a few words in a low tone to his bugler, saluted, and rode straight forward into the Notch, where, presently, at the summit of the road, his field-glass at his eyes, he showed against the sky, he and his horse, sharply defined and statuesque. The bugler had dashed down the speed and disappeared behind a wood.   Presently his bugle was heard singing in the cedars, and in an incredibly short time a single gun with its caisson, each drawn by six horses and manned by its full complement of gunners, came bounding and banging up the grade in a storm of dust, unlimbered under cover, and was run forward by hand to the fatal crest among the dead horses.   A gesture of the captain's arm, some strangely agile movements of the men in loading, and almost before the troops along the way had ceased to hear the rattle of the wheels, a great white cloud sprang forward down the slope, and with a deafening report the affair at Coulter's Notch had begun.

It is not intended to relate in detail the progress and incidents of that ghastly contest—a contest without vicissitudes, its alternations only different degrees of despair.   Almost at the instant when Captain Coulter's gun blew its challenging cloud twelve answering clouds rolled upward from among the trees about the plantation house, a deep multiple report roared back like a broken echo, and thenceforth to the end the Federal cannoneers fought their hopeless battle in an atmosphere of living iron whose thoughts were lightnings and whose deeds were death.

Unwilling to see the efforts which he could not aid and the slaughter which he could not stay, the colonel ascended the ridge at a point a quarter of a mile to the left, whence the Notch, itself invisible, but pushing up successive masses of smoke, seemed the crater of a volcano in thundering eruption. With his glass he watched the enemy's guns, noting as he could the effects of Coulter's fire—if Coulter still lived to direct it. He saw that the Federal gunners, ignoring those of the enemy's pieces whose positions could be determined by their smoke only, gave their whole attention to the one that maintained its place in the open—the lawn in front of the house. Over and about that hardy piece the shells exploded at intervals of a few seconds. Some exploded in the house, as could be seen by thin ascensions of smoke from the breached roof. Figures of prostrate men and horses were plainly visible.

"If our fellows are doing so good work with a single gun," said the colonel to an aide who happened to be nearest, "they must be suffering like the devil from twelve. Go down and present the commander of that piece with my congratulations on the accuracy of his fire."

Turning to his adjutant-general he said, "Did you observe Coulter's damned reluctance to obey orders?"

"Yes, sir, I did."

"Well, say nothing about it, please. I don't think the general will care to make any accusations. He will probably have enough to do in explaining his own connection with this uncommon way of amusing the rear-guard of a retreating enemy."

A young officer approached from below, climbing breathless up the acclivity. Almost before he had saluted, he gasped out:

"Colonel, I am directed by Colonel Harmon to say that the enemy's guns are within easy reach of our rifles, and most of them visible from several points along the ridge."

The brigade commander looked at him without a trace of interest in his expression. "I know it," he said quietly.

The young adjutant was visibly embarrassed. "Colonel Harmon would like to have permission to silence those guns," he stammered.

"So should I," the colonel said in the same tone. "Present my compliments to Colonel

Harmon and say to him that the general's orders for the infantry not to fire are still in force."

The adjutant saluted and retired. The colonel ground his heel into the earth and turned to look again at the enemy's guns.

"Colonel," said the adjutant-general, "I don't know that I ought to say anything, but there is something wrong in all this. Do you happen to know that Captain Coulter is from the South?"

"No; *was* he, indeed?"

"I heard that last summer the division which the general then commanded was in the vicinity of Coulter's home—camped there for weeks, and——"

"Listen!" said the colonel, interrupting with an upward gesture. "Do you hear *that?*"

"That" was the silence of the Federal gun. The staff, the orderlies, the lines of infantry behind the crest—all had "heard," and were looking curiously in the direction of the crater, whence no smoke now ascended except desultory cloudlets from the enemy's shells. Then came the blare of a bugle, a faint rattle of wheels; a minute later the sharp reports recommenced with double activity. The demolished gun had been replaced with a sound one.

" Yes," said the adjutant-general, resuming his narrative, " the general made the acquaintance of Coulter's family. There was trouble —I don't know the exact nature of it—something about Coulter's wife. She is a red-hot Secessionist, as they all are, except Coulter himself, but she is a good wife and high-bred lady. There was a complaint to army headquarters. The general was transferred to this division. It is odd that Coulter's battery should afterward have been assigned to it."

The colonel had risen from the rock upon which they had been sitting. His eyes were blazing with a generous indignation.

" See here, Morrison," said he, looking his gossiping staff officer straight in the face, " did you get that story from a gentleman or a liar? "

" I don't want to say how I got it, Colonel, unless it is necessary "—he was blushing a trifle—" but I'll stake my life upon its truth in the main."

The colonel turned toward a small knot of officers some distance away. " Lieutenant Williams! " he shouted.

One of the officers detached himself from

the group and coming forward saluted, saying: "Pardon me, Colonel, I thought you had been informed. Williams is dead down there by the gun. What can I do, sir?"

Lieutenant Williams was the aide who had had the pleasure of conveying to the officer in charge of the gun his brigade commander's congratulations.

"Go," said the colonel, "and direct the withdrawal of that gun instantly. No—I'll go myself."

He strode down the declivity toward the rear of the Notch at a break-neck pace, over rocks and through brambles, followed by his little retinue in tumultuous disorder. At the foot of the declivity they mounted their waiting animals and took to the road at a lively trot, round a bend and into the Notch. The spectacle which they encountered there was appalling!

Within that defile, barely broad enough for a single gun, were piled the wrecks of no fewer than four. They had noted the silencing of only the last one disabled—there had been a lack of men to replace it quickly with another. The débris lay on both sides of the road; the men had managed to keep an open way between, through which the fifth piece was now firing.   The men?—they looked like demons of the pit! All were hatless, all stripped to the waist, their reeking skins black with blotches of powder and spattered with gouts of blood. They worked like madmen, with rammer and cartridge, lever and lanyard. They set their swollen shoulders and bleeding hands against the wheels at each recoil and heaved the heavy gun back to its place. There were no commands; in that awful environment of whooping shot, exploding shells, shrieking fragments of iron, and flying splinters of wood, none could have been heard. Officers, if officers there were, were indistinguishable; all worked together—each while he lasted—governed by the eye. When the gun was sponged, it was loaded; when loaded, aimed and fired. The colonel observed something new to his military experience—something horrible and unnatural: the gun was bleeding at the mouth!   In temporary default of water, the man sponging had dipped his sponge into a pool of comrade's blood.   In all this work there was no clashing; the duty of the instant was obvious. When one fell, another, looking a trifle cleaner, seemed to rise from the earth in the dead man's tracks, to fall in his turn.

With the ruined guns lay the ruined men—
alongside the wreckage, under it and atop of
it; and back down the road—a ghastly procession!—crept on hands and knees such of the
wounded as were able to move. The colonel
—he had compassionately sent his cavalcade
to the right about—had to ride over those who
were entirely dead in order not to crush those
who were partly alive. Into that hell he tranquilly held his way, rode up alongside the
gun, and, in the obscurity of the last discharge,
tapped upon the cheek the man holding the
rammer—who straightway fell, thinking himself killed. A fiend seven times damned
sprang out of the smoke to take his place, but
paused and gazed up at the mounted officer
with an unearthly regard, his teeth flashing
between his black lips, his eyes, fierce and
expanded, burning like coals beneath his
bloody brow. The colonel made an author-
itative gesture and pointed to the rear. The
fiend bowed in token of obedience. It was
Captain Coulter.

Simultaneously with the colonel's arresting
sign, silence fell upon the whole field of action.
The procession of missiles no longer streamed
into that defile of death, for the enemy also had
ceased firing. His army had been gone for

hours, and the commander of his rear-guard, who had held his position perilously long in hope to silence the Federal fire, at that strange moment had silenced his own. "I was not aware of the breadth of my authority," said the colonel to anybody, riding forward to the crest to see what had really happened.

An hour later his brigade was in bivouac on the enemy's ground, and its idlers were examining, with something of awe, as the faithful inspect a saint's relics, a score of straddling dead horses and three disabled guns, all spiked. The fallen men had been carried away; their torn and broken bodies would have given too great satisfaction.

Naturally, the colonel established himself and his military family in the plantation house. It was somewhat shattered, but it was better than the open air. The furniture was greatly deranged and broken. Walls and ceilings were knocked away here and there, and a lingering odor of powder smoke was everywhere. The beds, the closets of women's clothing, the cupboards were not greatly damaged. The new tenants for a night made themselves comfortable, and the virtual effacement of Coulter's battery supplied them with an interesting topic.

During supper an orderly of the escort showed himself into the dining-room and asked permission to speak to the colonel.

"What is it, Barbour?" said that officer pleasantly, having overheard the request.

"Colonel, there is something wrong in the cellar; I don't know what—somebody there. I was down there rummaging about."

"I will go down and see," said a staff officer, rising.

"So will I," the colonel said; "let the others remain. Lead on, orderly."

They took a candle from the table and descended the cellar stairs, the orderly in visible trepidation. The candle made but a feeble light, but presently, as they advanced, its narrow circle of illumination revealed a human figure seated on the ground against the black stone wall which they were skirting, its knees elevated, its head bowed sharply forward. The face, which should have been seen in profile, was invisible, for the man was bent so far forward that his long hair concealed it; and, strange to relate, the beard, of a much darker hue, fell in a great tangled mass and lay along the ground at his side. They involuntarily paused; then the colonel, taking the candle from the orderly's shaking hand, approached the man and attentively considered him. The long dark beard was the hair of a woman—dead. The dead woman clasped in her arms a dead babe. Both were clasped in the arms of the man, pressed against his breast, against his lips. There was blood in the hair of the woman; there was blood in the hair of the man. A yard away, near an irregular depression in the beaten earth which formed the cellar's floor— a fresh excavation with a convex bit of iron, having jagged edges, visible in one of the sides—lay an infant's foot. The colonel held the light as high as he could. The floor of the room above was broken through, the splinters pointing at all angles downward. "This casemate is not bomb-proof," said the colonel gravely. It did not occur to him that his summing up of the matter had any levity in it.

They stood about the group awhile in silence; the staff officer was thinking of his unfinished supper, the orderly of what might possibly be in one of the casks on the other side of the cellar. Suddenly the man whom they had thought dead raised his head and gazed tranquilly into their faces. His complexion was coal black; the cheeks were apparently tattooed in irregular sinuous lines from the eyes downward. The lips, too, were white, like those of a stage negro. There was blood upon his forehead.

The staff officer drew back a pace, the orderly two paces.

"What are you doing here, my man?" said the colonel, unmoved.

"This house belongs to me, sir," was the reply, civilly delivered.

"To you? Ah, I see! And these?"

"My wife and child. I am Captain Coulter."

THE COUP DE GRÂCE

THE fighting had been hard and continuous; that was attested by all the senses. The very taste of battle was in the air. All was now over; it remained only to succor the wounded and bury the dead—to " tidy up a bit," as the humorist of a burial squad put it. A good deal of " tidying up " was required. As far as one could see through the forests, among the splintered trees, lay wrecks of men and horses. Among them moved the stretcher-bearers, gathering and carrying away the few who showed signs of life. Most of the wounded had died of neglect while the right to minister to their wants was in dispute. It is an army regulation that the wounded must wait; the best way to care for them is to win the battle. It must be confessed that victory is a distinct advantage to a man requiring attention, but many do not live to avail themselves of it.

The dead were collected in groups of a dozen or a score and laid side by side in rows while the trenches were dug to receive them.

Some, found at too great a distance from these rallying points, were buried where they lay. There was little attempt at identification, though in most cases, the burial parties being detailed to glean the same ground which they had assisted to reap, the names of the victorious dead were known and listed. The enemy's fallen had to be content with counting. But of that they got enough: many of them were counted several times, and the total, as given afterward in the official report of the victorious commander, denoted rather a hope than a result.

At some little distance from the spot where one of the burial parties had established its "bivouac of the dead," a man in the uniform of a Federal officer stood leaning against a tree. From his feet upward to his neck his attitude was that of weariness reposing; but he turned his head uneasily from side to side; his mind was apparently not at rest. He was perhaps uncertain in which direction to go; he was not likely to remain long where he was, for already the level rays of the setting sun straggled redly through the open spaces of the wood and the weary soldiers were quitting their task for the day. He would hardly make a night of it alone there among the dead.

Nine men in ten whom you meet after a battle inquire the way to some fraction of the army —as if any one could know. Doubtless this officer was lost. After resting himself a moment he would presumably follow one of the retiring burial squads.

When all were gone he walked straight away into the forest toward the red west, its light staining his face like blood. The air of confidence with which he now strode along showed that he was on familiar ground; he had recovered his bearings. The dead on his right and on his left were unregarded as he passed. An occasional low moan from some sorely-stricken wretch whom the relief-parties had not reached, and who would have to pass a comfortless night beneath the stars with his thirst to keep him company, was equally unheeded. What, indeed, could the officer have done, being no surgeon and having no water?

At the head of a shallow ravine, a mere depression of the ground, lay a small group of bodies. He saw, and swerving suddenly from his course walked rapidly toward them. Scanning each one sharply as he passed, he stopped at last above one which lay at a slight remove from the others, near a clump of small trees. He looked at it narrowly. It seemed to stir. He stooped and laid his hand upon its face. It screamed.

The officer was Captain Downing Madwell, of a Massachusetts regiment of infantry, a daring and intelligent soldier, an honorable man.

In the regiment were two brothers named Halcrow—Caffal and Creede Halcrow. Caffal Halcrow was a sergeant in Captain Madwell's company, and these two men, the sergeant and the captain, were devoted friends. In so far as disparity of rank, difference in duties and considerations of military discipline would permit they were commonly together. They had, indeed, grown up together from childhood. A habit of the heart is not easily broken off. Caffal Halcrow had nothing military in his taste nor disposition, but the thought of separation from his friend was disagreeable; he enlisted in the company in which Madwell was second-lieutenant. Each had taken two steps upward in rank, but between the highest non-commissioned and the lowest commissioned officer the gulf is deep and wide and the old relation was maintained with difficulty and a difference.

Creede Halcrow, the brother of Caffal, was

the major of the regiment—a cynical, saturnine man, between whom and Captain Madwell there was a natural antipathy which circumstances had nourished and strengthened to an active animosity. But for the restraining influence of their mutual relation to Caffal these two patriots would doubtless have endeavored to deprive their country of each other's services.

At the opening of the battle that morning the regiment was performing outpost duty a mile away from the main army. It was attacked and nearly surrounded in the forest, but stubbornly held its ground. During a lull in the fighting, Major Halcrow came to Captain Madwell. The two exchanged formal salutes, and the major said: "Captain, the colonel directs that you push your company to the head of this ravine and hold your place there until recalled. I need hardly apprise you of the dangerous character of the movement, but if you wish, you can, I suppose, turn over the command to your first-lieutenant. I was not, however, directed to authorize the substitution; it is merely a suggestion of my own, unofficially made."

To this deadly insult Captain Madwell coolly replied:

" Sir, I invite you to accompany the movement. A mounted officer would be a conspicuous mark, and I have long held the opinion that it would be better if you were dead."

The art of repartee was cultivated in military circles as early as 1862.

A half-hour later Captain Madwell's company was driven from its position at the head of the ravine, with a loss of one-third its number. Among the fallen was Sergeant Halcrow. The regiment was soon afterward forced back to the main line, and at the close of the battle was miles away. The captain was now standing at the side of his subordinate and friend.

Sergeant Halcrow was mortally hurt. His clothing was deranged; it seemed to have been violently torn apart, exposing the abdomen. Some of the buttons of his jacket had been pulled off and lay on the ground beside him and fragments of his other garments were strewn about. His leather belt was parted and had apparently been dragged from beneath him as he lay. There had been no great effusion of blood. The only visible wound was a wide, ragged opening in the abdomen.

It was defiled with earth and dead leaves. Protruding from it was a loop of small intestine. In all his experience Captain Madwell had not seen a wound like this. He could neither conjecture how it was made nor explain the attendant circumstances—the strangely torn clothing, the parted belt, the besmirching of the white skin. He knelt and made a closer examination. When he rose to his feet, he turned his eyes in different directions as if looking for an enemy. Fifty yards away, on the crest of a low, thinly wooded hill, he saw several dark objects moving about among the fallen men—a herd of swine. One stood with its back to him, its shoulders sharply elevated. Its forefeet were upon a human body, its head was depressed and invisible. The bristly ridge of its chine showed black against the red west. Captain Madwell drew away his eyes and fixed them again upon the thing which had been his friend.

The man who had suffered these monstrous mutilations was alive. At intervals he moved his limbs; he moaned at every breath. He stared blankly into the face of his friend and if touched screamed. In his giant agony he had torn up the ground on which he lay; his clenched hands were full of leaves and twigs and earth. Articulate speech was beyond his power; it was impossible to know if he were sensible to anything but pain. The expression of his face was an appeal; his eyes were full of prayer. For what?

There was no misreading that look; the captain had too frequently seen it in eyes of those whose lips had still the power to formulate it by an entreaty for death. Consciously or unconsciously, this writhing fragment of humanity, this type and example of acute sensation, this handiwork of man and beast, this humble, unheroic Prometheus, was imploring everything, all, the whole non-ego, for the boon of oblivion. To the earth and the sky alike, to the trees, to the man, to whatever took form in sense or consciousness, this incarnate suffering addressed that silent plea.

For what, indeed? For that which we accord to even the meanest creature without sense to demand it, denying it only to the wretched of our own race: for the blessed release, the rite of uttermost compassion, the *coup de grâce*.

Captain Madwell spoke the name of his friend. He repeated it over and over without effect until emotion choked his utterance.

His tears plashed upon the livid face beneath
his own and blinded himself. He saw nothing but a blurred and moving object, but
the moans were more distinct than ever, interrupted at briefer intervals by sharper shrieks.
He turned away, struck his hand upon his
forehead, and strode from the spot. The
swine, catching sight of him, threw up their
crimson muzzles, regarding him suspiciously
a second, and then with a gruff, concerted
grunt, raced away out of sight. A horse, its
foreleg splintered by a cannon-shot, lifted its
head sidewise from the ground and neighed
piteously. Madwell stepped forward, drew
his revolver and shot the poor beast between
the eyes, narrowly observing its death-
struggle, which, contrary to his expectation,
was violent and long; but at last it lay still.
The tense muscles of its lips, which had uncovered the teeth in a horrible grin, relaxed;
the sharp, clean-cut profile took on a look of
profound peace and rest.

Along the distant, thinly wooded crest to
westward the fringe of sunset fire had now
nearly burned itself out. The light upon the
trunks of the trees had faded to a tender gray;
shadows were in their tops, like great dark
birds aperch. Night was coming and there

were miles of haunted forest between Captain Madwell and camp. Yet he stood there at the side of the dead animal, apparently lost to all sense of his surroundings. His eyes were bent upon the earth at his feet; his left hand hung loosely at his side, his right still held the pistol. Presently he lifted his face, turned it toward his dying friend and walked rapidly back to his side. He knelt upon one knee, cocked the weapon, placed the muzzle against the man's forehead, and turning away his eyes pulled the trigger. There was no report. He had used his last cartridge for the horse.

The sufferer moaned and his lips moved convulsively. The froth that ran from them had a tinge of blood.

Captain Madwell rose to his feet and drew his sword from the scabbard. He passed the fingers of his left hand along the edge from hilt to point. He held it out straight before him, as if to test his nerves. There was no visible tremor of the blade; the ray of bleak skylight that it reflected was steady and true. He stooped and with his left hand tore away the dying man's shirt, rose and placed the point of the sword just over the heart. This time he did not withdraw his eyes. Grasping the hilt with both hands, he thrust downward with all his strength and weight. The blade sank into the man's body—through his body into the earth; Captain Madwell came near falling forward upon his work. The dying man drew up his knees and at the same time threw his right arm across his breast and grasped the steel so tightly that the knuckles of the hand visibly whitened. By a violent but vain effort to withdraw the blade the wound was enlarged; a rill of blood escaped, running sinuously down into the deranged clothing. At that moment three men stepped silently forward from behind the clump of young trees which had concealed their approach. Two were hospital attendants and carried a stretcher.

The third was Major Creede Halcrow.

PARKER ADDERSON,
PHILOSOPHER

PRISONER, what is your name?"

"As I am to lose it at daylight to-morrow morning it is hardly worth while concealing it. Parker Adderson."

"Your rank?"

"A somewhat humble one; commissioned officers are too precious to be risked in the perilous business of a spy. I am a sergeant."

"Of what regiment?"

"You must excuse me; my answer might, for anything I know, give you an idea of whose forces are in your front. Such knowledge as that is what I came into your lines to obtain, not to impart."

"You are not without wit."

"If you have the patience to wait you will find me dull enough to-morrow."

"How do you know that you are to die to-morrow morning?"

"Among spies captured by night that is the custom. It is one of the nice observances of the profession."

The general so far laid aside the dignity appropriate to a Confederate officer of high rank and wide renown as to smile. But no one in his power and out of his favor would have drawn any happy augury from that outward and visible sign of approval. It was neither genial nor infectious; it did not communicate itself to the other persons exposed to it—the caught spy who had provoked it and the armed guard who had brought him into the tent and now stood a little apart, watching his prisoner in the yellow candle-light. It was no part of that warrior's duty to smile; he had been detailed for another purpose. The conversation was resumed; it was in character a trial for a capital offense.

"You admit, then, that you are a spy— that you came into my camp, disguised as you are in the uniform of a Confederate soldier, to obtain information secretly regarding the numbers and disposition of my troops."

"Regarding, particularly, their numbers. Their disposition I already knew. It is morose."

The general brightened again; the guard, with a severer sense of his responsibility, accentuated the austerity of his expression and stood a trifle more erect than before. Twirling his gray slouch hat round and round upon his forefinger, the spy took a leisurely survey of his surroundings. They were simple enough. The tent was a common "wall tent," about eight feet by ten in dimensions, lighted by a single tallow candle stuck into the haft of a bayonet, which was itself stuck into a pine table at which the general sat, now busily writing and apparently forgetful of his unwilling guest. An old rag carpet covered the earthen floor; an older leather trunk, a second chair and a roll of blankets were about all else that the tent contained; in General Clavering's command Confederate simplicity and penury of "pomp and circumstance" had attained their highest development. On a large nail driven into the tent pole at the entrance was suspended a sword-belt supporting a long sabre, a pistol in its holster and, absurdly enough, a bowie-knife. Of that most unmilitary weapon it was the general's habit to explain that it was a souvenir of the peaceful days when he was a civilian.

It was a stormy night. The rain cascaded upon the canvas in torrents, with the dull, drum-like sound familiar to dwellers in tents. As the whooping blasts charged upon it the frail structure shook and swayed and strained at its confining stakes and ropes.

The general finished writing, folded the half-sheet of paper and spoke to the soldier guarding Adderson: "Here, Tassman, take that to the adjutant-general; then return."

"And the prisoner, General?" said the soldier, saluting, with an inquiring glance in the direction of that unfortunate.

"Do as I said," replied the officer, curtly.

The soldier took the note and ducked himself out of the tent. General Clavering turned his handsome face toward the Federal spy, looked him in the eyes, not unkindly, and said: "It is a bad night, my man."

"For me, yes."

"Do you guess what I have written?"

"Something worth reading, I dare say. And—perhaps it is my vanity—I venture to suppose that I am mentioned in it."

"Yes; it is a memorandum for an order to be read to the troops at *reveille* concerning your execution. Also some notes for the guidance of the provost-marshal in arranging the details of that event."

"I hope, General, the spectacle will be intelligently arranged, for I shall attend it myself."

"Have you any arrangements of your own that you wish to make? Do you wish to see a chaplain, for example?"

"I could hardly secure a longer rest for myself by depriving him of some of his."

"Good God, man! do you mean to go to your death with nothing but jokes upon your lips? Do you know that this is a serious matter?"

"How can I know that? I have never been dead in all my life. I have heard that death is a serious matter, but never from any of those who have experienced it."

The general was silent for a moment; the man interested, perhaps amused him—a type not previously encountered.

"Death," he said, "is at least a loss—a loss of such happiness as we have, and of opportunities for more."

"A loss of which we shall never be conscious can be borne with composure and therefore expected without apprehension. You must have observed, General, that of all the dead men with whom it is your soldierly pleasure to strew your path none shows signs of regret."

"If the being dead is not a regrettable condition, yet the becoming so—the act of dying

—appears to be distinctly disagreeable to one who has not lost the power to feel."

"Pain is disagreeable, no doubt. I never suffer it without more or less discomfort. But he who lives longest is most exposed to it. What you call dying is simply the last pain— there is really no such thing as dying. Suppose, for illustration, that I attempt to escape. You lift the revolver that you are courteously concealing in your lap, and——"

The general blushed like a girl, then laughed softly, disclosing his brilliant teeth, made a slight inclination of his handsome head and said nothing. The spy continued: "You fire, and I have in my stomach what I did not swallow. I fall, but am not dead. After a half-hour of agony I am dead. But at any given instant of that half-hour I was either alive or dead. There is no transition period.

"When I am hanged to-morrow morning it will be quite the same; while conscious I shall be living; when dead, unconscious. Nature appears to have ordered the matter quite in my interest—the way that I should have ordered it myself. It is so simple," he added with a smile, "that it seems hardly worth while to be hanged at all."

At the finish of his remarks there was a long silence. The general sat impassive, looking into the man's face, but apparently not attentive to what had been said. It was as if his eyes had mounted guard over the prisoner while his mind concerned itself with other matters. Presently he drew a long, deep breath, shuddered, as one awakened from a dreadful dream, and exclaimed almost inaudibly: "Death is horrible!"—this man of death.

"It was horrible to our savage ancestors," said the spy, gravely, "because they had not enough intelligence to dissociate the idea of consciousness from the idea of the physical forms in which it is manifested—as an even lower order of intelligence, that of the monkey, for example, may be unable to imagine a house without inhabitants, and seeing a ruined hut fancies a suffering occupant. To us it is horrible because we have inherited the tendency to think it so, accounting for the notion by wild and fanciful theories of another world—as names of places give rise to legends explaining them and reasonless conduct to philosophies in justification. You can hang me, General, but there your power of evil ends; you cannot condemn me to heaven."

The general appeared not to have heard; the spy's talk had merely turned his thoughts into an unfamiliar channel, but there they pursued their will independently to conclusions of their own. The storm had ceased, and something of the solemn spirit of the night had imparted itself to his reflections, giving them the sombre tinge of a supernatural dread. Perhaps there was an element of prescience in it. "I should not like to die," he said—"not to-night."

He was interrupted—if, indeed, he had intended to speak further—by the entrance of an officer of his staff, Captain Hasterlick, the provost-marshal. This recalled him to himself; the absent look passed away from his face.

"Captain," he said, acknowledging the officer's salute, "this man is a Yankee spy captured inside our lines with incriminating papers on him. He has confessed. How is the weather?"

"The storm is over, sir, and the moon shining."

"Good; take a file of men, conduct him at once to the parade ground, and shoot him."

A sharp cry broke from the spy's lips. He

threw himself forward, thrust out his neck, expanded his eyes, clenched his hands.

"Good God!" he cried hoarsely, almost inarticulately; "you do not mean that! You forget—I am not to die until morning."

"I have said nothing of morning," replied the general, coldly; "that was an assumption of your own. You die now."

"But, General, I beg—I implore you to remember; I am to hang! It will take some time to erect the gallows—two hours—an hour. Spies are hanged; I have rights under military law. For Heaven's sake, General, consider how short——"

"Captain, observe my directions."

The officer drew his sword and fixing his eyes upon the prisoner pointed silently to the opening of the tent. The prisoner hesitated; the officer grasped him by the collar and pushed him gently forward. As he approached the tent pole the frantic man sprang to it and with cat-like agility seized the handle of the bowie-knife, plucked the weapon from the scabbard and thrusting the captain aside leaped upon the general with the fury of a madman, hurling him to the ground and falling headlong upon him as he lay. The table was overturned, the candle extinguished and they fought blindly in the darkness. The provost-marshal sprang to the assistance of his superior officer and was himself prostrated upon the struggling forms. Curses and inarticulate cries of rage and pain came from the welter of limbs and bodies; the tent came down upon them and beneath its hampering and enveloping folds the struggle went on. Private Tassman, returning from his errand and dimly conjecturing the situation, threw down his rifle and laying hold of the flouncing canvas at random vainly tried to drag it off the men under it; and the sentinel who paced up and down in front, not daring to leave his beat though the skies should fall, discharged his rifle. The report alarmed the camp; drums beat the long roll and bugles sounded the assembly, bringing swarms of half-clad men into the moonlight, dressing as they ran, and falling into line at the sharp commands of their officers. This was well; being in line the men were under control; they stood at arms while the general's staff and the men of his escort brought order out of confusion by lifting off the fallen tent and pulling apart the breathless and bleeding actors in that strange contention.

Breathless, indeed, was one: the captain was

dead; the handle of the bowie-knife, protruding from his throat, was pressed back beneath his chin until the end had caught in the angle of the jaw and the hand that delivered the blow had been unable to remove the weapon. In the dead man's hand was his sword, clenched with a grip that defied the strength of the living. Its blade was streaked with red to the hilt.

Lifted to his feet, the general sank back to the earth with a moan and fainted. Besides his bruises he had two sword-thrusts—one through the thigh, the other through the shoulder.

The spy had suffered the least damage. Apart from a broken right arm, his wounds were such only as might have been incurred in an ordinary combat with nature's weapons. But he was dazed and seemed hardly to know what had occurred. He shrank away from those attending him, cowered upon the ground and uttered unintelligible remonstrances. His face, swollen by blows and stained with gouts of blood, nevertheless showed white beneath his disheveled hair—as white as that of a corpse.

" The man is not insane," said the surgeon, preparing bandages and replying to a question; "he is suffering from fright. Who and what is he?"

Private Tassman began to explain. It was the opportunity of his life; he omitted nothing that could in any way accentuate the importance of his own relation to the night's events. When he had finished his story and was ready to begin it again nobody gave him any attention.

The general had now recovered consciousness. He raised himself upon his elbow, looked about him, and, seeing the spy crouching by a camp-fire, guarded, said simply:

"Take that man to the parade ground and shoot him."

"The general's mind wanders," said an officer standing near.

"His mind does *not* wander," the adjutant-general said. "I have a memorandum from him about this business; he had given that same order to Hasterlick"—with a motion of the hand toward the dead provost-marshal—"and, by God! it shall be executed."

Ten minutes later Sergeant Parker Adderson, of the Federal army, philosopher and wit, kneeling in the moonlight and begging incoherently for his life, was shot to death by twenty men. As the volley rang out upon the keen air of the midnight, General Clavering, lying white and still in the red glow of the camp-fire, opened his big blue eyes, looked pleasantly upon those about him and said: "How silent it all is!"

The surgeon looked at the adjutant-general, gravely and significantly. The patient's eyes slowly closed, and thus he lay for a few moments; then, his face suffused with a smile of ineffable sweetness, he said, faintly: "I suppose this must be death," and so passed away.

AN AFFAIR OF OUTPOSTS

I

CONCERNING THE WISH TO BE DEAD

TWO men sat in conversation. One was the Governor of the State. The year was 1861; the war was on and the Governor already famous for the intelligence and zeal with which he directed all the powers and resources of his State to the service of the Union.

"What! *you?*" the Governor was saying in evident surprise—"you too want a military commission? Really, the fifing and drumming must have effected a profound alteration in your convictions. In my character of recruiting sergeant I suppose I ought not to be fastidious, but"—there was a touch of irony in his manner—"well, have you forgotten that an oath of allegiance is required?"

"I have altered neither my convictions nor my sympathies," said the other, tranquilly. "While my sympathies are with the South, as you do me the honor to recollect, I have never doubted that the North was in the right. I am a Southerner in fact and in feeling, but it is my habit in matters of importance to act as I think, not as I feel."

The Governor was absently tapping his desk with a pencil; he did not immediately reply. After a while he said: "I have heard that there are all kinds of men in the world, so I suppose there are some like that, and doubtless you think yourself one. I've known you a long time and—pardon me—I don't think so."

"Then I am to understand that my application is denied?"

"Unless you can remove my belief that your Southern sympathies are in some degree a disqualification, yes. I do not doubt your good faith, and I know you to be abundantly fitted by intelligence and special training for the duties of an officer. Your convictions, you say, favor the Union cause, but I prefer a man with his heart in it. The heart is what men fight with."

"Look here, Governor," said the younger man, with a smile that had more light than warmth: "I have something up my sleeve— a qualification which I had hoped it would not be necessary to mention. A great military authority has given a simple recipe for being a good soldier: 'Try always to get yourself killed.' It is with that purpose that I wish to enter the service. I am not, perhaps, much of a patriot, but I wish to be dead."

The Governor looked at him rather sharply, then a little coldly. "There is a simpler and franker way," he said.

"In my family, sir," was the reply, "we do not do that—no Armisted has ever done that."

A long silence ensued and neither man looked at the other. Presently the Governor lifted his eyes from the pencil, which had resumed its tapping, and said:

"Who is she?"

"My wife."

The Governor tossed the pencil into the desk, rose and walked two or three times across the room. Then he turned to Armisted, who also had risen, looked at him more coldly than before and said: "But the man—would it not be better that he—could not the country spare him better than it can spare you? Or are the Armisteds opposed to 'the unwritten law'?"

The Armisteds, apparently, could feel an insult: the face of the younger man flushed, then paled, but he subdued himself to the service of his purpose.

"The man's identity is unknown to me," he said, calmly enough.

"Pardon me," said the Governor, with even less of visible contrition than commonly underlies those words. After a moment's reflection he added: "I shall send you to-morrow a captain's commission in the Tenth Infantry, now at Nashville, Tennessee. Good night."

"Good night, sir. I thank you."

Left alone, the Governor remained for a time motionless, leaning against his desk. Presently he shrugged his shoulders as if throwing off a burden. "This is a bad business," he said.

Seating himself at a reading-table before the fire, he took up the book nearest his hand, absently opening it. His eyes fell upon this sentence:

"When God made it necessary for an unfaithful wife to lie about her husband in justification of her own sins He had the tenderness to endow men with the folly to believe her."

He looked at the title of the book; it was, *His Excellency the Fool*.

He flung the volume into the fire.

II

HOW TO SAY WHAT IS WORTH HEARING

The enemy, defeated in two days of battle at Pittsburg Landing, had sullenly retired to Corinth, whence he had come. For manifest incompetence Grant, whose beaten army had been saved from destruction and capture by Buell's soldierly activity and skill, had been relieved of his command, which nevertheless had not been given to Buell, but to Halleck, a man of unproved powers, a theorist, sluggish, irresolute. Foot by foot his troops, always deployed in line-of-battle to resist the enemy's bickering skirmishers, always entrenching against the columns that never came, advanced across the thirty miles of forest and swamp toward an antagonist prepared to vanish at contact, like a ghost at cock-crow. It was a campaign of "excursions and alarums," of reconnoissances and countermarches, of cross-purposes and countermanded orders. For weeks the solemn farce held attention, luring distinguished civilians from fields of political ambition to see what they safely could of the horrors of war. Among these was our friend the Governor. At the headquarters of the army and in the camps of the troops from his State he was a familiar figure, attended by the several members of his personal staff, showily horsed, faultlessly betailored and bravely silk-hatted. Things of charm they were, rich in suggestions of peaceful lands beyond a sea of strife. The bedraggled soldier looked up from his trench as they passed, leaned upon his spade and audibly damned them to signify his sense of their ornamental irrelevance to the austerities of his trade.

"I think, Governor," said General Masterson one day, going into informal session atop of his horse and throwing one leg across the pommel of his saddle, his favorite posture— "I think I would not ride any farther in that direction if I were you. We've nothing out there but a line of skirmishers. That, I presume, is why I was directed to put these siege guns here: if the skirmishers are driven in the enemy will die of dejection at being unable to haul them away—they're a trifle heavy."

There is reason to fear that the unstrained quality of this military humor dropped not as the gentle rain from heaven upon the place beneath the civilian's silk hat. Anyhow he abated none of his dignity in recognition.

"I understand," he said, gravely, "that some of my men are out there—a company of the Tenth, commanded by Captain Armisted. I should like to meet him if you do not mind."

"He is worth meeting. But there's a bad bit of jungle out there, and I should advise that you leave your horse and "—with a look at the Governor's retinue—"your other impedimenta."

The Governor went forward alone and on foot. In a half-hour he had pushed through a tangled undergrowth covering a boggy soil and entered upon firm and more open ground. Here he found a half-company of infantry lounging behind a line of stacked rifles. The men wore their accoutrements—their belts, cartridge-boxes, haversacks and canteens. Some lying at full length on the dry leaves were fast asleep: others in small groups gossiped idly of this and that; a few played at cards; none was far from the line of stacked arms. To the civilian's eye the scene was one of carelessness, confusion, indifference; a soldier would have observed expectancy and readiness.

At a little distance apart an officer in fatigue uniform, armed, sat on a fallen tree noting the approach of the visitor, to whom a sergeant, rising from one of the groups, now came forward.

"I wish to see Captain Armisted," said the Governor.

The sergeant eyed him narrowly, saying nothing, pointed to the officer, and taking a rifle from one of the stacks, accompanied him.

"This man wants to see you, sir," said the sergeant, saluting. The officer rose.

It would have been a sharp eye that would have recognized him. His hair, which but a few months before had been brown, was streaked with gray. His face, tanned by exposure, was seamed as with age. A long livid scar across the forehead marked the stroke of a sabre; one cheek was drawn and puckered by the work of a bullet. Only a woman of the loyal North would have thought the man handsome.

"Armisted—Captain," said the Governor, extending his hand, "do you not know me?"

"I know you, sir, and I salute you—as the Governor of my State."

Lifting his right hand to the level of his eyes he threw it outward and downward. In the code of military etiquette there is no provision for shaking hands. That of the civilian was withdrawn. If he felt either surprise or chagrin his face did not betray it.

"It is the hand that signed your commission," he said.

"And it is the hand——"

The sentence remains unfinished. The sharp report of a rifle came from the front, followed by another and another. A bullet hissed through the forest and struck a tree near by. The men sprang from the ground and even before the captain's high, clear voice was done intoning the command "At-ten-tion!" had fallen into line in rear of the stacked arms. Again—and now through the din of a crackling fusillade—sounded the strong, deliberate sing-song of authority: "Take . . . arms!" followed by the rattle of unlocking bayonets.

Bullets from the unseen enemy were now flying thick and fast, though mostly well spent and emitting the humming sound which signified interference by twigs and rotation in the plane of flight. Two or three of the men in the line were already struck and down. A few wounded men came limping awkwardly out of the undergrowth from the skirmish line in front; most of them did not pause, but held their way with white faces and set teeth to the rear.

Suddenly there was a deep, jarring report in front, followed by the startling rush of a shell, which passing overhead exploded in the edge of a thicket, setting afire the fallen leaves. Penetrating the din—seeming to float above it like the melody of a soaring bird—rang the slow, aspirated monotones of the captain's several commands, without emphasis, without accent, musical and restful as an evensong under the harvest moon. Familiar with this tranquilizing chant in moments of imminent peril, these raw soldiers of less than a year's training yielded themselves to the spell, executing its mandates with the composure and precision of veterans. Even the distinguished civilian behind his tree, hesitating between pride and terror, was accessible to its charm and suasion. He was conscious of a fortified resolution and ran away only when the skirmishers, under orders to rally on the reserve, came out of the woods like hunted hares and formed on the left of the stiff little line, breathing hard and thankful for the boon of breath.

III

THE FIGHTING OF ONE WHOSE HEART WAS NOT IN THE QUARREL

Guided in his retreat by that of the fugitive wounded, the Governor struggled bravely to the rear through the "bad bit of jungle." He was well winded and a trifle confused. Excepting a single rifle-shot now and again, there was no sound of strife behind him; the enemy was pulling himself together for a new onset against an antagonist of whose numbers and tactical disposition he was in doubt. The fugitive felt that he would probably be spared to his country, and only commended the arrangements of Providence to that end, but in leaping a small brook in more open ground one of the arrangements incurred the mischance of a disabling sprain at the ankle. He was unable to continue his flight, for he was too fat to hop, and after several vain attempts, causing intolerable pain, seated himself on the earth to nurse his ignoble disability and deprecate the military situation.

A brisk renewal of the firing broke out and stray bullets came flitting and droning by. Then came the crash of two clean, definite volleys, followed by a continuous rattle, through which he heard the yells and cheers of the combatants, punctuated by thunder-claps of cannon. All this told him that Armisted's little command was bitterly beset and fighting at close quarters. The wounded men whom he had distanced began to straggle by on either hand, their numbers visibly aug-mented by new levies from the line. Singly and by twos and threes, some supporting com-rades more desperately hurt than themselves, but all deaf to his appeals for assistance, they sifted through the underbrush and disap-peared. The firing was increasingly louder and more distinct, and presently the ailing fugitives were succeeded by men who strode with a firmer tread, occasionally facing about and discharging their pieces, then doggedly resuming their retreat, reloading as they walked. Two or three fell as he looked, and lay motionless. One had enough of life left in him to make a pitiful attempt to drag him-self to cover. A passing comrade paused beside him long enough to fire, appraised the poor devil's disability with a look and moved sullenly on, inserting a cartridge in his weapon.

In all this was none of the pomp of war

—no hint of glory. Even in his distress and
peril the helpless civilian could not forbear to
contrast it with the gorgeous parades and
reviews held in honor of himself—with the
brilliant uniforms, the music, the banners, and
the marching. It was an ugly and sickening
business: to all that was artistic in his nature,
revolting, brutal, in bad taste.

"Ugh!" he grunted, shuddering—"this is
beastly! Where is the charm of it all?
Where are the elevated sentiments, the devotion, the heroism, the——"

From a point somewhere near, in the direction of the pursuing enemy, rose the clear, deliberate sing-song of Captain Armisted.

"Stead-y, men—stead-y. Halt! Com-
mence fir-ing."

The rattle of fewer than a score of rifles
could be distinguished through the general
uproar, and again that penetrating falsetto:

"Cease fir-ing. In re-treat . . . .
maaarch!"

In a few moments this remnant had drifted
slowly past the Governor, all to the right of
him as they faced in retiring, the men deployed at intervals of a half-dozen paces. At
the extreme left and a few yards behind came
the captain. The civilian called out his name,

but he did not hear. A swarm of men in gray now broke out of cover in pursuit, making directly for the spot where the Governor lay —some accident of the ground had caused them to converge upon that point: their line had become a crowd. In a last struggle for life and liberty the Governor attempted to rise, and looking back the captain saw him. Promptly, but with the same slow precision as before, he sang his commands:

"Skirm-ish-ers, halt!" The men stopped and according to rule turned to face the enemy.

"Ral-ly on the right!"—and they came in at a run, fixing bayonets and forming loosely on the man at that end of the line.

"Forward . . to save the Gov-ern-or of your State . . doub-le quick . . . maaarch!"

Only one man disobeyed this astonishing command! He was dead. With a cheer they sprang forward over the twenty or thirty paces between them and their task. The captain having a shorter distance to go arrived first—simultaneously with the enemy. A half-dozen hasty shots were fired at him, and the foremost man—a fellow of heroic stature, hatless and bare-breasted—made a vicious sweep at his head with a clubbed rifle. The officer parried the blow at the cost of a broken arm and drove his sword to the hilt into the giant's breast. As the body fell the weapon was wrenched from his hand and before he could pluck his revolver from the scabbard at his belt another man leaped upon him like a tiger, fastening both hands upon his throat and bearing him backward upon the prostrate Governor, still struggling to rise. This man was promptly spitted upon the bayonet of a Federal sergeant and his death-gripe on the captain's throat loosened by a kick upon each wrist. When the captain had risen he was at the rear of his men, who had all passed over and around him and were thrusting fiercely at their more numerous but less coherent antagonists. Nearly all the rifles on both sides were empty and in the crush there was neither time nor room to reload. The Confederates were at a disadvantage in that most of them lacked bayonets; they fought by bludgeoning —and a clubbed rifle is a formidable arm. The sound of the conflict was a clatter like that of the interlocking horns of battling bulls —now and then the pash of a crushed skull, an oath, or a grunt caused by the impact of a rifle's muzzle against the abdomen transfixed by its bayonet. Through an opening made by the fall of one of his men Captain Armisted sprang, with his dangling left arm; in his right hand a full-charged revolver, which he fired with rapidity and terrible effect into the thick of the gray crowd: but across the bodies of the slain the survivors in the front were pushed forward by their comrades in the rear till again they breasted the tireless bayonets. There were fewer bayonets now to breast—a beggarly half-dozen, all told. A few minutes more of this rough work—a little fighting back to back—and all would be over.

Suddenly a lively firing was heard on the right and the left: a fresh line of Federal skirmishers came forward at a run, driving before them those parts of the Confederate line that had been separated by staying the advance of the centre. And behind these new and noisy combatants, at a distance of two or three hundred yards, could be seen, indistinct among the trees a line-of-battle!

Instinctively before retiring, the crowd in gray made a tremendous rush upon its hand-ful of antagonists, overwhelming them by mere momentum and, unable to use weapons in the crush, trampled them, stamped savagely on their limbs, their bodies, their necks, their faces; then retiring with bloody feet across its own dead it joined the general rout and the incident was at an end.

IV

THE GREAT HONOR THE GREAT

The Governor, who had been unconscious, opened his eyes and stared about him, slowly recalling the day's events. A man in the uniform of a major was kneeling beside him; he was a surgeon. Grouped about were the civilian members of the Governor's staff, their faces expressing a natural solicitude regarding their offices. A little apart stood General Masterson addressing another officer and gesticulating with a cigar. He was saying: "It was the beautifulest fight ever made—by God, sir, it was great!"

The beauty and greatness were attested by a row of dead, trimly disposed, and another of wounded, less formally placed, restless, half-naked, but bravely bebandaged.

"How do you feel, sir?" said the surgeon. "I find no wound."

"I think I am all right," the patient replied, sitting up. "It is that ankle."

The surgeon transferred his attention to the

ankle, cutting away the boot. All eyes followed the knife.

In moving the leg a folded paper was uncovered. The patient picked it up and carelessly opened it. It was a letter three months old, signed "Julia." Catching sight of his name in it he read it. It was nothing very remarkable—merely a weak woman's confession of unprofitable sin—the penitence of a faithless wife deserted by her betrayer. The letter had fallen from the pocket of Captain Armisted; the reader quietly transferred it to his own.

An aide-de-camp rode up and dismounted. Advancing to the Governor he saluted.

"Sir," he said, "I am sorry to find you wounded—the Commanding General has not been informed. He presents his compliments and I am directed to say that he has ordered for to-morrow a grand review of the reserve corps in your honor. I venture to add that the General's carriage is at your service if you are able to attend."

"Be pleased to say to the Commanding General that I am deeply touched by his kindness. If you have the patience to wait a few moments you shall convey a more definite reply."

He smiled brightly and glancing at the surgeon and his assistants added: "At present—if you will permit an allusion to the horrors of peace—I am 'in the hands of my friends.'"

The humor of the great is infectious; all laughed who heard.

"Where is Captain Armisted?" the Governor asked, not altogether carelessly.

The surgeon looked up from his work, pointing silently to the nearest body in the row of dead, the features discreetly covered with a handkerchief. It was so near that the great man could have laid his hand upon it, but he did not. He may have feared that it would bleed.

THE STORY OF A CONSCIENCE

I

CAPTAIN PARROL HARTROY stood at the advanced post of his picket-guard, talking in low tones with the sentinel. This post was on a turnpike which bisected the captain's camp, a half-mile in rear, though the camp was not in sight from that point. The officer was apparently giving the soldier certain instructions— was perhaps merely inquiring if all were quiet in front. As the two stood talking a man approached them from the direction of the camp, carelessly whistling, and was promptly halted by the soldier. He was evidently a civilian—a tall person, coarsely clad in the home-made stuff of yellow gray, called " butternut," which was men's only wear in the latter days of the Confederacy. On his head was a slouch felt hat, once white, from beneath which hung masses of uneven hair, seemingly unacquainted with either scissors or comb. The man's face was rather striking; a broad forehead, high nose, and thin cheeks, the mouth invisible in the full dark beard, which seemed as neglected as the hair. The eyes were large and had that steadiness and fixity of attention which so frequently mark a considering intelligence and a will not easily turned from its purpose—so say those physiognomists who have that kind of eyes. On the whole, this was a man whom one would be likely to observe and be observed by. He carried a walking-stick freshly cut from the forest and his ailing cowskin boots were white with dust.

"Show your pass," said the Federal soldier, a trifle more imperiously perhaps than he would have thought necessary if he had not been under the eye of his commander, who with folded arms looked on from the roadside.

"'Lowed you'd rec'lect me, Gineral," said the wayfarer tranquilly, while producing the paper from the pocket of his coat. There was something in his tone—perhaps a faint suggestion of irony—which made his elevation of his obstructor to exalted rank less agreeable to that worthy warrior than promotion is commonly found to be. "You-all have to be purty pertickler, I reckon," he added, in a more conciliatory tone, as if in half-apology for being halted.

Having read the pass, with his rifle resting on the ground, the soldier handed the document back without a word, shouldered his weapon, and returned to his commander. The civilian passed on in the middle of the road, and when he had penetrated the circumjacent Confederacy a few yards resumed his whistling and was soon out of sight beyond an angle in the road, which at that point entered a thin forest. Suddenly the officer undid his arms from his breast, drew a revolver from his belt and sprang forward at a run in the same direction, leaving his sentinel in gaping astonishment at his post. After making to the various visible forms of nature a solemn promise to be damned, that gentleman resumed the air of stolidity which is supposed to be appropriate to a state of alert military attention.

II

Captain Hartroy held an independent command. His force consisted of a company of infantry, a squadron of cavalry, and a section of artillery, detached from the army to which they belonged, to defend an important defile in the Cumberland Mountains in Tennessee. It was a field officer's command held by a line officer promoted from the ranks, where he had quietly served until "discovered." His post was one of exceptional peril; its defense entailed a heavy responsibility and he had wisely been given corresponding discretionary powers, all the more necessary because of his distance from the main army, the precarious nature of his communications and the lawless character of the enemy's irregular troops infesting that region. He had strongly fortified his little camp, which embraced a village of a half-dozen dwellings and a country store, and had collected a considerable quantity of supplies. To a few resident civilians of known loyalty, with whom it was desirable to trade, and of whose services in various ways he sometimes availed himself, he had given written passes admitting them within his lines. It is easy to understand that an abuse of this privilege in the interest of the enemy might entail serious consequences. Captain Hartroy had made an order to the effect that any one so abusing it would be summarily shot.

While the sentinel had been examining the civilian's pass the captain had eyed the latter narrowly. He thought his appearance familiar and had at first no doubt of having given him the pass which had satisfied the sentinel. It was not until the man had got out of sight and hearing that his identity was disclosed by a revealing light from memory. With soldierly promptness of decision the officer had acted on the revelation.

III

To any but a singularly self-possessed man the apparition of an officer of the military forces, formidably clad, bearing in one hand a sheathed sword and in the other a cocked revolver, and rushing in furious pursuit, is no doubt disquieting to a high degree; upon the man to whom the pursuit was in this instance directed it appeared to have no other effect than somewhat to intensify his tranquillity. He might easily enough have escaped into the forest to the right or the left, but chose another course of action—turned and quietly faced the captain, saying as he came up: "I reckon ye must have something to say to me, which ye disremembered. What mout it be, neighbor?"

But the "neighbor" did not answer, being engaged in the unneighborly act of covering him with a cocked pistol.

"Surrender," said the captain as calmly as a slight breathlessness from exertion would permit, "or you die."

There was no menace in the manner of this demand; that was all in the matter and in the means of enforcing it. There was, too, something not altogether reassuring in the cold gray eyes that glanced along the barrel of the weapon. For a moment the two men stood looking at each other in silence; then the civilian, with no appearance of fear—with as great apparent unconcern as when complying with the less austere demand of the sentinel— slowly pulled from his pocket the paper which had satisfied that humble functionary and held it out, saying:

"I reckon this 'ere parss from Mister Hartroy is——"

"The pass is a forgery," the officer said, interrupting. "I am Captain Hartroy—and you are Dramer Brune."

It would have required a sharp eye to observe the slight pallor of the civilian's face at these words, and the only other manifestation attesting their significance was a voluntary relaxation of the thumb and fingers holding the dishonored paper, which, falling to the road, unheeded, was rolled by a gentle wind and then lay still, with a coating of dust, as in humiliation for the lie that it bore. A moment later the civilian, still looking unmoved into the barrel of the pistol, said:

"Yes, I am Dramer Brune, a Confederate spy, and your prisoner. I have on my person, as you will soon discover, a plan of your fort and its armament, a statement of the distribution of your men and their number, a map of the approaches, showing the positions of all your outposts. My life is fairly yours, but if you wish it taken in a more formal way than by your own hand, and if you are willing to spare me the indignity of marching into camp at the muzzle of your pistol, I promise you that I will neither resist, escape, nor remonstrate, but will submit to whatever penalty may be imposed."

The officer lowered his pistol, uncocked it, and thrust it into its place in his belt. Brune advanced a step, extending his right hand.

"It is the hand of a traitor and a spy," said the officer coldly, and did not take it. The other bowed.

"Come," said the captain, "let us go to camp; you shall not die until to-morrow morning."

He turned his back upon his prisoner, and

these two enigmatical men retraced their
steps and soon passed the sentinel, who expressed his general sense of things by a needless and exaggerated salute to his commander.

IV

Early on the morning after these events the
two men, captor and captive, sat in the tent
of the former. A table was between them on
which lay, among a number of letters, official
and private, which the captain had written
during the night, the incriminating papers
found upon the spy. That gentleman had
slept through the night in an adjoining tent,
unguarded. Both, having breakfasted, were
now smoking.

"Mr. Brune," said Captain Hartroy, "you
probably do not understand why I recognized
you in your disguise, nor how I was aware of
your name."

"I have not sought to learn, Captain," the
prisoner said with quiet dignity.

"Nevertheless I should like you to know—
if the story will not offend. You will perceive
that my knowledge of you goes back to the
autumn of 1861. At that time you were a
private in an Ohio regiment—a brave and
trusted soldier. To the surprise and grief of

your officers and comrades you deserted and went over to the énemy. Soon afterward you were captured in a skirmish, recognized, tried by court-martial and sentenced to be shot. Awaiting the execution of the sentence you were confined, unfettered, in a freight car standing on a side track of a railway."

"At Grafton, Virginia," said Brune, pushing the ashes from his cigar with the little finger of the hand holding it, and without looking up.

"At Grafton, Virginia," the captain repeated. "One dark and stormy night a soldier who had just returned from a long, fatiguing march was put on guard over you. He sat on a cracker box inside the car, near the door, his rifle loaded and the bayonet fixed. You sat in a corner and his orders were to kill you if you attempted to rise."

"But if I *asked* to rise he might call the corporal of the guard."

"Yes. As the long silent hours wore away the soldier yielded to the demands of nature: he himself incurred the death penalty by sleeping at his post of duty."

"You did."

"What! you recognize me? you have known me all along?"

The captain had risen and was walking the floor of his tent, visibly excited. His face was flushed, the gray eyes had lost the cold, pitiless look which they had shown when Brune had seen them over the pistol barrel; they had softened wonderfully.

"I knew you," said the spy, with his customary tranquillity, "the moment you faced me, demanding my surrender. In the circumstances it would have been hardly becoming in me to recall these matters. I am perhaps a traitor, certainly a spy; but I should not wish to seem a suppliant."

The captain had paused in his walk and was facing his prisoner. There was a singular huskiness in his voice as he spoke again.

"Mr. Brune, whatever your conscience may permit you to be, you saved my life at what you must have believed the cost of your own. Until I saw you yesterday when halted by my sentinel I believed you dead—thought that you had suffered the fate which through my own crime you might easily have escaped. You had only to step from the car and leave me to take your place before the firing-squad. You had a divine compassion. You pitied my fatigue. You let me sleep, watched over me, and as the time drew near for the relief-guard to come and detect me in my crime, you gently waked me. Ah, Brune, Brune, that was well done—that was great—that——"

The captain's voice failed him; the tears were running down his face and sparkled upon his beard and his breast. Resuming his seat at the table, he buried his face in his arms and sobbed. All else was silence.

Suddenly the clear warble of a bugle was heard sounding the "assembly." The captain started and raised his wet face from his arms; it had turned ghastly pale. Outside, in the sunlight, were heard the stir of the men falling into line; the voices of the sergeants calling the roll; the tapping of the drummers as they braced their drums. The captain spoke again:

"I ought to have confessed my fault in order to relate the story of your magnanimity; it might have procured you a pardon. A hundred times I resolved to do so, but shame prevented. Besides, your sentence was just and righteous. Well, Heaven forgive me! I said nothing, and my regiment was soon afterward ordered to Tennessee and I never heard about you."

"It was all right, sir," said Brune, without visible emotion; "I escaped and returned to

my colors—the Confederate colors. I should
like to add that before deserting from the Federal service I had earnestly asked a discharge,
on the ground of altered convictions. I was
answered by punishment."

"Ah, but if I had suffered the penalty of
my crime—if you had not generously given
me the life that I accepted without gratitude
you would not be again in the shadow and
imminence of death."

The prisoner started slightly and a look of
anxiety came into his face. One would
have said, too, that he was surprised. At
that moment a lieutenant, the adjutant, appeared at the opening of the tent and saluted.
"Captain," he said, "the battalion is
formed."

Captain Hartroy had recovered his composure. He turned to the officer and said:
"Lieutenant, go to Captain Graham and say
that I direct him to assume command of the
battalion and parade it outside the parapet.
This gentleman is a deserter and a spy; he is
to be shot to death in the presence of the
troops. He will accompany you, unbound and
unguarded."

While the adjutant waited at the door the
two men inside the tent rose and exchanged

ceremonious bows, Brune immediately retiring.

Half an hour later an old negro cook, the only person left in camp except the commander, was so startled by the sound of a volley of musketry that he dropped the kettle that he was lifting from a fire. But for his consternation and the hissing which the contents of the kettle made among the embers, he might also have heard, nearer at hand, the single pistol shot with which Captain Hartroy renounced the life which in conscience he could no longer keep.

In compliance with the terms of a note that he left for the officer who succeeded him in command, he was buried, like the deserter and spy, without military honors; and in the solemn shadow of the mountain which knows no more of war the two sleep well in long-forgotten graves.

ONE KIND OF OFFICER

I

OF THE USES OF CIVILITY

CAPTAIN RANSOME, it is not permitted to you to know *anything*. It is sufficient that you obey my order—which permit me to repeat. If you perceive any movement of troops in your front you are to open fire, and if attacked hold this position as long as you can. Do I make myself understood, sir?"

"Nothing could be plainer. Lieutenant Price,"—this to an officer of his own battery, who had ridden up in time to hear the order —"the general's meaning is clear, is it not?"

"Perfectly."

The lieutenant passed on to his post. For a moment General Cameron and the commander of the battery sat in their saddles, looking at each other in silence. There was no more to say; apparently too much had already been said. Then the superior officer nodded coldly and turned his horse to ride away. The artillerist saluted slowly, gravely, and with extreme formality. One acquainted with the niceties of military etiquette would have said that by his manner he attested a sense of the rebuke that he had incurred. It is one of the important uses of civility to signify resentment.

When the general had joined his staff and escort, awaiting him at a little distance, the whole cavalcade moved off toward the right of the guns and vanished in the fog. Captain Ransome was alone, silent, motionless as an equestrian statue. The gray fog, thickening every moment, closed in about him like a visible doom.

II

UNDER WHAT CIRCUMSTANCES MEN DO NOT WISH TO BE SHOT

The fighting of the day before had been desultory and indecisive. At the points of collision the smoke of battle had hung in blue sheets among the branches of the trees till beaten into nothing by the falling rain. In the softened earth the wheels of cannon and ammunition wagons cut deep, ragged furrows, and movements of infantry seemed impeded by the mud that clung to the soldiers' feet as,

with soaken garments and rifles imperfectly
protected by capes of overcoats they went
dragging in sinuous lines hither and thither
through dripping forest and flooded field.
Mounted officers, their heads protruding from
rubber ponchos that glittered like black
armor, picked their way, singly and in loose
groups, among the men, coming and going
with apparent aimlessness and commanding
attention from nobody but one another. Here
and there a dead man, his clothing defiled
with earth, his face covered with a blanket or
showing yellow and claylike in the rain, added
his dispiriting influence to that of the other
dismal features of the scene and augmented
the general discomfort with a particular dejection. Very repulsive these wrecks looked
—not at all heroic, and nobody was accessible
to the infection of their patriotic example.
Dead upon the field of honor, yes; but the
field of honor was so very wet! It makes a
difference.

The general engagement that all expected
did not occur, none of the small advantages
accruing, now to this side and now to that, in
isolated and accidental collisions being followed up. Half-hearted attacks provoked a
sullen resistance which was satisfied with mere

repulse.   Orders were obeyed with mechanical fidelity; no one did any more than his duty.

"The army is cowardly to-day," said General Cameron, the commander of a Federal brigade, to his adjutant-general.

"The army is cold," replied the officer addressed, "and—yes, it doesn't wish to be like that."

He pointed to one of the dead bodies, lying in a thin pool of yellow water, its face and clothing bespattered with mud from hoof and wheel.

The army's weapons seemed to share its military delinquency. The rattle of rifles sounded flat and contemptible. It had no meaning and scarcely roused to attention and expectancy the unengaged parts of the line-of-battle and the waiting reserves. Heard at a little distance, the reports of cannon were feeble in volume and *timbre:* they lacked sting and resonance. The guns seemed to be fired with light charges, unshotted. And so the futile day wore on to its dreary close, and then to a night of discomfort succeeded a day of apprehension.

An army has a personality. Beneath the individual thoughts and emotions of its component parts it thinks and feels as a unit. And in this large, inclusive sense of things lies a wiser wisdom than the mere sum of all that it knows. On that dismal morning this great brute force, groping at the bottom of a white ocean of fog among trees that seemed as sea weeds, had a dumb consciousness that all was not well; that a day's manœuvring had resulted in a faulty disposition of its parts, a blind diffusion of its strength. The men felt insecure and talked among themselves of such tactical errors as with their meager military vocabulary they were able to name. Field and line officers gathered in groups and spoke more learnedly of what they apprehended with no greater clearness. Commanders of brigades and divisions looked anxiously to their connections on the right and on the left, sent staff officers on errands of inquiry and pushed skirmish lines silently and cautiously forward into the dubious region between the known and the unknown. At some points on the line the troops, apparently of their own volition, constructed such defenses as they could without the silent spade and the noisy ax.

One of these points was held by Captain Ransome's battery of six guns. Provided always with intrenching tools, his men had labored with diligence during the night, and now his guns thrust their black muzzles through the embrasures of a really formidable earthwork. It crowned a slight acclivity devoid of undergrowth and providing an unobstructed fire that would sweep the ground for an unknown distance in front. The position could hardly have been better chosen. It had this peculiarity, which Captain Ransome, who was greatly addicted to the use of the compass, had not failed to observe: it faced northward, whereas he knew that the general line of the army must face eastward. In fact, that part of the line was " refused "— that is to say, bent backward, away from the enemy. This implied that Captain Ransome's battery was somewhere near the left flank of the army; for an army in line of battle retires its flanks if the nature of the ground will permit, they being its vulnerable points. Actually, Captain Ransome appeared to hold the extreme left of the line, no troops being visible in that direction beyond his own. Immediately in rear of his guns occurred that conversation between him and his brigade commander, the concluding and more picturesque part of which is reported above.

III

HOW TO PLAY THE CANNON WITHOUT NOTES

Captain Ransome sat motionless and silent on horseback. A few yards away his men were standing at their guns. Somewhere— everywhere within a few miles—were a hundred thousand men, friends and enemies. Yet he was alone. The mist had isolated him as completely as if he had been in the heart of a desert. His world was a few square yards of wet and trampled earth about the feet of his horse. His comrades in that ghostly domain were invisible and inaudible. These were conditions favorable to thought, and he was thinking. Of the nature of his thoughts his clear-cut handsome features yielded no attesting sign. His face was as inscrutable as that of the sphinx. Why should it have made a record which there was none to observe? At the sound of a footstep he merely turned his eyes in the direction whence it came; one of his sergeants, looking a giant in stature in the false perspective of the fog, approached, and when clearly defined and reduced to his true dimensions by propinquity, saluted and stood at attention.

"Well, Morris," said the officer, returning his subordinate's salute.

"Lieutenant Price directed me to tell you, sir, that most of the infantry has been withdrawn. We have not sufficient support."

"Yes, I know."

"I am to say that some of our men have been out over the works a hundred yards and report that our front is not picketed."

"Yes."

"They were so far forward that they heard the enemy."

"Yes."

"They heard the rattle of the wheels of artillery and the commands of officers."

"Yes."

"The enemy is moving toward our works."

Captain Ransome, who had been facing to the rear of his line—toward the point where the brigade commander and his cavalcade had been swallowed up by the fog—reined his horse about and faced the other way. Then he sat motionless as before.

"Who are the men who made that statement?" he inquired, without looking at the sergeant; his eyes were directed straight into the fog over the head of his horse.

"Corporal Hassman and Gunner Manning."

Captain Ransome was a moment silent. A slight pallor came into his face, a slight compression affected the lines of his lips, but it would have required a closer observer than Sergeant Morris to note the change. There was none in the voice.

"Sergeant, present my compliments to Lieutenant Price and direct him to open fire with all the guns. Grape."

The sergeant saluted and vanished in the fog.

IV

TO INTRODUCE GENERAL MASTERSON

Searching for his division commander, General Cameron and his escort had followed the line of battle for nearly a mile to the right of Ransome's battery, and there learned that the division commander had gone in search of the corps commander. It seemed that everybody was looking for his immediate superior — an ominous circumstance. It meant that nobody was quite at ease. So General Cameron rode on for another half-mile, where by good luck he met General Masterson, the division commander, returning.

"Ah, Cameron," said the higher officer, reining up, and throwing his right leg across

the pommel of his saddle in a most unmilitary
way—"anything up? Found a good position
for your battery, I hope—if one place is better
than another in a fog."

"Yes, general," said the other, with the
greater dignity appropriate to his less exalted
rank, "my battery is very well placed. I wish
I could say that it is as well commanded."

"Eh, what's that? Ransome? I think him
a fine fellow. In the army we should be
proud of him."

It was customary for officers of the regular
army to speak of it as "the army." As the
greatest cities are most provincial, so the self-
complacency of aristocracies is most frankly
plebeian.

"He is too fond of his opinion. By the
way, in order to occupy the hill that he holds
I had to extend my line dangerously. The
hill is on my left—that is to say the left flank
of the army."

"Oh, no, Hart's brigade is beyond. It was
ordered up from Drytown during the night
and directed to hook on to you. Better go
and——"

The sentence was unfinished: a lively cannonade had broken out on the left, and both
officers, followed by their retinues of aides and
orderlies making a great jingle and clank,

rode rapidly toward the spot. But they were soon impeded, for they were compelled by the fog to keep within sight of the line-of-battle, behind which were swarms of men, all in motion across their way. Everywhere the line was assuming a sharper and harder definition, as the men sprang to arms and the officers, with drawn swords, "dressed" the ranks. Color-bearers unfurled the flags, buglers blew the "assembly," hospital attendants appeared with stretchers. Field officers mounted and sent their impedimenta to the rear in care of negro servants. Back in the ghostly spaces of the forest could be heard the rustle and murmur of the reserves, pulling themselves together.

Nor was all this preparation vain, for scarcely five minutes had passed since Captain Ransome's guns had broken the truce of doubt before the whole region was aroar: the enemy had attacked nearly everywhere.

V

HOW SOUNDS CAN FIGHT SHADOWS

Captain Ransome walked up and down behind his guns, which were firing rapidly but with steadiness. The gunners worked alertly, but without haste or apparent excitement. There was really no reason for excitement; it is not much to point a cannon into a fog and fire it. Anybody can do as much as that.

The men smiled at their noisy work, performing it with a lessening alacrity. They cast curious regards upon their captain, who had now mounted the banquette of the fortification and was looking across the parapet as if observing the effect of his fire. But the only visible effect was the substitution of wide, low-lying sheets of smoke for their bulk of fog. Suddenly out of the obscurity burst a great sound of cheering, which filled the intervals between the reports of the guns with startling distinctness! To the few with leisure and opportunity to observe, the sound was inexpressibly strange—so loud, so near, so menacing, yet nothing seen! The men who had smiled at their work smiled no more, but performed it with a serious and feverish activity.

From his station at the parapet Captain Ransome now saw a great multitude of dim gray figures taking shape in the mist below him and swarming up the slope. But the work of the guns was now fast and furious. They swept the populous declivity with gusts of grape and canister, the whirring of which could be heard through the thunder of the explosions. In this awful tempest of iron the assailants struggled forward foot by foot across their dead, firing into the embrasures, reloading, firing again, and at last falling in their turn, a little in advance of those who had fallen before. Soon the smoke was dense enough to cover all. It settled down upon the attack and, drifting back, involved the defense. The gunners could hardly see to serve their pieces, and when occasional figures of the enemy appeared upon the parapet—having had the good luck to get near enough to it, between two embrasures, to be protected from the guns—they looked so unsubstantial that it seemed hardly worth while for the few infantrymen to go to work upon them with the bayonet and tumble them back into the ditch.

As the commander of a battery in action can find something better to do than cracking individual skulls, Captain Ransome had retired from the parapet to his proper post in rear of his guns, where he stood with folded arms, his bugler beside him. Here, during the hottest of the fight, he was approached by Lieutenant Price, who had just sabred a daring assailant inside the work. A spirited colloquy ensued between the two officers—spirited, at least, on the part of the lieutenant, who gesticulated with energy and shouted again and again into his commander's ear in the attempt to make himself heard above the infernal din of the guns. His gestures, if coolly noted by an actor, would have been pronounced to be those of protestation: one would have said that he was opposed to the proceedings. Did he wish to surrender?

Captain Ransome listened without a change of countenance or attitude, and when the other man had finished his harangue, looked him coldly in the eyes and during a seasonable abatement of the uproar said:

"Lieutenant Price, it is not permitted to you to know *anything*. It is sufficient that you obey my orders."

The lieutenant went to his post, and the parapet being now apparently clear Captain Ransome returned to it to have a look over. As he mounted the banquette a man sprang upon the crest, waving a great brilliant flag. The captain drew a pistol from his belt and shot him dead. The body, pitching forward, hung over the inner edge of the embankment, the arms straight downward, both hands still grasping the flag. The man's few followers turned and fled down the slope. Looking over the parapet, the captain saw no living thing. He observed also that no bullets were coming into the work.

He made a sign to the bugler, who sounded the command to cease firing. At all other points the action had already ended with a repulse of the Confederate attack; with the cessation of this cannonade the silence was absolute.

VI

WHY, BEING AFFRONTED BY A, IT IS NOT BEST TO AFFRONT B

General Masterson rode into the redoubt. The men, gathered in groups, were talking loudly and gesticulating. They pointed at the dead, running from one body to another. They neglected their foul and heated guns and forgot to resume their outer clothing. They ran to the parapet and looked over, some of them leaping down into the ditch. A score were gathered about a flag rigidly held by a dead man.

"Well, my men," said the general cheerily, "you have had a pretty fight of it."

They stared; nobody replied; the presence

of the great man seemed to embarrass and alarm.

Getting no response to his pleasant condescension, the easy-mannered officer whistled a bar or two of a popular air, and riding forward to the parapet, looked over at the dead. In an instant he had whirled his horse about and was spurring along in rear of the guns, his eyes everywhere at once. An officer sat on the trail of one of the guns, smoking a cigar. As the general dashed up he rose and tranquilly saluted.

"Captain Ransome!"—the words fell sharp and harsh, like the clash of steel blades —"you have been fighting our own men—our own men, sir; do you hear? Hart's brigade!"

"General, I know that."

"You know it—you know that, and you sit here smoking? Oh, damn it, Hamilton, I'm losing my temper,"—this to his provost-marshal. "Sir—Captain Ransome, be good enough to say—to say why you fought our own men."

"That I am unable to say. In my orders that information was withheld."

Apparently the general did not comprehend.

"Who was the aggressor in this affair, you or General Hart?" he asked.

"I was."

"And could you not have known—could you not see, sir, that you were attacking our own men?"

The reply was astounding!

"I knew that, general. It appeared to be none of my business."

Then, breaking the dead silence that followed his answer, he said:

"I must refer you to General Cameron."

"General Cameron is dead, sir—as dead as he can be—as dead as any man in this army. He lies back yonder under a tree. Do you mean to say that he had anything to do with this horrible business?"

Captain Ransome did not reply. Observing the altercation his men had gathered about to watch the outcome. They were greatly excited. The fog, which had been partly dissipated by the firing, had again closed in so darkly about them that they drew more closely together till the judge on horseback and the accused standing calmly before him had but a narrow space free from intrusion. It was the most informal of courts-martial, but all felt that the formal one to follow would but affirm its judgment. It had no jurisdiction, but it had the significance of prophecy.

"Captain Ransome," the general cried impetuously, but with something in his voice that was almost entreaty, "if you can say anything to put a better light upon your incomprehensible conduct I beg you will do so."

Having recovered his temper this generous soldier sought for something to justify his naturally sympathetic attitude toward a brave man in the imminence of a dishonorable death.

"Where is Lieutenant Price?" the captain said.

That officer stood forward, his dark saturnine face looking somewhat forbidding under a bloody handkerchief bound about his brow. He understood the summons and needed no invitation to speak. He did not look at the captain, but addressed the general:

"During the engagement I discovered the state of affairs, and apprised the commander of the battery. I ventured to urge that the firing cease. I was insulted and ordered to my post."

"Do you know anything of the orders under which I was acting?" asked the captain.

"Of any orders under which the commander of the battery was acting," the lieutenant continued, still addressing the general, " I know nothing."

Captain Ransome felt his world sink away from his feet. In those cruel words he heard the murmur of the centuries breaking upon the shore of eternity. He heard the voice of doom; it said, in cold, mechanical, and measured tones: "Ready, aim, fire!" and he felt the bullets tear his heart to shreds. He heard the sound of the earth upon his coffin and (if the good God was so merciful) the song of a bird above his forgotten grave. Quietly detaching his sabre from its supports, he handed it up to the provost-marshal.

ONE OFFICER, ONE MAN

CAPTAIN GRAFFENREID stood at the head of his company. The regiment was not engaged. It formed a part of the front line-of-battle, which stretched away to the right with a visible length of nearly two miles through the open ground. The left flank was veiled by woods; to the right also the line was lost to sight, but it extended many miles. A hundred yards in rear was a second line; behind this, the reserve brigades and divisions in column. Batteries of artillery occupied the spaces between and crowned the low hills. Groups of horsemen—generals with their staffs and escorts, and field officers of regiments behind the colors—broke the regularity of the lines and columns. Numbers of these figures of interest had field-glasses at their eyes and sat motionless, stolidly scanning the country in front; others came and went at a slow canter, bearing orders. There were squads of stretcher-bearers, ambulances, wagon-trains with ammunition, and officers' servants in rear of all—of all that was visible—for still in rear of these, along the roads, extended for many miles all that vast multitude of non-combatants who with their various *impedimenta* are assigned to the inglorious but important duty of supplying the fighters' many needs.

An army in line-of-battle awaiting attack, or prepared to deliver it, presents strange contrasts. At the front are precision, formality, fixity, and silence. Toward the rear these characteristics are less and less conspicuous, and finally, in point of space, are lost altogether in confusion, motion and noise. The homogeneous becomes heterogeneous. Definition is lacking; repose is replaced by an apparently purposeless activity; harmony vanishes in hubbub, form in disorder. Commotion everywhere and ceaseless unrest. The men who do not fight are never ready.

From his position at the right of his company in the front rank, Captain Graffenreid had an unobstructed outlook toward the enemy. A half-mile of open and nearly level ground lay before him, and beyond it an irregular wood, covering a slight acclivity; not a human being anywhere visible. He could imagine nothing more peaceful than the appearance of that pleasant landscape with its long stretches of brown fields over which the atmosphere was beginning to quiver in the heat of the morning sun. Not a sound came from forest or field—not even the barking of a dog or the crowing of a cock at the half-seen plantation house on the crest among the trees. Yet every man in those miles of men knew that he and death were face to face.

Captain Graffenreid had never in his life seen an armed enemy, and the war in which his regiment was one of the first to take the field was two years old. He had had the rare advantage of a military education, and when his comrades had marched to the front he had been detached for administrative service at the capital of his State, where it was thought that he could be most useful. Like a bad soldier he protested, and like a good one obeyed. In close official and personal relations with the governor of his State, and enjoying his confidence and favor, he had firmly refused promotion and seen his juniors elevated above him. Death had been busy in his distant regiment; vacancies among the field officers had occurred again and again; but from a chivalrous feeling that war's rewards belonged of right to those who bore the storm and stress of battle he had held his humble rank and generously advanced the fortunes of others. His silent devotion to principle had conquered at last: he had been relieved of his hateful duties and ordered to the front, and now, untried by fire, stood in the van of battle in command of a company of hardy veterans, to whom he had been only a name, and that name a by-word. By none —not even by those of his brother officers in whose favor he had waived his rights—was his devotion to duty understood. They were too busy to be just; he was looked upon as one who had shirked his duty, until forced unwillingly into the field. Too proud to explain, yet not too insensible to feel, he could only endure and hope.

Of all the Federal Army on that summer morning none had accepted battle more joyously than Anderton Graffenreid. His spirit was buoyant, his faculties were riotous. He was in a state of mental exaltation and scarcely could endure the enemy's tardiness in advancing to the attack. To him this was opportunity—for the result he cared nothing. Victory or defeat, as God might will; in one or in the other he should prove himself a soldier and a hero; he should vindicate his right to the respect of his men and the companionship of his brother officers—to the consideration of his superiors. How his heart leaped in his breast as the bugle sounded the stirring notes of the " assembly"! With what a light tread, scarcely conscious of the earth beneath his feet, he strode forward at the head of his company, and how exultingly he noted the tactical dispositions which placed his regiment in the front line! And if perchance some memory came to him of a pair of dark eyes that might take on a tenderer light in reading the account of that day's doings, who shall blame him for the unmartial thought or count it a debasement of soldierly ardor?

Suddenly, from the forest a half-mile in front—apparently from among the upper branches of the trees, but really from the ridge beyond—rose a tall column of white smoke. A moment later came a deep, jarring explosion, followed—almost attended—by a hideous rushing sound that seemed to leap forward across the intervening space with inconceivable rapidity, rising from whisper to roar with too quick a gradation for attention to note the successive stages of its horrible progression! A visible tremor ran along the lines of men; all were startled into motion. Captain Graffenreid dodged and threw up his hands to one side of his head, palms outward.

As he did so he heard a keen, ringing report, and saw on a hillside behind the line a fierce roll of smoke and dust—the shell's explosion. It had passed a hundred feet to his left! He heard, or fancied he heard, a low, mocking laugh and turning in the direction whence it came saw the eyes of his first lieutenant fixed upon him with an unmistakable look of amusement. He looked along the line of faces in the front ranks. The men were laughing. At him? The thought restored the color to his bloodless face—restored too much of it. His cheeks burned with a fever of shame.

The enemy's shot was not answered: the officer in command at that exposed part of the line had evidently no desire to provoke a cannonade. For the forbearance Captain Graffenreid was conscious of a sense of gratitude. He had not known that the flight of a projectile was a phenomenon of so appalling character. His conception of war had already undergone a profound change, and he was conscious that his new feeling was manifesting itself in visible perturbation. His blood was boiling in his veins; he had a choking sensation and felt that if he had a command to give it would be inaudible, or at least unintelligible. The hand in which he held his sword trembled; the other moved automatically, clutching at various parts of his clothing. He found a difficulty in standing still and fancied that his men observed it. Was it fear? He feared it was.

From somewhere away to the right came, as the wind served, a low, intermittent murmur like that of ocean in a storm—like that of a distant railway train—like that of wind among the pines—three sounds so nearly alike that the ear, unaided by the judgment, cannot distinguish them one from another. The eyes of the troops were drawn in that direction; the mounted officers turned their field-glasses that way. Mingled with the sound was an irregular throbbing. He thought it, at first, the beating of his fevered blood in his ears; next, the distant tapping of a bass drum.

"The ball is opened on the right flank," said an officer.

Captain Graffenreid understood: the sounds were musketry and artillery. He nodded and tried to smile. There was apparently nothing infectious in the smile.

Presently a light line of blue smoke-puffs broke out along the edge of the wood in front, succeeded by a crackle of rifles. There were keen, sharp hissings in the air, terminating abruptly with a thump near by. The man at Captain Graffenreid's side dropped his rifle; his knees gave way and he pitched awkwardly forward, falling upon his face. Somebody shouted "Lie down!" and the dead man was hardly distinguishable from the living. It looked as if those few rifle-shots had slain ten thousand men. Only the field officers remained erect; their concession to the emergency consisted in dismounting and sending their horses to the shelter of the low hills immediately in rear.

Captain Graffenreid lay alongside the dead man, from beneath whose breast flowed a little rill of blood. It had a faint, sweetish odor that sickened him. The face was crushed into the earth and flattened. It looked yellow already, and was repulsive. Nothing suggested the glory of a soldier's death nor mitigated the loathsomeness of the incident. He could not turn his back upon the body without facing away from his company.

He fixed his eyes upon the forest, where all again was silent. He tried to imagine what was going on there—the lines of troops forming to attack, the guns being pushed forward by hand to the edge of the open. He fancied he could see their black muzzles protruding from the undergrowth, ready to deliver their storm of missiles—such missiles as the one whose shriek had so unsettled his nerves. The distension of his eyes became painful; a mist seemed to gather before them; he could no longer see across the field, yet would not withdraw his gaze lest he see the dead man at his side.

The fire of battle was not now burning very brightly in this warrior's soul. From inaction had come introspection. He sought rather to analyze his feelings than distinguish himself by courage and devotion. The result was profoundly disappointing. He covered his face with his hands and groaned aloud.

The hoarse murmur of battle grew more and more distinct upon the right; the murmur had, indeed, become a roar, the throbbing, a thunder. The sounds had worked round obliquely to the front; evidently the enemy's left was being driven back, and the propitious moment to move against the salient angle of his line would soon arrive. The silence and mystery in front were ominous; all felt that they boded evil to the assailants.

Behind the prostrate lines sounded the hoof-

beats of galloping horses; the men turned to
look. A dozen staff officers were riding to
the various brigade and regimental commanders, who had remounted. A moment
more and there was a chorus of voices, all uttering out of time the same words—"Attention, battalion!" The men sprang to their
feet and were aligned by the company commanders. They awaited the word "forward"—awaited, too, with beating hearts and
set teeth the gusts of lead and iron that were
to smite them at their first movement in obedience to that word. The word was not given;
the tempest did not break out. The delay was
hideous, maddening! It unnerved like a
respite at the guillotine.

Captain Graffenreid stood at the head of
his company, the dead man at his feet. He
heard the battle on the right—rattle and crash
of musketry, ceaseless thunder of cannon,
desultory cheers of invisible combatants. He
marked ascending clouds of smoke from distant forests. He noted the sinister silence of
the forest in front. These contrasting ex-
tremes affected the whole range of his sensibilities. The strain upon his nervous organ-
ization was insupportable. He grew hot and
cold by turns. He panted like a dog, and

then forgot to breathe until reminded by vertigo.

Suddenly he grew calm. Glancing downward, his eyes had fallen upon his naked sword, as he held it, point to earth. Foreshortened to his view, it resembled somewhat, he thought, the short heavy blade of the ancient Roman. The fancy was full of suggestion, malign, fateful, heroic!

The sergeant in the rear rank, immediately behind Captain Graffenreid, now observed a strange sight. His attention drawn by an uncommon movement made by the captain—a sudden reaching forward of the hands and their energetic withdrawal, throwing the elbows out, as in pulling an oar—he saw spring from between the officer's shoulders a bright point of metal which prolonged itself outward, nearly a half-arm's length—a blade! It was faintly streaked with crimson, and its point approached so near to the sergeant's breast, and with so quick a movement, that he shrank backward in alarm. That moment Captain Graffenreid pitched heavily forward upon the dead man and died.

A week later the major-general commanding the left corps of the Federal Army submitted the following official report:

" SIR: I have the honor to report, with regard to the action of the 19th inst., that owing to the enemy's withdrawal from my front to reinforce his beaten left, my command was not seriously engaged. My loss was as follows: Killed, one officer, one man."

GEORGE THURSTON

THREE INCIDENTS IN THE LIFE OF A MAN

GEORGE THURSTON was a first lieutenant and aide-de-camp on the staff of Colonel Brough, commanding a Federal brigade. Colonel Brough was only temporarily in command, as senior colonel, the brigadier-general having been severely wounded and granted a leave of absence to recover. Lieutenant Thurston was, I believe, of Colonel Brough's regiment, to which, with his chief, he would naturally have been relegated had he lived till our brigade commander's recovery. The aide whose place Thurston took had been killed in battle; Thurston's advent among us was the only change in the *personnel* of our staff consequent upon the change in commanders. We did not like him; he was unsocial. This, however, was more observed by others than by me. Whether in camp or on the march, in barracks, in tents, or *en bivouac,* my duties as topographical engineer kept me working like a beaver—all day in the saddle and half the night at my drawing-table, platting my surveys. It was hazardous work; the nearer to the enemy's lines I could penetrate, the more valuable were my field notes and the resulting maps. It was a business in which the lives of men counted as nothing against the chance of defining a road or sketching a bridge. Whole squadrons of cavalry escort had sometimes to be sent thundering against a powerful infantry outpost in order that the brief time between the charge and the inevitable retreat might be utilized in sounding a ford or determining the point of intersection of two roads.

In some of the dark corners of England and Wales they have an immemorial custom of "beating the bounds" of the parish. On a certain day of the year the whole population turns out and travels in procession from one landmark to another on the boundary line. At the most important points lads are soundly beaten with rods to make them remember the place in after life. They become authorities. Our frequent engagements with the Confederate outposts, patrols, and scouting parties had, incidentally, the same educating value; they fixed in my memory a vivid and apparently imperishable picture of the locality—a picture serving instead of accurate field notes, which, indeed, it was not always convenient to take, with carbines cracking, sabers clashing, and horses plunging all about. These spirited encounters were observations entered in red.

One morning as I set out at the head of my escort on an expedition of more than the usual hazard Lieutenant Thurston rode up alongside and asked if I had any objection to his accompanying me, the colonel commanding having given him permission.

"None whatever," I replied rather gruffly; "but in what capacity will you go? You are not a topographical engineer, and Captain Burling commands my escort."

"I will go as a spectator," he said. Removing his sword-belt and taking the pistols from his holsters he handed them to his servant, who took them back to headquarters. I realized the brutality of my remark, but not clearly seeing my way to an apology, said nothing.

That afternoon we encountered a whole regiment of the enemy's cavalry in line and a field-piece that dominated a straight mile of the turnpike by which we had approached. My escort fought deployed in the woods on both sides, but Thurston remained in the center of the road, which at intervals of a few seconds was swept by gusts of grape and canister that tore the air wide open as they passed. He had dropped the rein on the neck of his horse and sat bolt upright in the saddle, with folded arms. Soon he was down, his horse torn to pieces. From the side of the road, my pencil and field book idle, my duty forgotten, I watched him slowly disengaging himself from the wreck and rising. At that instant, the cannon having ceased firing, a burly Confederate trooper on a spirited horse dashed like a thunderbolt down the road with drawn saber. Thurston saw him coming, drew himself up to his full height, and again folded his arms. He was too brave to retreat before the word, and my uncivil words had disarmed him. He was a spectator. Another moment and he would have been split like a mackerel, but a blessed bullet tumbled his assailant into the dusty road so near that the impetus sent the body rolling to Thurston's feet. That evening, while platting my hasty survey, I found time to frame an apology, which I think took the rude, primitive form of a confession that I had spoken like a malicious idiot.

A few weeks later a part of our army made an assault upon the enemy's left. The attack, which was made upon an unknown position and across unfamiliar ground, was led by our brigade. The ground was so broken and the underbrush so thick that all mounted officers and men were compelled to fight on foot—the brigade commander and his staff included. In the *mêlée* Thurston was parted from the rest of us, and we found him, horribly wounded, only when we had taken the enemy's last defense. He was some months in hospital at Nashville, Tennessee, but finally rejoined us. He said little about his misadventure, except that he had been bewildered and had strayed into the enemy's lines and been shot down; but from one of his captors, whom we in turn had captured, we learned the particulars. "He came walking right upon us as we lay in line," said this man. "A whole company of us instantly sprang up and leveled our rifles at his breast, some of them almost touching him. 'Throw down that sword and surrender, you damned Yank!' shouted some one in authority. The fellow ran his eyes along the line of rifle barrels, folded his arms across his breast, his right hand still clutching his sword, and deliberately replied, 'I will not.' If we had

all fired he would have been torn to shreds.
Some of us didn't. I didn't, for one; nothing
could have induced me."

When one is tranquilly looking death in the
eye and refusing him any concession one
naturally has a good opinion of one's self. I
don't know if it was this feeling that in Thurston found expression in a stiffish attitude and
folded arms; at the mess table one day, in his
absence, another explanation was suggested by
our quartermaster, an irreclaimable stammerer when the wine was in: "It's h—is
w—ay of m-m-mastering a c-c-consti-t-tu-
tional t-tendency to r—un aw—ay."

"What!" I flamed out, indignantly rising;
"you intimate that Thurston is a coward—
and in his absence?"

"If he w—ere a cow—wow-ard h—e
w—wouldn't t-try to m-m-master it; and if he
w—ere p-present I w—wouldn't d-d-dare to
d-d-discuss it," was the mollifying reply.

This intrepid man, George Thurston, died
an ignoble death. The brigade was in camp,
with headquarters in a grove of immense trees.
To an upper branch of one of these a venturesome climber had attached the two ends of a
long rope and made a swing with a length of
not less than one hundred feet. Plunging

downward from a height of fifty feet, along
the arc of a circle with such a radius, soaring
to an equal altitude, pausing for one breathless instant, then sweeping dizzily backward
—no one who has not tried it can conceive the
terrors of such sport to the novice. Thurston
came out of his tent one day and asked for in-
struction in the mystery of propelling the
swing—the art of rising and sitting, which
every boy has mastered. In a few moments
he had acquired the trick and was swinging
higher than the most experienced of us had
dared. We shuddered to look at his fearful
flights.

" St-t-top him," said the quartermaster,
snailing lazily along from the mess-tent,
where he had been lunching; " h—e d-doesn't
know that if h—e g-g-goes c-clear over h—e'll
w—ind up the sw—ing."

With such energy was that strong man cannonading himself through the air that at each
extremity of his increasing arc his body,
standing in the swing, was almost horizontal.
Should he once pass above the level of the
rope's attachment he would be lost; the rope
would slacken and he would fall vertically to
a point as far below as he had gone above,
and then the sudden tension of the rope would

wrest it from his hands. All saw the peril—
all cried out to him to desist, and gesticulated
at him as, indistinct and with a noise like the
rush of a cannon shot in flight, he swept past
us through the lower reaches of his hideous
oscillation. A woman standing at a little distance away fainted and fell unobserved.
Men from the camp of a regiment near by ran
in crowds to see, all shouting. Suddenly, as
Thurston was on his upward curve, the shouts
all ceased.

Thurston and the swing had parted—that is
all that can be known; both hands at once
had released the rope. The impetus of the
light swing exhausted, it was falling back;
the man's momentum was carrying him, almost erect, upward and forward, no longer in
his arc, but with an outward curve. It could
have been but an instant, yet it seemed an age.
I cried out, or thought I cried out: "My
God! will he never stop going up?" He
passed close to the branch of a tree. I remember a feeling of delight as I thought he
would clutch it and save himself. I specu-
lated on the possibility of it sustaining his
weight. He passed above it, and from my
point of view was sharply outlined against the
blue. At this distance of many years I can

distinctly recall that image of a man in the sky, its head erect, its feet close together, its hands—I do not see its hands.   All at once, with astonishing suddenness and rapidity, it turns clear over and pitches downward. There is another cry from the crowd, which has rushed instinctively forward.   The man has become merely a whirling object, mostly legs.   Then there is an indescribable sound— the sound of an impact that shakes the earth, and these men, familiar with death in its most awful aspects, turn sick.   Many walk unsteadily away from the spot; others support themselves against the trunks of trees or sit at the roots.   Death has taken an unfair advantage; he has struck with an unfamiliar weapon; he has executed a new and disquieting stratagem.   We did not know that he had so ghastly resources, possibilities of terror so dismal.

Thurston's body lay on its back.   One leg, bent beneath, was broken above the knee and the bone driven into the earth.   The abdomen had burst; the bowels protruded.   The neck was broken.

The arms were folded tightly across the breast.

THE MOCKING-BIRD

THE time, a pleasant Sunday after-noon in the early autumn of 1861. The place, a forest's heart in the mountain region of southwestern Virginia. Private Grayrock of the Federal Army is discovered seated comfortably at the root of a great pine tree, against which he leans, his legs extended straight along the ground, his rifle lying across his thighs, his hands (clasped in order that they may not fall away to his sides) resting upon the barrel of the weapon. The contact of the back of his head with the tree has pushed his cap downward over his eyes, almost concealing them; one seeing him would say that he slept.

Private Grayrock did not sleep; to have done so would have imperiled the interests of the United States, for he was a long way outside the lines and subject to capture or death at the hands of the enemy. Moreover, he was in a frame of mind unfavorable to repose. The cause of his perturbation of spirit was this: during the previous night he had served on the picket-guard, and had been posted as a sentinel in this very forest. The night was clear, though moonless, but in the gloom of the wood the darkness was deep. Grayrock's post was at a considerable distance from those to right and left, for the pickets had been thrown out a needless distance from the camp, making the line too long for the force detailed to occupy it. The war was young, and military camps entertained the error that while sleeping they were better protected by thin lines a long way out toward the enemy than by thicker ones close in. And surely they needed as long notice as possible of an enemy's approach, for they were at that time addicted to the practice of undressing—than which nothing could be more unsoldierly. On the morning of the memorable 6th of April, at Shiloh, many of Grant's men when spitted on Confederate bayonets were as naked as civilians; but it should be allowed that this was not because of any defect in their picket line. Their error was of another sort: they had no pickets. This is perhaps a vain digression. I should not care to undertake to interest the reader in the fate of an army; what we have here to consider is that of Private Grayrock.

For two hours after he had been left at his

lonely post that Saturday night he stood stock-still, leaning against the trunk of a large tree, staring into the darkness in his front and trying to recognize known objects; for he had been posted at the same spot during the day. But all was now different; he saw nothing in detail, but only groups of things, whose shapes, not observed when there was something more of them to observe, were now unfamiliar. They seemed not to have been there before. A landscape that is all trees and undergrowth, moreover, lacks definition, is confused and without accentuated points upon which attention can gain a foothold. Add the gloom of a moonless night, and something more than great natural intelligence and a city education is required to preserve one's knowledge of direction. And that is how it occurred that Private Grayrock, after vigilantly watching the spaces in his front and then imprudently executing a circumspection of his whole dimly visible environment (silently walking around his tree to accomplish it) lost his bearings and seriously impaired his usefulness as a sentinel. Lost at his post—unable to say in which direction to look for an enemy's approach, and in which lay the sleeping camp for whose security he was account-

able with his life—conscious, too, of many
another awkward feature of the situation and
of considerations affecting his own safety,
Private Grayrock was profoundly disquieted.
Nor was he given time to recover his tranquillity, for almost at the moment that he
realized his awkward predicament he heard a
stir of leaves and a snap of fallen twigs, and
turning with a stilled heart in the direction
whence it came, saw in the gloom the indistinct outlines of a human figure.

"Halt!" shouted Private Grayrock, peremptorily as in duty bound, backing up the
command with the sharp metallic snap of his
cocking rifle—"who goes there?"

There was no answer; at least there was an
instant's hesitation, and the answer, if it came,
was lost in the report of the sentinel's rifle. In
the silence of the night and the forest the
sound was deafening, and hardly had it died
away when it was repeated by the pieces
of the pickets to right and left, a sympathetic fusillade. For two hours every un-
converted civilian of them had been evolving
enemies from his imagination, and peopling
the woods in his front with them, and Grayrock's shot had started the whole encroaching
host into visible existence. Having fired, all

retreated, breathless, to the reserves—all but Grayrock, who did not know in what direction to retreat. When, no enemy appearing, the roused camp two miles away had undressed and got itself into bed again, and the picket line was cautiously re-established, he was discovered bravely holding his ground, and was complimented by the officer of the guard as the one soldier of that devoted band who could rightly be considered the moral equivalent of that uncommon unit of value, "a whoop in hell."

In the mean time, however, Grayrock had made a close but unavailing search for the mortal part of the intruder at whom he had fired, and whom he had a marksman's intuitive sense of having hit; for he was one of those born experts who shoot without aim by an instinctive sense of direction, and are nearly as dangerous by night as by day. During a full half of his twenty-four years he had been a terror to the targets of all the shooting-galleries in three cities. Unable now to produce his dead game he had the discretion to hold his tongue, and was glad to observe in his officer and comrades the natural assumption that not having run away he had seen nothing hostile. His "honorable mention"

had been earned by not running away anyhow.

Nevertheless, Private Grayrock was far
from satisfied with the night's adventure, and
when the next day he made some fair enough
pretext to apply for a pass to go outside the
lines, and the general commanding promptly
granted it in recognition of his bravery the
night before, he passed out at the point where
that had been displayed. Telling the sentinel
then on duty there that he had lost something,
—which was true enough—he renewed the
search for the person whom he supposed
himself to have shot, and whom if only
wounded he hoped to trail by the blood.
He was no more successful by daylight than he had been in the darkness, and
after covering a wide area and boldly penetrating a long distance into "the Confederacy" he gave up the search, somewhat
fatigued, seated himself at the root of the
great pine tree, where we have seen him, and
indulged his disappointment.

It is not to be inferred that Grayrock's was
the chagrin of a cruel nature balked of its
bloody deed. In the clear large eyes, finely
wrought lips, and broad forehead of that
young man one could read quite another story,

and in point of fact his character was a singularly felicitous compound of boldness and sensibility, courage and conscience.

"I find myself disappointed," he said to himself, sitting there at the bottom of the golden haze submerging the forest like a subtler sea—"disappointed in failing to discover a fellow-man dead by my hand! Do I then really wish that I had taken life in the performance of a duty as well performed without? What more could I wish? If any danger threatened, my shot averted it; that is what I was there to do. No, I am glad indeed if no human life was needlessly extinguished by me. But I am in a false position. I have suffered myself to be complimented by my officers and envied by my comrades. The camp is ringing with praise of my courage. That is not just; I know myself courageous, but this praise is for specific acts which I did not perform, or performed—otherwise. It is believed that I remained at my post bravely, without firing, whereas it was I who began the fusillade, and I did not retreat in the general alarm because bewildered. What, then, shall I do? Explain that I saw an enemy and fired? They have all said that of themselves, yet none believes it. Shall I tell a truth

which, discrediting my courage, will have the
effect of a lie? Ugh! it is an ugly business
altogether. I wish to God I could find my
man!"

And so wishing, Private Grayrock, overcome at last by the languor of the afternoon
and lulled by the stilly sounds of insects droning and prosing in certain fragrant shrubs, so
far forgot the interests of the United States
as to fall asleep and expose himself to capture.
And sleeping he dreamed.

He thought himself a boy, living in a far,
fair land by the border of a great river upon
which the tall steamboats moved grandly up
and down beneath their towering evolutions
of black smoke, which announced them long
before they had rounded the bends and
marked their movements when miles out of
sight. With him always, at his side as he
watched them, was one to whom he gave his
heart and soul in love—a twin brother. Together they strolled along the banks of the
stream; together explored the fields lying
farther away from it, and gathered pungent
mints and sticks of fragrant sassafras in the
hills overlooking all—beyond which lay the
Realm of Conjecture, and from which, looking southward across the great river, they

caught glimpses of the Enchanted Land. Hand in hand and heart in heart they two, the only children of a widowed mother, walked in paths of light through valleys of peace, seeing new things under a new sun. And through all the golden days floated one unceasing sound—the rich, thrilling melody of a mocking-bird in a cage by the cottage door. It pervaded and possessed all the spiritual intervals of the dream, like a musical benediction. The joyous bird was always in song; its infinitely various notes seemed to flow from its throat, effortless, in bubbles and rills at each heart-beat, like the waters of a pulsing spring. That fresh, clear melody seemed, indeed, the spirit of the scene, the meaning and interpretation to sense of the mysteries of life and love.

But there came a time when the days of the dream grew dark with sorrow in a rain of tears. The good mother was dead, the meadowside home by the great river was broken up, and the brothers were parted between two of their kinsmen. William (the dreamer) went to live in a populous city in the Realm of Conjecture, and John, crossing the river into the Enchanted Land, was taken to a distant region whose people in their lives

and ways were said to be strange and wicked.
To him, in the distribution of the dead
mother's estate, had fallen all that they
deemed of value—the mocking-bird. They
could be divided, but it could not, so it
was carried away into the strange country,
and the world of William knew it no more
forever. Yet still through the aftertime of
his loneliness its song filled all the dream, and
seemed always sounding in his ear and in his
heart.

The kinsmen who had adopted the boys
were enemies, holding no communication.
For a time letters full of boyish bravado and
boastful narratives of the new and larger experience—grotesque descriptions of their
widening lives and the new worlds they had
conquered—passed between them; but these
gradually became less frequent, and with William's removal to another and greater city
ceased altogether. But ever through it all ran
the song of the mocking-bird, and when the
dreamer opened his eyes and stared through
the vistas of the pine forest the cessation of its
music first apprised him that he was awake.

The sun was low and red in the west; the
level rays projected from the trunk of each
giant pine a wall of shadow traversing the

golden haze to eastward until light and shade were blended in undistinguishable blue.

Private Grayrock rose to his feet, looked cautiously about him, shouldered his rifle and set off toward camp. He had gone perhaps a half-mile, and was passing a thicket of laurel, when a bird rose from the midst of it and perching on the branch of a tree above, poured from its joyous breast so inexhaustible floods of song as but one of all God's creatures can utter in His praise. There was little in that—it was only to open the bill and breathe; yet the man stopped as if struck—stopped and let fall his rifle, looked upward at the bird, covered his eyes with his hands and wept like a child! For the moment he was, indeed, a child, in spirit and in memory, dwelling again by the great river, over-against the Enchanted Land! Then with an effort of the will he pulled himself together, picked up his weapon and audibly damning himself for an idiot strode on. Passing an opening that reached into the heart of the little thicket he looked in, and there, supine upon the earth, its arms all abroad, its gray uniform stained with a single spot of blood upon the breast, its white face turned sharply upward and backward, lay the image of himself!—the body of John Grayrock, dead of a gunshot wound, and still warm! He had found his man.

As the unfortunate soldier knelt beside that masterwork of civil war the shrilling bird upon the bough overhead stilled her song and, flushed with sunset's crimson glory, glided silently away through the solemn spaces of the wood. At roll-call that evening in the Federal camp the name William Grayrock brought no response, nor ever again thereafter.

CIVILIANS

THE MAN OUT OF THE NOSE

A T the intersection of two certain streets in that part of San Francisco known by the rather loosely applied name of North Beach, is a vacant lot, which is rather more nearly level than is usually the case with lots, vacant or otherwise, in that region. Immediately at the back of it, to the south, however, the ground slopes steeply upward, the acclivity broken by three terraces cut into the soft rock. It is a place for goats and poor persons, several families of each class having occupied it jointly and amicably "from the foundation of the city." One of the humble habitations of the lowest terrace is noticeable for its rude resemblance to the human face, or rather to such a simulacrum of it as a boy might cut out of a hollowed pumpkin, meaning no offense to his race. The eyes are two circular windows, the nose is a door, the mouth an aperture caused by removal of a board below. There are no doorsteps. As a face, this house is too large; as a dwelling, too small. The blank, unmeaning stare of its lidless and browless eyes is uncanny.

Sometimes a man steps out of the nose, turns, passes the place where the right ear should be and making his way through the throng of children and goats obstructing the narrow walk between his neighbors' doors and the edge of the terrace gains the street by descending a flight of rickety stairs. Here he pauses to consult his watch and the stranger who happens to pass wonders why such a man as that can care what is the hour. Longer observations would show that the time of day is an important element in the man's movements, for it is at precisely two o'clock in the afternoon that he comes forth 365 times in every year.

Having satisfied himself that he has made no mistake in the hour he replaces the watch and walks rapidly southward up the street two squares, turns to the right and as he approaches the next corner fixes his eyes on an upper window in a three-story building across the way. This is a somewhat dingy structure, originally of red brick and now gray. It shows the touch of age and dust. Built for a dwelling, it is now a factory. I do not know what is made there; the things that are com-

monly made in a factory, I suppose. I only
know that at two o'clock in the afternoon of
every day but Sunday it is full of activity and
clatter; pulsations of some great engine shake
it and there are recurrent screams of wood tor-
mented by the saw. At the window on which
the man fixes an intensely expectant gaze nothing ever appears; the glass, in truth, has such
a coating of dust that it has long ceased to be
transparent. The man looks at it without
stopping; he merely keeps turning his head
more and more backward as he leaves the
building behind. Passing along to the next
corner, he turns to the left, goes round the
block, and comes back till he reaches the point
diagonally across the street from the factory—
a point on his former course, which he then
retraces, looking frequently backward over his
right shoulder at the window while it is in
sight. For many years he has not been known
to vary his route nor to introduce a single in-
novation into his action. In a quarter of an
hour he is again at the mouth of his dwelling,
and a woman, who has for some time been
standing in the nose, assists him to enter. He
is seen no more until two o'clock the next day.

The woman is his wife. She supports herself and him by washing for the poor people

among whom they live, at rates which destroy Chinese and domestic competition.

This man is about fifty-seven years of age, though he looks greatly older. His hair is dead white. He wears no beard, and is always newly shaven. His hands are clean, his nails well kept. In the matter of dress he is distinctly superior to his position, as indicated by his surroundings and the business of his wife. He is, indeed, very neatly, if not quite fashionably, clad. His silk hat has a date no earlier than the year before the last, and his boots, scrupulously polished, are innocent of patches. I am told that the suit which he wears during his daily excursions of fifteen minutes is not the one that he wears at home. Like everything else that he has, this is provided and kept in repair by the wife, and is renewed as frequently as her scanty means permit.

Thirty years ago John Hardshaw and his wife lived on Rincon Hill in one of the finest residences of that once aristocratic quarter. He had once been a physician, but having inherited a considerable estate from his father concerned himself no more about the ailments of his fellow-creatures and found as much work as he cared for in managing his own affairs. Both he and his wife were highly cultivated persons, and their house was frequented by a small set of such men and women as persons of their tastes would think worth knowing. So far as these knew, Mr. and Mrs. Hardshaw lived happily together; certainly the wife was devoted to her handsome and accomplished husband and exceedingly proud of him.

Among their acquaintances were the Barwells—man, wife and two young children—of Sacramento. Mr. Barwell was a civil and mining engineer, whose duties took him much from home and frequently to San Francisco. On these occasions his wife commonly accompanied him and passed much of her time at the house of her friend, Mrs. Hardshaw, always with her two children, of whom Mrs. Hardshaw, childless herself, grew fond. Unluckily, her husband grew equally fond of their mother—a good deal fonder. Still more unluckily, that attractive lady was less wise than weak.

At about three o'clock one autumn morning Officer No. 13 of the Sacramento police saw a man stealthily leaving the rear entrance of a gentleman's residence and promptly arrested him. The man—who wore a slouch hat and shaggy overcoat—offered the policeman one hundred, then five hundred, then one thousand dollars to be released. As he had less than the first mentioned sum on his person the officer treated his proposal with virtuous contempt. Before reaching the station the prisoner agreed to give him a check for ten thousand dollars and remain ironed in the willows along the river bank until it should be paid. As this only provoked new derision he would say no more, merely giving an obviously fictitious name. When he was searched at the station nothing of value was found on him but a miniature portrait of Mrs. Barwell—the lady of the house at which he was caught. The case was set with costly diamonds; and something in the quality of the man's linen sent a pang of unavailing regret through the severely incorruptible bosom of Officer No. 13. There was nothing about the prisoner's clothing nor person to identify him and he was booked for burglary under the name that he had given, the honorable name of John K. Smith. The K. was an inspiration upon which, doubtless, he greatly prided himself.

In the mean time the mysterious disappearance of John Hardshaw was agitating the gossips of Rincon Hill in San Francisco, and was even mentioned in one of the newspapers. It did not occur to the lady whom that journal considerately described as his "widow," to look for him in the city prison at Sacramento —a town which he was not known ever to have visited. As John K. Smith he was arraigned and, waiving examination, committed for trial.

About two weeks before the trial, Mrs. Hardshaw, accidentally learning that her husband was held in Sacramento under an assumed name on a charge of burglary, hastened to that city without daring to mention the matter to any one and presented herself at the prison, asking for an interview with her husband, John K. Smith. Haggard and ill with anxiety, wearing a plain traveling wrap which covered her from neck to foot, and in which she had passed the night on the steamboat, too anxious to sleep, she hardly showed for what she was, but her manner pleaded for her more strongly than anything that she chose to say in evidence of her right to admittance. She was permitted to see him alone.

What occurred during that distressing interview has never transpired; but later events

prove that Hardshaw had found means to subdue her will to his own. She left the prison,
a broken-hearted woman, refusing to answer
a single question, and returning to her desolate
home renewed, in a half-hearted way, her in-
quiries for her missing husband.   A week
later she was herself missing: she had "gone
back to the States"—nobody knew any more
than that.

On his trial the prisoner pleaded guilty—
"by advice of his counsel," so his counsel said.
Nevertheless, the judge, in whose mind several unusual circumstances had created a
doubt, insisted on the district attorney placing
Officer No. 13 on the stand, and the deposition of Mrs. Barwell, who was too ill to attend, was read to the jury. It was very brief:
she knew nothing of the matter except that the
likeness of herself was her property, and had,
she thought, been left on the parlor table
when she had retired on the night of the
arrest. She had intended it as a present to her
husband, then and still absent in Europe on
business for a mining company.

This witness's manner when making the
deposition at her residence was afterward described by the district attorney as most extraordinary. Twice she had refused to testify,
and once, when the deposition lacked noth-

ing but her signature, she had caught it from
the clerk's hands and torn it in pieces. She
had called her children to the bedside and
embraced them with streaming eyes, then suddenly sending them from the room, she veri-
fied her statement by oath and signature, and
fainted—"slick away," said the district attorney. It was at that time that her physician,
arriving upon the scene, took in the situation
at a glance and grasping the representative of
the law by the collar chucked him into the
street and kicked his assistant after him. The
insulted majesty of the law was not vindic-
ated; the victim of the indignity did not even
mention anything of all this in court. He was
ambitious to win his case, and the circumstances of the taking of that deposition were
not such as would give it weight if related;
and after all, the man on trial had committed
an offense against the law's majesty only
less heinous than that of the irascible physician.

By suggestion of the judge the jury rendered a verdict of guilty; there was nothing
else to do, and the prisoner was sentenced to
the penitentiary for three years. His counsel,
who had objected to nothing and had made
no plea for lenity—had, in fact, hardly said a
word—wrung his client's hand and left the

room. It was obvious to the whole bar that
he had been engaged only to prevent the court
from appointing counsel who might possibly
insist on making a defense.

John Hardshaw served out his term at San
Quentin, and when discharged was met at the
prison gates by his wife, who had returned
from "the States" to receive him. It is
thought they went straight to Europe; anyhow, a general power-of-attorney to a lawyer
still living among us—from whom I have
many of the facts of this simple history—was
executed in Paris. This lawyer in a short
time sold everything that Hardshaw owned in
California, and for years nothing was heard
of the unfortunate couple; though many to
whose ears had come vague and inaccurate
intimations of their strange story, and who
had known them, recalled their personality
with tenderness and their misfortunes with
compassion.

Some years later they returned, both broken
in fortune and spirits and he in health. The
purpose of their return I have not been able
to ascertain. For some time they lived, under
the name of Johnson, in a respectable enough
quarter south of Market Street, pretty well
out, and were never seen away from the vicin-

ity of their dwelling. They must have had a
little money left, for it is not known that the
man had any occupation, the state of his health
probably not permitting. The woman's devotion to her invalid husband was matter of remark among their neighbors; she seemed
never absent from his side and always supporting and cheering him. They would sit
for hours on one of the benches in a little public park, she reading to him, his hand in hers,
her light touch occasionally visiting his pale
brow, her still beautiful eyes frequently lifted
from the book to look into his as she made
some comment on the text, or closed the vol·
ume to beguile his mood with talk of—what?
Nobody ever overheard a conversation between these two. The reader who has had the
patience to follow their history to this point
may possibly find a pleasure in conjecture:
there was probably something to be avoided.
The bearing of the man was one of profound
dejection; indeed, the unsympathetic youth of
the neighborhood, with that keen sense for
visible characteristics which ever distinguishes
the young male of our species, sometimes mentioned him among themselves by the name of
Spoony Glum.

It occurred one day that John Hardshaw

was possessed by the spirit of unrest. God knows what led him whither he went, but he crossed Market Street and held his way northward over the hills, and downward into the region known as North Beach. Turning aimlessly to the left he followed his toes along an unfamiliar street until he was opposite what for that period was a rather grand dwelling, and for this is a rather shabby factory. Casting his eyes casually upward he saw at an open window what it had been better that he had not seen—the face and figure of Elvira Barwell. Their eyes met. With a sharp exclamation, like the cry of a startled bird, the lady sprang to her feet and thrust her body half out of the window, clutching the casing on each side. Arrested by the cry, the people in the street below looked up. Hardshaw stood motionless, speechless, his eyes two flames. "Take care!" shouted some one in the crowd, as the woman strained further and further forward, defying the silent, implacable law of gravitation, as once she had defied that other law which God thundered from Sinai. The suddenness of her movements had tumbled a torrent of dark hair down her shoulders, and now it was blown about her cheeks, almost concealing her face. A

moment so, and then—! A fearful cry rang
through the street, as, losing her balance, she
pitched headlong from the window, a confused and whirling mass of skirts, limbs, hair,
and white face, and struck the pavement with
a horrible sound and a force of impact that
was felt a hundred feet away. For a moment
all eyes refused their office and turned from
the sickening spectacle on the sidewalk.
Drawn again to that horror, they saw it
strangely augmented. A man, hatless, seated
flat upon the paving stones, held the broken,
bleeding body against his breast, kissing the
mangled cheeks and streaming mouth through
tangles of wet hair, his own features indis-
tinguishably crimson with the blood that half-
strangled him and ran in rills from his soaken
beard.

The reporter's task is nearly finished. The
Barwells had that very morning returned
from a two years' absence in Peru. A week
later the widower, now doubly desolate, since
there could be no missing the significance of
Hardshaw's horrible demonstration, had
sailed for I know not what distant port; he has
never come back to stay. Hardshaw—as Johnson no longer—passed a year in the Stockton
asylum for the insane, where also, through the

influence of pitying friends, his wife was admitted to care for him. When he was discharged, not cured but harmless, they returned to the city; it would seem ever to have had some dreadful fascination for them. For a time they lived near the Mission Dolores, in poverty only less abject than that which is their present lot; but it was too far away from the objective point of the man's daily pilgrimage. They could not afford car fare. So that poor devil of an angel from Heaven—wife to this convict and lunatic—obtained, at a fair enough rental, the blank-faced shanty on the lower terrace of Goat Hill. Thence to the structure that was a dwelling and is a factory the distance is not so great; it is, in fact, an agreeable walk, judging from the man's eager and cheerful look as he takes it. The return journey appears to be a trifle wearisome.

AN ADVENTURE AT BROWNVILLE*

I TAUGHT a little country school near Brownville, which, as every one knows who has had the good luck to live there, is the capital of a considerable expanse of the finest scenery in California. The town is somewhat frequented in summer by a class of persons whom it is the habit of the local journal to call "pleasure seekers," but who by a juster classification would be known as "the sick and those in adversity." Brownville itself might rightly enough be described, indeed, as a summer place of last resort. It is fairly well endowed with boarding-houses, at the least pernicious of which I performed twice a day (lunching at the schoolhouse) the humble rite of cementing the alliance between soul and body. From this "hostelry" (as the local journal preferred to call it when it did not call it a "caravanserai") to the schoolhouse the distance by the wagon road was about a mile and a half; but there was a trail, very little used, which led over an interven-

*This story was written in collaboration with Miss Ina Lillian Peterson, to whom is rightly due the credit for whatever merit it may have.

ing range of low, heavily wooded hills, considerably shortening the distance. By this trail I was returning one evening later than usual. It was the last day of the term and I had been detained at the schoolhouse until almost dark, preparing an account of my stewardship for the trustees—two of whom, I proudly reflected, would be able to read it, and the third (an instance of the dominion of mind over matter) would be overruled in his customary antagonism to the schoolmaster of his own creation.

I had gone not more than a quarter of the way when, finding an interest in the antics of a family of lizards which dwelt thereabout and seemed full of reptilian joy for their immunity from the ills incident to life at the Brownville House, I sat upon a fallen tree to observe them. As I leaned wearily against a branch of the gnarled old trunk the twilight deepened in the somber woods and the faint new moon began casting visible shadows and gilding the leaves of the trees with a tender but ghostly light.

I heard the sound of voices—a woman's, angry, impetuous, rising against deep masculine tones, rich and musical. I strained my eyes, peering through the dusky shadows of the wood, hoping to get a view of the intruders on my solitude, but could see no one. For some yards in each direction I had an uninterrupted view of the trail, and knowing of no other within a half mile thought the persons heard must be approaching from the wood at one side. There was no sound but that of the voices, which were now so distinct that I could catch the words. That of the man gave me an impression of anger, abundantly confirmed by the matter spoken.

"I will have no threats; you are powerless, as you very well know. Let things remain as they are or, by God! you shall both suffer for it."

"What do you mean?"—this was the voice of the woman, a cultivated voice, the voice of a lady. "You would not—murder us."

There was no reply, at least none that was audible to me. During the silence I peered into the wood in hope to get a glimpse of the speakers, for I felt sure that this was an affair of gravity in which ordinary scruples ought not to count. It seemed to me that the woman was in peril; at any rate the man had not dis-avowed a willingness to murder. When a man is enacting the rôle of potential assassin he has not the right to choose his audience.

After some little time I saw them, indistinct in the moonlight among the trees. The man, tall and slender, seemed clothed in black; the woman wore, as nearly as I could make out, a gown of gray stuff. Evidently they were still unaware of my presence in the shadow, though for some reason when they renewed their conversation they spoke in lower tones and I could no longer understand. As I looked the woman seemed to sink to the ground and raise her hands in supplication, as is frequently done on the stage and never, so far as I knew, anywhere else, and I am now not altogether sure that it was done in this instance. The man fixed his eyes upon her; they seemed to glitter bleakly in the moonlight with an expression that made me apprehensive that he would turn them upon me. I do not know by what impulse I was moved, but I sprang to my feet out of the shadow. At that instant the figures vanished. I peered in vain through the spaces among the trees and clumps of undergrowth. The night wind rustled the leaves; the lizards had retired early, reptiles of exemplary habits. The little moon was already slipping behind a black hill in the west.

I went home, somewhat disturbed in mind,

half doubting that I had heard or seen any living thing excepting the lizards. It all seemed a trifle odd and uncanny. It was as if among the several phenomena, objective and subjective, that made the sum total of the incident there had been an uncertain element which had diffused its dubious character over all—had leavened the whole mass with unreality. I did not like it.

At the breakfast table the next morning there was a new face; opposite me sat a young woman at whom I merely glanced as I took my seat. In speaking to the high and mighty female personage who condescended to seem to wait upon us, this girl soon invited my attention by the sound of her voice, which was like, yet not altogether like, the one still murmuring in my memory of the previous evening's adventure. A moment later another girl, a few years older, entered the room and sat at the left of the other, speaking to her a gentle "good morning." By *her* voice I was startled: it was without doubt the one of which the first girl's had reminded me. Here was the lady of the sylvan incident sitting bodily before me, "in her habit as she lived."

Evidently enough the two were sisters.

With a nebulous kind of apprehension that I might be recognized as the mute inglorious hero of an adventure which had in my consciousness and conscience something of the character of eavesdropping, I allowed myself only a hasty cup of the lukewarm coffee thoughtfully provided by the prescient waitress for the emergency, and left the table. As I passed out of the house into the grounds I heard a rich, strong male voice singing an aria from "Rigoletto." I am bound to say that it was exquisitely sung, too, but there was something in the performance that displeased me, I could say neither what nor why, and I walked rapidly away.

Returning later in the day I saw the elder of the two young women standing on the porch and near her a tall man in black clothing—the man whom I had expected to see. All day the desire to know something of these persons had been uppermost in my mind and I now resolved to learn what I could of them in any way that was neither dishonorable nor low.

The man was talking easily and affably to his companion, but at the sound of my footsteps on the gravel walk he ceased, and turning about looked me full in the face. He was apparently of middle age, dark and uncommonly handsome. His attire was faultless, his bearing easy and graceful, the look which he turned upon me open, free, and devoid of any suggestion of rudeness. Nevertheless it affected me with a distinct emotion which on subsequent analysis in memory appeared to be compounded of hatred and dread—I am unwilling to call it fear. A second later the man and woman had disappeared. They seemed to have a trick of disappearing. On entering the house, however, I saw them through the open doorway of the parlor as I passed; they had merely stepped through a window which opened down to the floor.

Cautiously "approached" on the subject of her new guests my landlady proved not ungracious. Restated with, I hope, some small reverence for English grammar the facts were these: the two girls were Pauline and Eva Maynard of San Francisco; the elder was Pauline. The man was Richard Benning, their guardian, who had been the most intimate friend of their father, now deceased. Mr. Benning had brought them to Brownville in the hope that the mountain climate might benefit Eva, who was thought to be in danger of consumption.

Upon these short and simple annals the landlady wrought an embroidery of eulogium which abundantly attested her faith in Mr. Benning's will and ability to pay for the best that her house afforded. That he had a good heart was evident to her from his devotion to his two beautiful wards and his really touching solicitude for their comfort. The evidence impressed me as insufficient and I silently found the Scotch verdict, "Not proven."

Certainly Mr. Benning was most attentive to his wards. In my strolls about the country I frequently encountered them—sometimes in company with other guests of the hotel—exploring the gulches, fishing, rifle shooting, and otherwise wiling away the monotony of country life; and although I watched them as closely as good manners would permit I saw nothing that would in any way explain the strange words that I had overheard in the wood. I had grown tolerably well acquainted with the young ladies and could exchange looks and even greetings with their guardian without actual repugnance.

A month went by and I had almost ceased to interest myself in their affairs when one night our entire little community was thrown into excitement by an event which vividly recalled my experience in the forest.

This was the death of the elder girl, Pauline.

The sisters had occupied the same bedroom on the third floor of the house. Waking in the gray of the morning Eva had found Pauline dead beside her. Later, when the poor girl was weeping beside the body amid a throng of sympathetic if not very considerate persons, Mr. Benning entered the room and appeared to be about to take her hand. She drew away from the side of the dead and moved slowly toward the door.

"It is you," she said—"you who have done this. You—you—you!"

"She is raving," he said in a low voice. He followed her, step by step, as she retreated, his eyes fixed upon hers with a steady gaze in which there was nothing of tenderness nor of compassion. She stopped; the hand that she had raised in accusation fell to her side, her dilated eyes contracted visibly, the lids slowly dropped over them, veiling their strange wild beauty, and she stood motionless and almost as white as the dead girl lying near. The man took her hand and put his arm gently about her shoulders, as if to support her. Suddenly she burst into a passion of tears and clung to him as a child to its mother. He smiled with a smile that affected me most disagreeably— perhaps any kind of smile would have done so—and led her silently out of the room.

There was an inquest—and the customary verdict: the deceased, it appeared, came to her death through "heart disease." It was before the invention of heart *failure,* though the heart of poor Pauline had indubitably failed. The body was embalmed and taken to San Francisco by some one summoned thence for the purpose, neither Eva nor Benning accompanying it. Some of the hotel gossips ventured to think that very strange, and a few hardy spirits went so far as to think it very strange indeed; but the good landlady generously threw herself into the breach, saying it was owing to the precarious nature of the girl's health. It is not of record that either of the two persons most affected and apparently least concerned made any explanation.

One evening about a week after the death I went out upon the veranda of the hotel to get a book that I had left there. Under some vines shutting out the moonlight from a part of the space I saw Richard Benning, for whose apparition I was prepared by having previously heard the low, sweet voice of Eva Maynard, whom also I now discerned, standing before him with one hand raised to his shoulder and her eyes, as nearly as I could judge, gazing upward into his. He held her disengaged hand and his head was bent with a singular dignity and grace. Their attitude was that of lovers, and as I stood in deep shadow to observe I felt even guiltier than on that memorable night in the wood. I was about to retire, when the girl spoke, and the contrast between her words and her attitude was so surprising that I remained, because I had merely forgotten to go away.

"You will take my life," she said, "as you did Pauline's. I know your intention as well as I know your power, and I ask nothing, only that you finish your work without needless delay and let me be at peace."

He made no reply—merely let go the hand that he was holding, removed the other from his shoulder, and turning away descended the steps leading to the garden and disappeared in the shrubbery. But a moment later I heard, seemingly from a great distance, his fine clear voice in a barbaric chant, which as I listened brought before some inner spiritual sense a consciousness of some far, strange land peopled with beings having forbidden powers. The song held me in a kind of spell, but when it had died away I recovered and instantly perceived what I thought an opportunity. I walked out of my shadow to where the girl stood. She turned and stared at me with something of the look, it seemed to me, of a hunted hare. Possibly my intrusion had frightened her.

"Miss Maynard," I said, "I beg you to tell me who that man is and the nature of his power over you. Perhaps this is rude in me, but it is not a matter for idle civilities. When a woman is in danger any man has a right to act."

She listened without visible emotion— almost I thought without interest, and when I had finished she closed her big blue eyes as if unspeakably weary.

"You can do nothing," she said.

I took hold of her arm, gently shaking her as one shakes a person falling into a danger-ous sleep.

"You must rouse yourself," I said; "some-thing must be done and you must give me leave to act. You have said that that man killed your sister, and I believe it—that he will kill you, and I believe that."

She merely raised her eyes to mine.

"Will you not tell me all?" I added.

"There is nothing to be done, I tell you—nothing. And if I could do anything I would not. It does not matter in the least. We shall be here only two days more; we go away then, oh, so far! If you have observed anything, I beg you to be silent."

"But this is madness, girl." I was trying by rough speech to break the deadly repose of her manner. "You have accused him of murder. Unless you explain these things to me I shall lay the matter before the authorities."

This roused her, but in a way that I did not like. She lifted her head proudly and said: "Do not meddle, sir, in what does not concern you. This is my affair, Mr. Moran, not yours."

"It concerns every person in the country—in the world," I answered, with equal coldness. "If you had no love for your sister I, at least, am concerned for you."

"Listen," she interrupted, leaning toward me. "I loved her, yes, God knows! But more than that—beyond all, beyond expression, I love *him*. You have overheard a secret, but you shall not make use of it to harm him. I shall deny all. Your word against mine—it will be that. Do you think your 'authorities' will believe you?"

She was now smiling like an angel and, God help me! I was heels over head in love with her! Did she, by some of the many methods of divination known to her sex, read my feelings? Her whole manner had altered.

"Come," she said, almost coaxingly, "promise that you will not be impolite again." She took my arm in the most friendly way. "Come, I will walk with you. He will not know—he will remain away all night."

Up and down the veranda we paced in the moonlight, she seemingly forgetting her recent bereavement, cooing and murmuring girl-wise of every kind of nothing in all Brownville; I silent, consciously awkward and with something of the feeling of being concerned in an intrigue. It was a revelation—this most charming and apparently blameless creature coolly and confessedly deceiving the man for whom a moment before she had acknowledged and shown the supreme love which finds even death an acceptable endearment.

"Truly," I thought in my inexperience, "here is something new under the moon."

And the moon must have smiled.

Before we parted I had exacted a promise
that she would walk with me the next afternoon—before going away forever—to the Old
Mill, one of Brownville's revered antiquities,
erected in 1860.

"If he is not about," she added gravely, as
I let go the hand she had given me at parting,
and of which, may the good saints forgive me,
I strove vainly to repossess myself when she
had said it—so charming, as the wise French-
man has pointed out, do we find woman's in-
fidelity when we are its objects, not its victims. In apportioning his benefactions that
night the Angel of Sleep overlooked me.

The Brownville House dined early, and
after dinner the next day Miss Maynard, who
had not been at table, came to me on the
veranda, attired in the demurest of walking
costumes, saying not a word. "He" was evidently "not about." We went slowly up the
road that led to the Old Mill. She was apparently not strong and at times took my arm,
relinquishing it and taking it again rather
capriciously, I thought. Her mood, or rather
her succession of moods, was as mutable as
skylight in a rippling sea. She jested as if
she had never heard of such a thing as death,
and laughed on the lightest incitement, and

directly afterward would sing a few bars of some grave melody with such tenderness of expression that I had to turn away my eyes lest she should see the evidence of her success in art, if art it was, not artlessness, as then I was compelled to think it. And she said the oddest things in the most unconventional way, skirting sometimes unfathomable abysms of thought, where I had hardly the courage to set foot. In short, she was fascinating in a thousand and fifty different ways, and at every step I executed a new and profounder emotional folly, a hardier spiritual indiscretion, incurring fresh liability to arrest by the constabulary of conscience for infractions of my own peace.

Arriving at the mill, she made no pretense of stopping, but turned into a trail leading through a field of stubble toward a creek. Crossing by a rustic bridge we continued on the trail, which now led uphill to one of the most picturesque spots in the country. The Eagle's Nest, it was called—the summit of a cliff that rose sheer into the air to a height of hundreds of feet above the forest at its base. From this elevated point we had a noble view of another valley and of the opposite hills flushed with the last rays of the setting sun.

As we watched the light escaping to higher and higher planes from the encroaching flood of shadow filling the valley we heard footsteps, and in another moment were joined by Richard Benning.

"I saw you from the road," he said carelessly; "so I came up."

Being a fool, I neglected to take him by the throat and pitch him into the treetops below, but muttered some polite lie instead. On the girl the effect of his coming was immediate and unmistakable. Her face was suffused with the glory of love's transfiguration: the red light of the sunset had not been more obvious in her eyes than was now the lovelight that replaced it.

"I am so glad you came!" she said, giving him both her hands; and, God help me! it was manifestly true.

Seating himself upon the ground he began a lively dissertation upon the wild flowers of the region, a number of which he had with him. In the middle of a facetious sentence he suddenly ceased speaking and fixed his eyes upon Eva, who leaned against the stump of a tree, absently plaiting grasses. She lifted her eyes in a startled way to his, as if she had *felt* his look. She then rose, cast away her grasses, and moved slowly away from him. He also rose, continuing to look at her. He had still in his hand the bunch of flowers. The girl turned, as if to speak, but said nothing. I recall clearly now something of which I was but half-conscious then—the dreadful contrast between the smile upon her lips and the terrified expression in her eyes as she met his steady and imperative gaze. I know nothing of how it happened, nor how it was that I did not sooner understand; I only know that with the smile of an angel upon her lips and that look of terror in her beautiful eyes Eva Maynard sprang from the cliff and shot crashing into the tops of the pines below!

How and how long afterward I reached the place I cannot say, but Richard Benning was already there, kneeling beside the dreadful thing that had been a woman.

"She is dead—quite dead," he said coldly. "I will go to town for assistance. Please do me the favor to remain."

He rose to his feet and moved away, but in a moment had stopped and turned about.

"You have doubtless observed, my friend," he said, "that this was entirely her own act. I did not rise in time to prevent it, and you, not knowing her mental condition—you could not, of course, have suspected."

His manner maddened me.

"You are as much her assassin," I said, "as if your damnable hands had cut her throat."

He shrugged his shoulders without reply and, turning, walked away. A moment later I heard, through the deepening shadows of the wood into which he had disappeared, a rich, strong, baritone voice singing *"La donna e mobile,"* from "Rigoletto."

THE FAMOUS GILSON BEQUEST

IT was rough on Gilson. Such was the terse, cold, but not altogether unsympathetic judgment of the better public opinion at Mammon Hill—the dictum of respectability. The verdict of the opposite, or rather the opposing, element—the element that lurked red-eyed and restless about Moll Gurney's "deadfall," while respectability took it with sugar at Mr. Jo. Bentley's gorgeous "saloon"—was to pretty much the same general effect, though somewhat more ornately expressed by the use of picturesque expletives, which it is needless to quote. Virtually, Mammon Hill was a unit on the Gilson question. And it must be confessed that in a merely temporal sense all was not well with Mr. Gilson. He had that morning been led into town by Mr. Brentshaw and publicly charged with horse stealing; the sheriff meantime busying himself about The Tree with a new manila rope and Carpenter Pete being actively employed between drinks upon a pine box about the length and breadth of Mr. Gilson. Society having rendered its verdict, there remained between Gilson and eternity only the decent formality of a trial.

These are the short and simple annals of the prisoner: He had recently been a resident of New Jerusalem, on the north fork of the Little Stony, but had come to the newly discovered placers of Mammon Hill immediately before the "rush" by which the former place was depopulated. The discovery of the new diggings had occurred opportunely for Mr. Gilson, for it had only just before been intimated to him by a New Jerusalem vigilance committee that it would better his prospects in, and for, life to go somewhere; and the list of places to which he could safely go did not include any of the older camps; so he naturally established himself at Mammon Hill. Being eventually followed thither by all his judges, he ordered his conduct with considerable circumspection, but as he had never been known to do an honest day's work at any industry sanctioned by the stern local code of morality except draw poker he was still an object of suspicion. Indeed, it was conjectured that he was the author of the many daring depredations that had recently been committed with pan and brush on the sluice boxes.

Prominent among those in whom this suspicion had ripened into a steadfast conviction was Mr. Brentshaw. At all seasonable and unseasonable times Mr. Brentshaw avowed his belief in Mr. Gilson's connection with these unholy midnight enterprises, and his own willingness to prepare a way for the solar beams through the body of any one who might think it expedient to utter a different opinion —which, in his presence, no one was more careful not to do than the peace-loving person most concerned. Whatever may have been the truth of the matter, it is certain that Gilson frequently lost more "clean dust" at Jo. Bentley's faro table than it was recorded in local history that he had ever honestly earned at draw poker in all the days of the camp's existence. But at last Mr. Bentley— fearing, it may be, to lose the more profitable patronage of Mr. Brentshaw—peremptorily refused to let Gilson copper the queen, intimating at the same time, in his frank, forthright way, that the privilege of losing money at "this bank" was a blessing appertaining to, proceeding logically from, and coterminous with, a condition of notorious commercial righteousness and social good repute.

The Hill thought it high time to look after

a person whom its most honored citizen had felt it his duty to rebuke at a considerable personal sacrifice. The New Jerusalem contingent, particularly, began to abate something of the toleration begotten of amusement at their own blunder in exiling an objectionable neighbor from the place which they had left to the place whither they had come. Mammon Hill was at last of one mind. Not much was said, but that Gilson must hang was "in the air." But at this critical juncture in his affairs he showed signs of an altered life if not a changed heart. Perhaps it was only that "the bank" being closed against him he had no further use for gold dust. Anyhow the sluice boxes were molested no more forever. But it was impossible to repress the abounding energies of such a nature as his, and he continued, possibly from habit, the tortuous courses which he had pursued for profit of Mr. Bentley. After a few tentative and resultless undertakings in the way of highway robbery—if one may venture to designate road-agency by so harsh a name— he made one or two modest essays in horse-herding, and it was in the midst of a promising enterprise of this character, and just as he had taken the tide in his affairs at its flood, that he made shipwreck. For on a misty, moonlight night Mr. Brentshaw rode up alongside a person who was evidently leaving that part of the country, laid a hand upon the halter connecting Mr. Gilson's wrist with Mr. Harper's bay mare, tapped him familiarly on the cheek with the barrel of a navy revolver and requested the pleasure of his company in a direction opposite to that in which he was traveling.

It was indeed rough on Gilson.

On the morning after his arrest he was tried, convicted, and sentenced. It only remains, so far as concerns his earthly career, to hang him, reserving for more particular mention his last will and testament, which, with great labor, he contrived in prison, and in which, probably from some confused and imperfect notion of the rights of captors, he bequeathed everything he owned to his " lawfle execketer," Mr. Brentshaw. The bequest, however, was made conditional on the legatee taking the testator's body from The Tree and " planting it white."

So Mr. Gilson was—I was about to say " swung off," but I fear there has been already something too much of slang in this straightforward statement of facts; besides,

the manner in which the law took its course
is more accurately described in the terms employed by the judge in passing sentence: Mr.
Gilson was "strung up."

In due season Mr. Brentshaw, somewhat
touched, it may well be, by the empty compli-
ment of the bequest, repaired to The Tree to
pluck the fruit thereof. When taken down
the body was found to have in its waistcoat
pocket a duly attested codicil to the will already noted. The nature of its provisions accounted for the manner in which it had been
withheld, for had Mr. Brentshaw previously
been made aware of the conditions under
which he was to succeed to the Gilson estate
he would indubitably have declined the
responsibility. Briefly stated, the purport of
the codicil was as follows:

Whereas, at divers times and in sundry
places, certain persons had asserted that during his life the testator had robbed their sluice
boxes; therefore, if during the five years next
succeeding the date of this instrument any one
should make proof of such assertion before a
court of law, such person was to receive as
reparation the entire personal and real estate
of which the testator died seized and possessed, minus the expenses of court and a

stated compensation to the executor, Henry
Clay Brentshaw; provided, that if more than
one person made such proof the estate was to
be equally divided between or among them.
But in case none should succeed in so estab-
lishing the testator's guilt, then the whole
property, minus court expenses, as aforesaid,
should go to the said Henry Clay Brentshaw
for his own use, as stated in the will.

The syntax of this remarkable document
was perhaps open to critical objection, but that
was clearly enough the meaning of it. The
orthography conformed to no recognized system, but being mainly phonetic it was not
ambiguous. As the probate judge remarked,
it would take five aces to beat it. Mr. Brentshaw smiled good-humoredly, and after performing the last sad rites with amusing
ostentation, had himself duly sworn as executor and conditional legatee under the provisions of a law hastily passed (at the instance
of the member from the Mammon Hill district) by a facetious legislature; which law
was afterward discovered to have created also
three or four lucrative offices and authorized
the expenditure of a considerable sum of public money for the construction of a certain
railway bridge that with greater advantage

might perhaps have been erected on the line of some actual railway.

Of course Mr. Brentshaw expected neither profit from the will nor litigation in consequence of its unusual provisions; Gilson, although frequently " flush," had been a man whom assessors and tax collectors were well satisfied to lose no money by. But a careless and merely formal search among his papers revealed title deeds to valuable estates in the East and certificates of deposit for incredible sums in banks less severely scrupulous than that of Mr. Jo. Bentley.

The astounding news got abroad directly, throwing the Hill into a fever of excitement. The Mammon Hill *Patriot,* whose editor had been a leading spirit in the proceedings that resulted in Gilson's departure from New Jerusalem, published a most complimentary obituary notice of the deceased, and was good enough to call attention to the fact that his degraded contemporary, the Squaw Gulch *Clarion,* was bringing virtue into contempt by beslavering with flattery the memory of one who in life had spurned the vile sheet as a nuisance from his door. Undeterred by the press, however, claimants under the will were not slow in presenting themselves with their evidence; and great as was the Gilson estate it appeared conspicuously paltry considering the vast number of sluice boxes from which it was averred to have been obtained. The country rose as one man!

Mr. Brentshaw was equal to the emergency. With a shrewd application of humble auxiliary devices, he at once erected above the bones of his benefactor a costly monument, overtopping every rough headboard in the cemetery, and on this he judiciously caused to be inscribed an epitaph of his own composing, eulogizing the honesty, public spirit and cognate virtues of him who slept beneath, "a victim to the unjust aspersions of Slander's viper brood."

Moreover, he employed the best legal talent in the Territory to defend the memory of his departed friend, and for five long years the Territorial courts were occupied with litigation growing out of the Gilson bequest. To fine forensic abilities Mr. Brentshaw opposed abilities more finely forensic; in bidding for purchasable favors he offered prices which utterly deranged the market; the judges found at his hospitable board entertainment for man and beast, the like of which had never been spread in the Territory; with mendacious witnesses he confronted witnesses of superior mendacity.

Nor was the battle confined to the temple of the blind goddess—it invaded the press, the pulpit, the drawing-room. It raged in the mart, the exchange, the school; in the gulches, and on the street corners. And upon the last day of the memorable period to which legal action under the Gilson will was limited, the sun went down upon a region in which the moral sense was dead, the social conscience callous, the intellectual capacity dwarfed, enfeebled, and confused! But Mr. Brentshaw was victorious all along the line.

On that night it so happened that the cemetery in one corner of which lay the now honored ashes of the late Milton Gilson, Esq., was partly under water. Swollen by incessant rains, Cat Creek had spilled over its banks an angry flood which, after scooping out unsightly hollows wherever the soil had been disturbed, had partly subsided, as if ashamed of the sacrilege, leaving exposed much that had been piously concealed. Even the famous Gilson monument, the pride and glory of Mammon Hill, was no longer a standing rebuke to the "viper brood"; succumbing to the sapping current it had toppled

prone to earth. The ghoulish flood had ex-
humed the poor, decayed pine coffin, which
now lay half-exposed, in pitiful contrast to the
pompous monolith which, like a giant note of
admiration, emphasized the disclosure.

To this depressing spot, drawn by some
subtle influence he had sought neither to resist
nor analyze, came Mr. Brentshaw. An altered man was Mr. Brentshaw. Five years
of toil, anxiety, and wakefulness had dashed
his black locks with streaks and patches of
gray, bowed his fine figure, drawn sharp and
angular his face, and debased his walk to a
doddering shuffle. Nor had this lustrum of
fierce contention wrought less upon his heart
and intellect. The careless good humor that
had prompted him to accept the trust of the
dead man had given place to a fixed habit of
melancholy. The firm, vigorous intellect had
overripened into the mental mellowness of
second childhood. His broad understanding
had narrowed to the accommodation of a
single idea; and in place of the quiet, cynical
incredulity of former days, there was in him a
haunting faith in the supernatural, that flitted
and fluttered about his soul, shadowy, batlike,
ominous of insanity. Unsettled in all else, his
understanding clung to one conviction with

the tenacity of a wrecked intellect. That was an unshaken belief in the entire blamelessness of the dead Gilson. He had so often sworn to this in court and asserted it in private conversation—had so frequently and so triumphantly established it by testimony that had come expensive to him (for that very day he had paid the last dollar of the Gilson estate to Mr. Jo. Bentley, the last witness to the Gilson good character)—that it had become to him a sort of religious faith. It seemed to him the one great central and basic truth of life—the sole serene verity in a world of lies.

On that night, as he seated himself pensively upon the prostrate monument, trying by the uncertain moonlight to spell out the epitaph which five years before he had composed with a chuckle that memory had not recorded, tears of remorse came into his eyes as he remembered that he had been mainly instrumental in compassing by a false accusation this good man's death; for during some of the legal proceedings, Mr. Harper, for a consideration (forgotten) had come forward and sworn that in the little transaction with his bay mare the deceased had acted in strict accordance with the Harperian wishes, confidentially communicated to the deceased and by him faithfully concealed at the cost of his life. All that Mr. Brentshaw had since done for the dead man's memory seemed pitifully inadequate—most mean, paltry, and debased with selfishness!

As he sat there, torturing himself with futile regrets, a faint shadow fell across his eyes. Looking toward the moon, hanging low in the west, he saw what seemed a vague, watery cloud obscuring her; but as it moved so that her beams lit up one side of it he perceived the clear, sharp outline of a human figure. The apparition became momentarily more distinct, and grew, visibly; it was drawing near. Dazed as were his senses, half locked up with terror and confounded with dreadful imaginings, Mr. Brentshaw yet could but perceive, or think he perceived, in this unearthly shape a strange similitude to the mortal part of the late Milton Gilson, as that person had looked when taken from The Tree five years before. The likeness was indeed complete, even to the full, stony eyes, and a certain shadowy circle about the neck. It was without coat or hat, precisely as Gilson had been when laid in his poor, cheap casket by the not ungentle hands of Carpenter Pete —for whom some one had long since performed the same neighborly office. The spectre, if such it was, seemed to bear something in its hands which Mr. Brentshaw could not clearly make out. It drew nearer, and paused at last beside the coffin containing the ashes of the late Mr. Gilson, the lid of which was awry, half disclosing the uncertain interior. Bending over this, the phantom seemed to shake into it from a basin some dark substance of dubious consistency, then glided stealthily back to the lowest part of the cemetery. Here the retiring flood had stranded a number of open coffins, about and among which it gurgled with low sobbings and stilly whispers. Stooping over one of these, the apparition carefully brushed its contents into the basin, then returning to its own casket, emptied the vessel into that, as before. This mysterious operation was repeated at every exposed coffin, the ghost sometimes dipping its laden basin into the running water, and gently agitating it to free it of the baser clay, always hoarding the residuum in its own private box. In short, the immortal part of the late Milton Gilson was cleaning up the dust of its neighbors and providently adding the same to its own.

Perhaps it was a phantasm of a disordered

mind in a fevered body. Perhaps it was a solemn farce enacted by pranking existences that throng the shadows lying along the border of another world. God knows; to us is permitted only the knowledge that when the sun of another day touched with a grace of gold the ruined cemetery of Mammon Hill his kindliest beam fell upon the white, still face of Henry Brentshaw, dead among the dead.

THE APPLICANT

PUSHING his adventurous shins through the deep snow that had fallen overnight, and encouraged by the glee of his little sister, following in the open way that he made, a sturdy small boy, the son of Grayville's most distinguished citizen, struck his foot against something of which there was no visible sign on the surface of the snow. It is the purpose of this narrative to explain how it came to be there.

No one who has had the advantage of passing through Grayville by day can have failed to observe the large stone building crowning the low hill to the north of the railway station —that is to say, to the right in going toward Great Mowbray. It is a somewhat dull-looking edifice, of the Early Comatose order, and appears to have been designed by an architect who shrank from publicity, and although unable to conceal his work—even compelled, in this instance, to set it on an eminence in the sight of men—did what he honestly could to insure it against a second look. So far as concerns its outer and visible aspect, the Aber-

sush Home for Old Men is unquestionably in-
hospitable to human attention. But it is a
building of great magnitude, and cost its
benevolent founder the profit of many a cargo
of the teas and silks and spices that his ships
brought up from the under-world when he
was in trade in Boston; though the main ex-
pense was its endowment. Altogether, this
reckless person had robbed his heirs-at-law of
no less a sum than half a million dollars and
flung it away in riotous giving. Possibly it
was with a view to get out of sight of the silent big witness to his extravagance that he
shortly afterward disposed of all his Grayville property that remained to him, turned
his back upon the scene of his prodigality and
went off across the sea in one of his own ships.
But the gossips who got their inspiration most
directly from Heaven declared that he went in
search of a wife—a theory not easily recon-
ciled with that of the village humorist, who
solemnly averred that the bachelor philanthropist had departed this life (left Grayville,
to wit) because the marriageable maidens had
made it too hot to hold him. However this
may have been, he had not returned, and although at long intervals there had come to
Grayville, in a desultory way, vague rumors

of his wanderings in strange lands, no one seemed certainly to know about him, and to the new generation he was no more than a name. But from above the portal of the Home for Old Men the name shouted in stone.

Despite its unpromising exterior, the Home is a fairly commodious place of retreat from the ills that its inmates have incurred by being poor and old and men. At the time embraced in this brief chronicle they were in number about a score, but in acerbity, querulousness, and general ingratitude they could hardly be reckoned at fewer than a hundred; at least that was the estimate of the superintendent, Mr. Silas Tilbody. It was Mr. Tilbody's steadfast conviction that always, in admitting new old men to replace those who had gone to another and a better Home, the trustees had distinctly in will the infraction of his peace, and the trial of his patience. In truth, the longer the institution was connected with him, the stronger was his feeling that the founder's scheme of benevolence was sadly impaired by providing any inmates at all. He had not much imagination, but with what he had he was addicted to the reconstruction of the Home for Old Men into a kind of " castle in

Spain," with himself as castellan, hospitably entertaining about a score of sleek and prosperous middle-aged gentlemen, consummately good-humored and civilly willing to pay for their board and lodging. In this revised project of philanthropy the trustees, to whom he was indebted for his office and responsible for his conduct, had not the happiness to appear. As to them, it was held by the village humorist aforementioned that in their management of the great charity Providence had thoughtfully supplied an incentive to thrift. With the inference which he expected to be drawn from that view we have nothing to do; it had neither support nor denial from the inmates, who certainly were most concerned. They lived out their little remnant of life, crept into graves neatly numbered, and were succeeded by other old men as like them as could be desired by the Adversary of Peace. If the Home was a place of punishment for the sin of unthrift the veteran offenders sought justice with a persistence that attested the sincerity of their penitence. It is to one of these that the reader's attention is now invited.

In the matter of attire this person was not altogether engaging. But for this season, which was midwinter, a careless observer might have looked upon him as a clever device of the husbandman indisposed to share the fruits of his toil with the crows that toil not, neither spin—an error that might not have been dispelled without longer and closer observation than he seemed to court; for his progress up Abersush Street, toward the Home in the gloom of the winter evening, was not visibly faster than what might have been expected of a scarecrow blessed with youth, health, and discontent. The man was indisputably ill-clad, yet not without a certain fitness and good taste, withal; for he was obviously an applicant for admittance to the Home, where poverty was a qualification. In the army of indigence the uniform is rags; they serve to distinguish the rank and file from the recruiting officers.

As the old man, entering the gate of the grounds, shuffled up the broad walk, already white with the fast-falling snow, which from time to time he feebly shook from its various coigns of vantage on his person, he came under inspection of the large globe lamp that burned always by night over the great door of the building. As if unwilling to incur its revealing beams, he turned to the left and, passing a considerable distance along the face of the building, rang at a smaller door emitting a dimmer ray that came from within, through the fanlight, and expended itself incuriously overhead. The door was opened by no less a personage than the great Mr. Tilbody himself. Observing his visitor, who at once uncovered, and somewhat shortened the radius of the permanent curvature of his back, the great man gave visible token of neither surprise nor displeasure. Mr. Tilbody was, indeed, in an uncommonly good humor, a phenomenon ascribable doubtless to the cheerful influence of the season; for this was Christmas Eve, and the morrow would be that blessed 365th part of the year that all Christian souls set apart for mighty feats of goodness and joy. Mr. Tilbody was so full of the spirit of the season that his fat face and pale blue eyes, whose ineffectual fire served to distinguish it from an untimely summer squash, effused so genial a glow that it seemed a pity that he could not have lain down in it, basking in the consciousness of his own identity. He was hatted, booted, overcoated, and umbrellaed, as became a person who was about to expose himself to the night and the storm on an errand of charity; for Mr. Tilbody had just parted from his wife and children to go

"down town" and purchase the wherewithal
to confirm the annual falsehood about the
hunch-bellied saint who frequents the chim-
neys to reward little boys and girls who are
good, and especially truthful. So he did not
invite the old man in, but saluted him cheerily:

"Hello! just in time; a moment later and
you would have missed me. Come, I have
no time to waste; we'll walk a little way together."

"Thank you," said the old man, upon
whose thin and white but not ignoble face the
light from the open door showed an expression that was perhaps disappointment; "but
if the trustees—if my application——"

"The trustees," Mr. Tilbody said, closing
more doors than one, and cutting off two kinds
of light, "have agreed that your application
disagrees with them."

Certain sentiments are inappropriate to
Christmastide, but Humor, like Death, has all
seasons for his own.

"Oh, my God!" cried the old man, in so
thin and husky a tone that the invocation was
anything but impressive, and to at least one
of his two auditors sounded, indeed, somewhat
ludicrous. To the Other—but that is a mat-

ter which laymen are devoid of the light to expound.

"Yes," continued Mr. Tilbody, accommodating his gait to that of his companion, who was mechanically, and not very successfully, retracing the track that he had made through the snow; "they have decided that, under the circumstances—under the very peculiar circumstances, you understand—it would be inexpedient to admit you. As superintendent and *ex officio* secretary of the honorable board"—as Mr. Tilbody "read his title clear" the magnitude of the big building, seen through its veil of falling snow, appeared to suffer somewhat in comparison—"it is my duty to inform you that, in the words of Deacon Byram, the chairman, your presence in the Home would—under the circumstances—be peculiarly embarrassing. I felt it my duty to submit to the honorable board the statement that you made to me yesterday of your needs, your physical condition, and the trials which it has pleased Providence to send upon you in your very proper effort to present your claims in person; but, after careful, and I may say prayerful, consideration of your case—with something too, I trust, of the large charitableness appropriate to the season—it was decided that we would not be justified in doing anything likely to impair the usefulness of the institution intrusted (under Providence) to our care."

They had now passed out of the grounds; the street lamp opposite the gate was dimly visible through the snow. Already the old man's former track was obliterated, and he seemed uncertain as to which way he should go. Mr. Tilbody had drawn a little away from him, but paused and turned half toward him, apparently reluctant to forego the continuing opportunity.

"Under the circumstances," he resumed, "the decision——"

But the old man was inaccessible to the suasion of his verbosity; he had crossed the street into a vacant lot and was going forward, rather deviously toward nowhere in particular —which, he having nowhere in particular to go to, was not so reasonless a proceeding as it looked.

And that is how it happened that the next morning, when the church bells of all Grayville were ringing with an added unction appropriate to the day, the sturdy little son of Deacon Byram, breaking a way through the snow to the place of worship, struck his foot against the body of Amasa Abersush, philanthropist.

A WATCHER BY THE DEAD

I

IN an upper room of an unoccupied dwelling in the part of San Francisco known as North Beach lay the body of a man, under a sheet. The hour was near nine in the evening; the room was dimly lighted by a single candle. Although the weather was warm, the two windows, contrary to the custom which gives the dead plenty of air, were closed and the blinds drawn down. The furniture of the room consisted of but three pieces—an arm-chair, a small reading-stand supporting the candle, and a long kitchen table, supporting the body of the man. All these, as also the corpse, seemed to have been recently brought in, for an observer, had there been one, would have seen that all were free from dust, whereas everything else in the room was pretty thickly coated with it, and there were cobwebs in the angles of the walls.

Under the sheet the outlines of the body could be traced, even the features, these having that unnaturally sharp definition which seems to belong to faces of the dead, but is really characteristic of those only that have been wasted by disease. From the silence of the room one would rightly have inferred that it was not in the front of the house, facing a street. It really faced nothing but a high breast of rock, the rear of the building being set into a hill.

As a neighboring church clock was striking nine with an indolence which seemed to imply such an indifference to the flight of time that one could hardly help wondering why it took the trouble to strike at all, the single door of the room was opened and a man entered, advancing toward the body. As he did so the door closed, apparently of its own volition; there was a grating, as of a key turned with difficulty, and the snap of the lock bolt as it shot into its socket. A sound of retiring footsteps in the passage outside ensued, and the man was to all appearance a prisoner. Advancing to the table, he stood a moment looking down at the body; then with a slight shrug of the shoulders walked over to one of the windows and hoisted the blind. The darkness outside was absolute, the panes were covered with dust, but by wiping this away he could see that the window was fortified with strong iron bars crossing it within a few inches of the glass and imbedded in the masonry on each side. He examined the other window. It was the same. He manifested no great curiosity in the matter, did not even so much as raise the sash. If he was a prisoner he was apparently a tractable one. Having completed his examination of the room, he seated himself in the arm-chair, took a book from his pocket, drew the stand with its candle alongside and began to read.

The man was young—not more than thirty —dark in complexion, smooth-shaven, with brown hair. His face was thin and high-nosed, with a broad forehead and a "firmness" of the chin and jaw which is said by those having it to denote resolution. The eyes were gray and steadfast, not moving except with definitive purpose. They were now for the greater part of the time fixed upon his book, but he occasionally withdrew them and turned them to the body on the table, not, apparently, from any dismal fascination which under such circumstances it might be supposed to exercise upon even a courageous person, nor with a conscious rebellion against the contrary influence which might dominate a timid one. He looked at it as if in his read-

ing he had come upon something recalling
him to a sense of his surroundings.   Clearly
this watcher by the dead was discharging his
trust with intelligence and composure, as became him.

After reading for perhaps a half-hour he
seemed to come to the end of a chapter and
quietly laid away the book.   He then rose and
taking the reading-stand from the floor
carried it into a corner of the room near one
of the windows, lifted the candle from it and
returned to the empty fireplace before which
he had been sitting.

A moment later he walked over to the body
on the table, lifted the sheet and turned it
back from the head, exposing a mass of dark
hair and a thin face-cloth, beneath which the
features showed with even sharper definition
than before.   Shading his eyes by interposing
his free hand between them and the candle, he
stood looking at his motionless companion with
a serious and tranquil regard.   Satisfied with
his inspection, he pulled the sheet over the
face again and returning to the chair, took
some matches off the candlestick, put them in
the side pocket of his sack-coat and sat down.
He then lifted the candle from its socket and
looked at it critically, as if calculating how

long it would last. It was barely two inches long; in another hour he would be in darkness. He replaced it in the candlestick and blew it out.

II

In a physician's office in Kearny Street three men sat about a table, drinking punch and smoking. It was late in the evening, almost midnight, indeed, and there had been no lack of punch. The gravest of the three, Dr. Helberson, was the host—it was in his rooms they sat. He was about thirty years of age; the others were even younger; all were physicians.

"The superstitious awe with which the living regard the dead," said Dr. Helberson, "is hereditary and incurable. One needs no more be ashamed of it than of the fact that he inherits, for example, an incapacity for mathematics, or a tendency to lie."

The others laughed. "Oughtn't a man to be ashamed to lie?" asked the youngest of the three, who was in fact a medical student not yet graduated.

"My dear Harper, I said nothing about that. The tendency to lie is one thing; lying is another."

"But do you think," said the third man,

"that this superstitious feeling, this fear of the dead, reasonless as we know it to be, is universal? I am myself not conscious of it."

"Oh, but it is 'in your system' for all that," replied Helberson; "it needs only the right conditions—what Shakespeare calls the 'confederate season'—to manifest itself in some very disagreeable way that will open your eyes. Physicians and soldiers are of course more nearly free from it than others."

"Physicians and soldiers!—why don't you add hangmen and headsmen?   Let us have in all the assassin classes."

"No, my dear Mancher; the juries will not let the public executioners acquire sufficient familiarity with death to be altogether unmoved by it."

Young Harper, who had been helping himself to a fresh cigar at the sideboard, resumed his seat. "What would you consider conditions under which any man of woman born would become insupportably conscious of his share of our common weakness in this regard?" he asked, rather verbosely.

"Well, I should say that if a man were locked up all night with a corpse—alone—in a dark room—of a vacant house—with no bed covers to pull over his head—and lived

through it without going altogether mad, he
might justly boast himself not of woman born,
nor yet, like Macduff, a product of Cæsarean
section."

"I thought you never would finish piling
up conditions," said Harper, "but I know a
man who is neither a physician nor a soldier
who will accept them all, for any stake you
like to name."

"Who is he?"

"His name is Jarette—a stranger here;
comes from my town in New York. I have
no money to back him, but he will back himself with loads of it."

"How do you know that?"

"He would rather bet than eat. As for
fear—I dare say he thinks it some cutaneous
disorder, or possibly a particular kind of religious heresy."

"What does he look like?" Helberson
was evidently becoming interested.

"Like Mancher, here—might be his twin
brother."

"I accept the challenge," said Helberson,
promptly.

"Awfully obliged to you for the compli-
ment, I'm sure," drawled Mancher, who was
growing sleepy. "Can't I get into this?"

"Not against me," Helberson said. "I don't want *your* money."

"All right," said Mancher; "I'll be the corpse."

The others laughed.

The outcome of this crazy conversation we have seen.

III

In extinguishing his meagre allowance of candle Mr. Jarette's object was to preserve it against some unforeseen need. He may have thought, too, or half thought, that the darkness would be no worse at one time than another, and if the situation became insupportable it would be better to have a means of relief, or even release. At any rate it was wise to have a little reserve of light, even if only to enable him to look at his watch.

No sooner had he blown out the candle and set it on the floor at his side than he settled himself comfortably in the arm-chair, leaned back and closed his eyes, hoping and expecting to sleep. In this he was disappointed; he had never in his life felt less sleepy, and in a few minutes he gave up the attempt. But what could he do? He could not go groping about in absolute darkness at the risk of bruising himself—at the risk, too, of blundering against the table and rudely disturbing the dead. We all recognize their right to lie at rest, with immunity from all that is harsh and violent. Jarette almost succeeded in making himself believe that considerations of this kind restrained him from risking the collision and fixed him to the chair.

While thinking of this matter he fancied that he heard a faint sound in the direction of the table—what kind of sound he could hardly have explained. He did not turn his head. Why should he—in the darkness? But he listened—why should he not? And listening he grew giddy and grasped the arms of the chair for support. There was a strange ringing in his ears; his head seemed bursting; his chest was oppressed by the constriction of his clothing. He wondered why it was so, and whether these were symptoms of fear. Then, with a long and strong expiration, his chest appeared to collapse, and with the great gasp with which he refilled his exhausted lungs the vertigo left him and he knew that so intently had he listened that he had held his breath almost to suffocation. The revelation was vexatious; he arose, pushed away the chair with his foot and strode to the centre of the room. But one does not stride far in darkness; he began to grope, and finding the wall followed it to an angle, turned, followed it past the two windows and there in another corner came into violent contact with the reading-stand, overturning it. It made a clatter that startled him. He was annoyed. "How the devil could I have forgotten where it was?" he muttered, and groped his way along the third wall to the fireplace. "I must put things to rights," said he, feeling the floor for the candle.

Having recovered that, he lighted it and instantly turned his eyes to the table, where, naturally, nothing had undergone any change. The reading-stand lay unobserved upon the floor: he had forgotten to "put it to rights." He looked all about the room, dispersing the deeper shadows by movements of the candle in his hand, and crossing over to the door tested it by turning and pulling the knob with all his strength. It did not yield and this seemed to afford him a certain satisfaction; indeed, he secured it more firmly by a bolt which he had not before observed. Returning to his chair, he looked at his watch; it was half-past nine. With a start of surprise he held the watch at his ear. It had not stopped. The candle was now visibly shorter. He again extinguished it, placing it on the floor at his side as before.

Mr. Jarette was not at his ease; he was distinctly dissatisfied with his surroundings, and with himself for being so. "What have I to fear?" he thought. "This is ridiculous and disgraceful; I will not be so great a fool." But courage does not come of saying, "I will be courageous," nor of recognizing its appropriateness to the occasion. The more Jarette condemned himself, the more reason he gave himself for condemnation; the greater the number of variations which he played upon the simple theme of the harmlessness of the dead, the more insupportable grew the discord of his emotions. "What!" he cried aloud in the anguish of his spirit, "what! shall I, who have not a shade of superstition in my nature —I, who have no belief in immortality—I, who know (and never more clearly than now) that the after-life is the dream of a desire— shall I lose at once my bet, my honor and my self-respect, perhaps my reason, because certain savage ancestors dwelling in caves and burrows conceived the monstrous notion that the dead walk by night?—that——" Distinctly, unmistakably, Mr. Jarette heard behind him a light, soft sound of footfalls, deliberate, regular, successively nearer!

IV

Just before daybreak the next morning Dr. Helberson and his young friend Harper were driving slowly through the streets of North Beach in the doctor's coupé.

"Have you still the confidence of youth in the courage or stolidity of your friend?" said the elder man. "Do you believe that I have lost this wager?"

"I *know* you have," replied the other, with enfeebling emphasis.

"Well, upon my soul, I hope so."

It was spoken earnestly, almost solemnly. There was a silence for a few moments.

"Harper," the doctor resumed, looking very serious in the shifting half-lights that entered the carriage as they passed the street lamps, "I don't feel altogether comfortable about this business. If your friend had not irritated me by the contemptuous manner in which he treated my doubt of his endurance —a purely physical quality—and by the cool incivility of his suggestion that the corpse be that of a physician, I should not have gone on with it. If anything should happen we are ruined, as I fear we deserve to be."

"What can happen? Even if the matter should be taking a serious turn, of which I am not at all afraid, Mancher has only to 'resurrect' himself and explain matters. With a genuine 'subject' from the dissecting-room, or one of your late patients, it might be different."

Dr. Mancher, then, had been as good as his promise; he was the "corpse."

Dr. Helberson was silent for a long time, as the carriage, at a snail's pace, crept along the same street it had traveled two or three times already. Presently he spoke: "Well, let us hope that Mancher, if he has had to rise from the dead, has been discreet about it. A mistake in that might make matters worse instead of better."

"Yes," said Harper, "Jarette would kill him. But, Doctor"—looking at his watch as the carriage passed a gas lamp—"it is nearly four o'clock at last."

A moment later the two had quitted the vehicle and were walking briskly toward the long-unoccupied house belonging to the doctor in which they had immured Mr. Jarette in accordance with the terms of the mad wager. As they neared it they met a man running. "Can you tell me," he cried, suddenly checking his speed, "where I can find a doctor?"

"What's the matter?" Helberson asked, non-committal.

"Go and see for yourself," said the man, resuming his running.

They hastened on. Arrived at the house, they saw several persons entering in haste and excitement. In some of the dwellings near by and across the way the chamber windows were thrown up, showing a protrusion of heads. All heads were asking questions, none heeding the questions of the others. A few of the windows with closed blinds were illuminated; the inmates of those rooms were dressing to come down. Exactly opposite the door of the house that they sought a street lamp threw a yellow, insufficient light upon the scene, seeming to say that it could disclose a good deal more if it wished. Harper paused at the door and laid a hand upon his companion's arm. "It is all up with us, Doctor," he said in extreme agitation, which contrasted strangely with his free-and-easy words; "the game has gone against us all. Let's not go in there; I'm for lying low."

"I'm a physician," said Dr. Helberson, calmly; "there may be need of one."

They mounted the doorsteps and were about to enter. The door was open; the street lamp opposite lighted the passage into which it opened. It was full of men. Some had ascended the stairs at the farther end, and, denied admittance above, waited for better fortune. All were talking, none listening. Suddenly, on the upper landing there was a great commotion; a man had sprung out of a door and was breaking away from those endeavoring to detain him. Down through the mass of affrighted idlers he came, pushing them aside, flattening them against the wall on one side, or compelling them to cling to the rail on the other, clutching them by the throat, striking them savagely, thrusting them back down the stairs and walking over the fallen. His clothing was in disorder, he was without a hat. His eyes, wild and restless, had in them something more terrifying than his apparently superhuman strength. His face, smooth-shaven, was bloodless, his hair frost-white.

As the crowd at the foot of the stairs, having more freedom, fell away to let him pass

Harper sprang forward. "Jarette! Jarette!"
he cried.

Dr. Helberson seized Harper by the collar
and dragged him back. The man looked
into their faces without seeming to see them
and sprang through the door, down the steps,
into the street, and away. A stout policeman,
who had had inferior success in conquering
his way down the stairway, followed a moment later and started in pursuit, all the heads
in the windows—those of women and children
now—screaming in guidance.

The stairway being now partly cleared,
most of the crowd having rushed down to
the street to observe the flight and pursuit, Dr.
Helberson mounted to the landing, followed
by Harper. At a door in the upper passage
an officer denied them admittance. "We are
physicians," said the doctor, and they passed
in. The room was full of men, dimly seen,
crowded about a table. The newcomers
edged their way forward and looked over the
shoulders of those in the front rank. Upon
the table, the lower limbs covered with a
sheet, lay the body of a man, brilliantly illuminated by the beam of a bull's-eye lantern
held by a policeman standing at the feet. The

others, excepting those near the head—the officer himself—all were in darkness. The face of the body showed yellow, repulsive, horrible! The eyes were partly open and upturned and the jaw fallen; traces of froth defiled the lips, the chin, the cheeks. A tall man, evidently a doctor, bent over the body with his hand thrust under the shirt front. He withdrew it and placed two fingers in the open mouth. "This man has been about six hours dead," said he. "It is a case for the coroner."

He drew a card from his pocket, handed it to the officer and made his way toward the door.

"Clear the room—out, all!" said the officer, sharply, and the body disappeared as if it had been snatched away, as shifting the lantern he flashed its beam of light here and there against the faces of the crowd. The effect was amazing! The men, blinded, confused, almost terrified, made a tumultuous rush for the door, pushing, crowding, and tumbling over one another as they fled, like the hosts of Night before the shafts of Apollo. Upon the struggling, trampling mass the officer poured his light without pity and without cessation. Caught in the current, Helberson and Harper were swept out of the room and cascaded down the stairs into the street.

"Good God, Doctor! did I not tell you that Jarette would kill him?" said Harper, as soon as they were clear of the crowd.

"I believe you did," replied the other, without apparent emotion.

They walked on in silence, block after block. Against the graying east the dwellings of the hill tribes showed in silhouette. The familiar milk wagon was already astir in the streets; the baker's man would soon come upon the scene; the newspaper carrier was abroad in the land.

"It strikes me, youngster," said Helberson, "that you and I have been having too much of the morning air lately. It is unwholesome; we need a change. What do you say to a tour in Europe?"

"When?"

"I'm not particular. I should suppose that four o'clock this afternoon would be early enough."

"I'll meet you at the boat," said Harper.

V

Seven years afterward these two men sat upon a bench in Madison Square, New York, in familiar conversation. Another man, who had been observing them for some time, himself unobserved, approached and, courteously lifting his hat from locks as white as frost, said: "I beg your pardon, gentlemen, but when you have killed a man by coming to life, it is best to change clothes with him, and at the first opportunity make a break for liberty."

Helberson and Harper exchanged significant glances. They were obviously amused. The former then looked the stranger kindly in the eye and replied:

"That has always been my plan. I entirely agree with you as to its advant——"

He stopped suddenly, rose and went white. He stared at the man, open-mouthed; he trembled visibly.

"Ah!" said the stranger, "I see that you are indisposed, Doctor. If you cannot treat yourself Dr. Harper can do something for you, I am sure."

"Who the devil are you?" said Harper, bluntly.

The stranger came nearer and, bending toward them, said in a whisper: "I call myself Jarette sometimes, but I don't mind telling you, for old friendship, that I am Dr. William Mancher."

The revelation brought Harper to his feet. "Mancher!" he cried; and Helberson added: "It is true, by God!"

"Yes," said the stranger, smiling vaguely, "it is true enough, no doubt."

He hesitated and seemed to be trying to recall something, then began humming a popular air. He had apparently forgotten their presence.

"Look here, Mancher," said the elder of the two, "tell us just what occurred that night —to Jarette, you know."

"Oh, yes, about Jarette," said the other. "It's odd I should have neglected to tell you —I tell it so often. You see I knew, by overhearing him talking to himself, that he was pretty badly frightened. So I couldn't resist the temptation to come to life and have a bit of fun out of him—I couldn't really. That was all right, though certainly I did not think he would take it so seriously; I did not, truly. And afterward—well, it was a tough job changing places with him, and then—damn you! you didn't let me out!"

Nothing could exceed the ferocity with which these last words were delivered. Both men stepped back in alarm.

"We?—why—why," Helberson stammered, losing his self-possession utterly, "we had nothing to do with it."

"Didn't I say you were Drs. Hell-born and Sharper?" inquired the man, laughing.

"My name is Helberson, yes; and this gentleman is Mr. Harper," replied the former, reassured by the laugh. "But we are not physicians now; we are—well, hang it, old man, we are gamblers."

And that was the truth.

"A very good profession—very good, indeed; and, by the way, I hope Sharper here paid over Jarette's money like an honest stakeholder. A very good and honorable profession," he repeated, thoughtfully, moving carelessly away; "but I stick to the old one. I am High Supreme Medical Officer of the Bloomingdale Asylum; it is my duty to cure the superintendent."

THE MAN AND THE SNAKE

It is of veritabyll report, and attested of so many that there be nowe of wyse and learned none to gaynsaye it, that yᵉ serpente hys eye hath a magnetick propertie that whosoe falleth into ·its svasion is drawn forwards in despyte of his wille, and perisheth miserabyll by yᵉ creature hys byte.

STRETCHED at ease upon a sofa, in gown and slippers, Harker Brayton smiled as he read the foregoing sentence in old Morryster's *Marvells of Science.* "The only marvel in the matter," he said to himself, "is that the wise and learned in Morryster's day should have believed such nonsense as is rejected by most of even the ignorant in ours."

A train of reflection followed—for Brayton was a man of thought—and he unconsciously lowered his book without altering the direction of his eyes. As soon as the volume had gone below the line of sight, something in an obscure corner of the room recalled his attention to his surroundings. What he saw, in the shadow under his bed, was two small points of light, apparently about an inch apart. They might have been reflections of the gas jet above him, in metal nail heads; he gave them but little thought and resumed his reading. A moment later something—some impulse which it did not occur to him to analyze—impelled him to lower the book again and seek for what he saw before. The points of light were still there. They seemed to have become brighter than before, shining with a greenish lustre that he had not at first observed. He thought, too, that they might have moved a trifle—were somewhat nearer. They were still too much in shadow, however, to reveal their nature and origin to an indolent attention, and again he resumed his reading. Suddenly something in the text suggested a thought that made him start and drop the book for the third time to the side of the sofa, whence, escaping from his hand, it fell sprawling to the floor, back upward. Brayton, half-risen, was staring intently into the obscurity beneath the bed, where the points of light shone with, it seemed to him, an added fire. His attention was now fully aroused, his gaze eager and imperative. It disclosed, almost directly under the foot-rail of the bed, the coils of a large serpent—the points of light were its eyes! Its horrible head, thrust flatly forth from the innermost coil and resting upon the outermost, was directed straight toward him, the definition of the wide, brutal jaw and the idiot-like forehead serving to show the direction of its malevolent gaze. The eyes were no longer merely luminous points; they looked into his own with a meaning, a malign significance.

II

A snake in a bedroom of a modern city dwelling of the better sort is, happily, not so common a phenomenon as to make explanation altogether needless. Harker Brayton, a bachelor of thirty-five, a scholar, idler and something of an athlete, rich, popular and of sound health, had returned to San Francisco from all manner of remote and unfamiliar countries. His tastes, always a trifle luxurious, had taken on an added exuberance from long privation; and the resources of even the Castle Hotel being inadequate to their perfect gratification, he had gladly accepted the hospitality of his friend, Dr. Druring, the distinguished scientist. Dr. Druring's house, a large, old-fashioned one in what is now an obscure quarter of the city, had an outer and

visible aspect of proud reserve. It plainly
would not associate with the contiguous elements of its altered environment, and appeared to have developed some of the eccen-
tricities which come of isolation. One of
these was a "wing," conspicuously irrelevant
in point of architecture, and no less rebellious
in matter of purpose; for it was a combination
of laboratory, menagerie and museum. It
was here that the doctor indulged the scientific side of his nature in the study of such
forms of animal life as engaged his interest
and comforted his taste—which, it must be
confessed, ran rather to the lower types. For
one of the higher nimbly and sweetly to re-
commend itself unto his gentle senses it had at
least to retain certain rudimentary characteristics allying it to such "dragons of the
prime" as toads and snakes. His scientific
sympathies were distinctly reptilian; he loved
nature's vulgarians and described himself as
the Zola of zoölogy. His wife and daughters
not having the advantage to share his enlight-
ened curiosity regarding the works and ways
of our ill-starred fellow-creatures, were with
needless austerity excluded from what he
called the Snakery and doomed to companionship with their own kind, though to soften the

rigors of their lot he had permitted them out of his great wealth to outdo the reptiles in the gorgeousness of their surroundings and to shine with a superior splendor.

Architecturally and in point of "furnishing" the Snakery had a severe simplicity befitting the humble circumstances of its occupants, many of whom, indeed, could not safely have been intrusted with the liberty that is necessary to the full enjoyment of luxury, for they had the troublesome peculiarity of being alive. In their own apartments, however, they were under as little personal restraint as was compatible with their protection from the baneful habit of swallowing one another; and, as Brayton had thoughtfully been apprised, it was more than a tradition that some of them had at divers times been found in parts of the premises where it would have embarrassed them to explain their presence. Despite the Snakery and its uncanny associations—to which, indeed, he gave little attention—Brayton found life at the Druring mansion very much to his mind.

III

Beyond a smart shock of surprise and a shudder of mere loathing Mr. Brayton was not greatly affected. His first thought was to

ring the call bell and bring a servant; but
although the bell cord dangled within easy
reach he made no movement toward it; it had
occurred to his mind that the act might subject him to the suspicion of fear, which he
certainly did not feel. He was more keenly
conscious of the incongruous nature of the situation than affected by its perils; it was revolting, but absurd.

The reptile was of a species with which
Brayton was unfamiliar. Its length he could
only conjecture; the body at the largest visible
part seemed about as thick as his forearm.
In what way was it dangerous, if in any way?
Was it venomous? Was it a constrictor? His
knowledge of nature's danger signals did not
enable him to say; he had never deciphered
the code.

If not dangerous the creature was at least
offensive. It was *de trop*—"matter out of
place"—an impertinence. The gem was unworthy of the setting. Even the barbarous
taste of our time and country, which had
loaded the walls of the room with pictures,
the floor with furniture and the furniture with
bric-a-brac, had not quite fitted the place for
this bit of the savage life of the jungle. Besides—insupportable thought!—the exhala-

tions of its breath mingled with the atmosphere which he himself was breathing.

These thoughts shaped themselves with greater or less definition in Brayton's mind and begot action. The process is what we call consideration and decision. It is thus that we are wise and unwise. It is thus that the withered leaf in an autumn breeze shows greater or less intelligence than its fellows, falling upon the land or upon the lake. The secret of human action is an open one: something contracts our muscles. Does it matter if we give to the preparatory molecular changes the name of will?

Brayton rose to his feet and prepared to back softly away from the snake, without disturbing it if possible, and through the door. Men retire so from the presence of the great, for greatness is power and power is a menace. He knew that he could walk backward without error. Should the monster follow, the taste which had plastered the walls with paintings had consistently supplied a rack of murderous Oriental weapons from which he could snatch one to suit the occasion. In the mean time the snake's eyes burned with a more pitiless malevolence than before.

Brayton lifted his right foot free of the

floor to step backward. That moment he felt a strong aversion to doing so.

"I am accounted brave," he thought; "is bravery, then, no more than pride? Because there are none to witness the shame shall I retreat?"

He was steadying himself with his right hand upon the back of a chair, his foot suspended.

"Nonsense!" he said aloud; "I am not so great a coward as to fear to seem to myself afraid."

He lifted the foot a little higher by slightly bending the knee and thrust it sharply to the floor—an inch in front of the other! He could not think how that occurred. A trial with the left foot had the same result; it was again in advance of the right. The hand upon the chair back was grasping it; the arm was straight, reaching somewhat backward. One might have said that he was reluctant to lose his hold. The snake's malignant head was still thrust forth from the inner coil as before, the neck level. It had not moved, but its eyes were now electric sparks, radiating an infinity of luminous needles.

The man had an ashy pallor. Again he took a step forward, and another, partly dragging the chair, which when finally released fell upon the floor with a crash. The man groaned; the snake made neither sound nor motion, but its eyes were two dazzling suns. The reptile itself was wholly concealed by them. They gave off enlarging rings of rich and vivid colors, which at their greatest expansion successively vanished like soap-bubbles; they seemed to approach his very face, and anon were an immeasurable distance away. He heard, somewhere, the continuous throbbing of a great drum, with desultory bursts of far music, inconceivably sweet, like the tones of an æolian harp. He knew it for the sunrise melody of Memnon's statue, and thought he stood in the Nileside reeds hearing with exalted sense that immortal anthem through the silence of the centuries.

The music ceased; rather, it became by insensible degrees the distant roll of a retreating thunder-storm. A landscape, glittering with sun and rain, stretched before him, arched with a vivid rainbow framing in its giant curve a hundred visible cities. In the middle distance a vast serpent, wearing a crown, reared its head out of its voluminous convolutions and looked at him with his dead mother's eyes. Suddenly this enchanting landscape seemed to rise swiftly upward like the drop scene at a theatre, and vanished in a blank. Something struck him a hard blow upon the face and breast. He had fallen to the floor; the blood ran from his broken nose and his bruised lips. For a time he was dazed and stunned, and lay with closed eyes, his face against the floor. In a few moments he had recovered, and then knew that this fall, by withdrawing his eyes, had broken the spell that held him. He felt that now, by keeping his gaze averted, he would be able to retreat. But the thought of the serpent within a few feet of his head, yet unseen—perhaps in the very act of springing upon him and throwing its coils about his throat—was too horrible! He lifted his head, stared again into those baleful eyes and was again in bondage.

The snake had not moved and appeared somewhat to have lost its power upon the imagination; the gorgeous illusions of a few moments before were not repeated. Beneath that flat and brainless brow its black, beady eyes simply glittered as at first with an ex- pression unspeakably malignant. It was as if the creature, assured of its triumph, had de- termined to practise no more alluring wiles.

Now ensued a fearful scene. The man,

prone upon the floor, within a yard of his enemy, raised the upper part of his body upon his elbows, his head thrown back, his legs extended to their full length. His face was white between its stains of blood; his eyes were strained open to their uttermost expansion. There was froth upon his lips; it dropped off in flakes. Strong convulsions ran through his body, making almost serpentile undulations. He bent himself at the waist, shifting his legs from side to side. And every movement left him a little nearer to the snake. He thrust his hands forward to brace himself back, yet constantly advanced upon his elbows.

IV

Dr. Druring and his wife sat in the library. The scientist was in rare good humor.

"I have just obtained by exchange with another collector," he said, "a splendid specimen of the *ophiophagus*."

"And what may that be?" the lady inquired with a somewhat languid interest.

"Why, bless my soul, what profound ignorance! My dear, a man who ascertains after marriage that his wife does not know Greek is entitled to a divorce. The *ophiophagus* is a snake that eats other snakes."

"I hope it will eat all yours," she said, absently shifting the lamp. "But how does it get the other snakes? By charming them, I suppose."

"That is just like you, dear," said the doctor, with an affectation of petulance. "You know how irritating to me is any allusion to that vulgar superstition about a snake's power of fascination."

The conversation was interrupted by a mighty cry, which rang through the silent house like the voice of a demon shouting in a tomb! Again and yet again it sounded, with terrible distinctness. They sprang to their feet, the man confused, the lady pale and speechless with fright. Almost before the echoes of the last cry had died away the doctor was out of the room, springing up the stairs two steps at a time. In the corridor in front of Brayton's chamber he met some servants who had come from the upper floor. Together they rushed at the door without knocking. It was unfastened and gave way. Brayton lay upon his stomach on the floor, dead. His head and arms were partly concealed under the foot rail of the bed. They pulled the body away, turning it upon the back. The face was daubed with blood and froth, the eyes were wide open, staring—a dreadful sight!

"Died in a fit," said the scientist, bending his knee and placing his hand upon the heart. While in that position, he chanced to look under the bed. "Good God!" he added, "how did this thing get in here?"

He reached under the bed, pulled out the snake and flung it, still coiled, to the center of the room, whence with a harsh, shuffling sound it slid across the polished floor till stopped by the wall, where it lay without motion. It was a stuffed snake; its eyes were two shoe buttons.

A HOLY TERROR

I

THERE was an entire lack of interest in the latest arrival at Hurdy-Gurdy. He was not even christened with the picturesquely descriptive nick-name which is so frequently a mining camp's word of welcome to the newcomer. In almost any other camp thereabout this circumstance would of itself have secured him some such appellation as "The White-headed Conundrum," or "No Sarvey"—an expression naïvely supposed to suggest to quick intelligences the Spanish *quien sabe*. He came without provoking a ripple of concern upon the social surface of Hurdy-Gurdy—a place which to the general Californian contempt of men's personal history superadded a local indifference of its own. The time was long past when it was of any importance who came there, or if anybody came. No one was living at Hurdy-Gurdy.

Two years before, the camp had boasted a stirring population of two or three thousand males and not fewer than a dozen females.

A majority of the former had done a few weeks' earnest work in demonstrating, to the disgust of the latter, the singularly mendacious character of the person whose ingenious tales of rich gold deposits had lured them thither— work, by the way, in which there was as little mental satisfaction as pecuniary profit; for a bullet from the pistol of a public-spirited citizen had put that imaginative gentleman beyond the reach of aspersion on the third day of the camp's existence. Still, his fiction had a certain foundation in fact, and many had lingered a considerable time in and about Hurdy-Gurdy, though now all had been long gone.

But they had left ample evidence of their sojourn. From the point where Injun Creek falls into the Rio San Juan Smith, up along both banks of the former into the cañon whence it emerges, extended a double row of forlorn shanties that seemed about to fall upon one another's neck to bewail their desolation; while about an equal number appeared to have straggled up the slope on either hand and perched themselves upon commanding eminences, whence they craned forward to get a good view of the affecting scene. Most of these habitations were emaciated as by famine to the condition of mere skeletons, about which clung unlovely tatters of what might have been skin, but was really canvas. The little valley itself, torn and gashed by pick and shovel, was unhandsome with long, bending lines of decaying flume resting here and there upon the summits of sharp ridges, and stilting awkwardly across the intervals upon unhewn poles. The whole place presented that raw and forbidding aspect of arrested development which is a new country's substitute for the solemn grace of ruin wrought by time. Wherever there remained a patch of the original soil a rank overgrowth of weeds and brambles had spread upon the scene, and from its dank, unwholesome shades the visitor curious in such matters might have obtained numberless souvenirs of the camp's former glory—fellowless boots mantled with green mould and plethoric of rotting leaves; an occasional old felt hat; desultory remnants of a flannel shirt; sardine boxes inhumanly mutilated and a surprising profusion of black bottles distributed with a truly catholic impartiality, everywhere.

II

The man who had now rediscovered Hurdy-Gurdy was evidently not curious as to its archæology. Nor, as he looked about him upon the dismal evidences of wasted work and broken hopes, their dispiriting significance accentuated by the ironical pomp of a cheap gilding by the rising sun, did he supplement his sigh of weariness by one of sensibility. He simply removed from the back of his tired burro a miner's outfit a trifle larger than the animal itself, picketed that creature and selecting a hatchet from his kit moved off at once across the dry bed of Injun Creek to the top of a low, gravelly hill beyond.

Stepping across a prostrate fence of brush and boards he picked up one of the latter, split it into five parts and sharpened them at one end. He then began a kind of search, occasionally stooping to examine something with close attention. At last his patient scrutiny appeared to be rewarded with success, for he suddenly erected his figure to its full height, made a gesture of satisfaction, pronounced the word " Scarry " and at once strode away with long, equal steps, which he counted. Then he stopped and drove one of his stakes into the earth. He then looked carefully about him, measured off a number of paces over a singularly uneven ground and hammered in another. Pacing off twice the distance at a right angle to his former course he drove down a third, and repeating the process sank home the fourth, and then a fifth. This he split at the top and in the cleft inserted an old letter envelope covered with an intricate system of pencil tracks. In short, he staked off a hill claim in strict accordance with the local mining laws of Hurdy-Gurdy and put up the customary notice.

It is necessary to explain that one of the adjuncts to Hurdy-Gurdy—one to which that metropolis became afterward itself an adjunct—was a cemetery. In the first week of the camp's existence this had been thoughtfully laid out by a committee of citizens. The day after had been signalized by a debate between two members of the committee, with reference to a more eligible site, and on the third day the necropolis was inaugurated by a double funeral. As the camp had waned the cemetery had waxed; and long before the ultimate inhabitant, victorious alike over the insidious malaria and the forthright revolver, had turned the tail of his pack-ass upon Injun Creek the outlying settlement had become a populous if not popular suburb. And now, when the town was fallen into the sere and yellow leaf of an unlovely senility, the graveyard—though somewhat marred by time and circumstance, and not altogether exempt from innovations in grammar and experiments in orthography, to say nothing of the devastating coyote—answered the humble needs of its denizens with reasonable completeness. It comprised a generous two acres of ground, which with commendable thrift but needless care had been selected for its mineral unworth, contained two or three skeleton trees (one of which had a stout lateral branch from which a weather-wasted rope still significantly dangled), half a hundred gravelly mounds, a score of rude headboards displaying the literary peculiarities above mentioned and a struggling colony of prickly pears. Altogether, God's Location, as with characteristic reverence it had been called, could justly boast of an indubitably superior quality of desolation. It was in the most thickly settled part of this interesting demesne that Mr. Jefferson Doman staked off his claim. If in the prosecution of his design he should deem it expedient to remove any of the dead they would have the right to be suitably reinterred.

III

This Mr. Jefferson Doman was from Elizabethtown, New Jersey, where six years before he had left his heart in the keeping of a golden-haired, demure-mannered young woman named Mary Matthews, as collateral security for his return to claim her hand.

"I just *know* you'll never get back alive—you never do succeed in anything," was the remark which illustrated Miss Matthews's notion of what constituted success and, inferentially, her view of the nature of encouragement. She added: "If you don't I'll go to California too. I can put the coins in little bags as you dig them out."

This characteristically feminine theory of auriferous deposits did not commend itself to the masculine intelligence: it was Mr. Doman's belief that gold was found in a liquid state. He deprecated her intent with considerable enthusiasm, suppressed her sobs with a light hand upon her mouth, laughed in her eyes as he kissed away her tears, and with a cheerful "Ta-ta" went to California to labor for her through the long, loveless years, with a strong heart, an alert hope and a steadfast fidelity that never for a moment forgot what it was about. In the mean time, Miss Matthews had granted a monopoly of her humble talent for sacking up coins to Mr. Jo. Seeman, of New York, gambler, by whom it was better appreciated than her commanding

genius for unsacking and bestowing them
upon his local rivals. Of this latter aptitude,
indeed, he manifested his disapproval by an
act which secured him the position of clerk
of the laundry in the State prison, and for her
the *sobriquet* of " Split-faced Moll." At
about this time she wrote to Mr. Doman a
touching letter of renunciation, inclosing her
photograph to prove that she had no longer
a right to indulge the dream of becoming
Mrs. Doman, and recounting so graphically
her fall from a horse that the staid " plug "
upon which Mr. Doman had ridden into Red
Dog to get the letter made vicarious atonement under the spur all the way back to camp.
The letter failed in a signal way to accomplish
its object; the fidelity which had before been
to Mr. Doman a matter of love and duty was
thenceforth a matter of honor also; and the
photograph, showing the once pretty face
sadly disfigured as by the slash of a knife, was
duly instated in his affections and its more
comely predecessor treated with contumelious
neglect. On being informed of this, Miss
Matthews, it is only fair to say, appeared less
surprised than from the apparently low estimate of Mr. Doman's generosity which the
tone of her former letter attested one would

naturally have expected her to be. Soon after, however, her letters grew infrequent, and then ceased altogether.

But Mr. Doman had another correspondent, Mr. Barney Bree, of Hurdy-Gurdy, formerly of Red Dog. This gentleman, although a notable figure among miners, was not a miner. His knowledge of mining consisted mainly in a marvelous command of its slang, to which he made copious contributions, enriching its vocabulary with a wealth of uncommon phrases more remarkable for their aptness than their refinement, and which impressed the unlearned "tenderfoot" with a lively sense of the profundity of their inventor's acquirements. When not entertaining a circle of admiring auditors from San Francisco or the East he could commonly be found pursuing the comparatively obscure industry of sweeping out the various dance houses and purifying the cuspidors.

Barney had apparently but two passions in life—love of Jefferson Doman, who had once been of some service to him, and love of whisky, which certainly had not. He had been among the first in the rush to Hurdy-Gurdy, but had not prospered, and had sunk by degrees to the position of grave digger.

This was not a vocation, but Barney in a desultory way turned his trembling hand to it whenever some local misunderstanding at the card table and his own partial recovery from a prolonged debauch occurred coincidently in point of time. One day Mr. Doman received, at Red Dog, a letter with the simple postmark, " Hurdy, Cal.," and being occupied with another matter, carelessly thrust it into a chink of his cabin for future perusal. Some two years later it was accidentally dislodged and he read it. It ran as follows:—

HURDY, June 6.

FRIEND JEFF: I've hit her hard in the boneyard. She's blind and lousy. I'm on the divvy—that's me, and mum's my lay till you toot. Yours,   BARNEY.

P. S.—I've clayed her with Scarry.

With some knowledge of the general mining camp *argot* and of Mr. Bree's private system for the communication of ideas Mr. Doman had no difficulty in understanding by this uncommon epistle that Barney while performing his duty as grave digger had uncovered a quartz ledge with no outcroppings; that it was visibly rich in free gold; that, moved by considerations of friendship, he was willing to accept Mr. Doman as a partner and awaiting that gentleman's declaration of his will in the matter would discreetly keep the discovery a secret. From the postscript it was plainly inferable that in order to conceal the treasure he had buried above it the mortal part of a person named Scarry.

From subsequent events, as related to Mr. Doman at Red Dog, it would appear that before taking this precaution Mr. Bree must have had the thrift to remove a modest competency of the gold; at any rate, it was at about that time that he entered upon that memorable series of potations and treatings which is still one of the cherished traditions of the San Juan Smith country, and is spoken of with respect as far away as Ghost Rock and Lone Hand. At its conclusion some former citizens of Hurdy-Gurdy, for whom he had performed the last kindly office at the cemetery, made room for him among them, and he rested well.

IV

Having finished staking off his claim Mr. Doman walked back to the centre of it and stood again at the spot where his search among the graves had expired in the exclamation, " Scarry." He bent again over the headboard that bore that name and as if to reinforce the senses of sight and hearing ran his forefinger along the rudely carved letters. Re-erecting himself he appended orally to the simple inscription the shockingly forthright epitaph, " She was a holy terror!"

Had Mr. Doman been required to make these words good with proof—as, considering their somewhat censorious character, he doubt-less should have been—he would have found himself embarrassed by the absence of reput-able witnesses, and hearsay evidence would have been the best he could command. At the time when Scarry had been prevalent in the mining camps thereabout—when, as the editor of the *Hurdy Herald* would have phrased it, she was " in the plenitude of her power "— Mr. Doman's fortunes had been at a low ebb, and he had led the vagrantly laborious life of a prospector. His time had been mostly spent in the mountains, now with one com-panion, now with another. It was from the admiring recitals of these casual partners, fresh from the various camps, that his judg-ment of Scarry had been made up; he him-self had never had the doubtful advantage of her acquaintance and the precarious distinc-tion of her favor. And when, finally, on the termination of her perverse career at Hurdy-Gurdy he had read in a chance copy of the

Herald her column-long obituary (written by the local humorist of that lively sheet in the highest style of his art) Doman had paid to her memory and to her historiographer's genius the tribute of a smile and chivalrously forgotten her. Standing now at the grave-side of this mountain Messalina he recalled the leading events of her turbulent career, as he had heard them celebrated at his several camp-fires, and perhaps with an unconscious attempt at self-justification repeated that she was a holy terror, and sank his pick into her grave up to the handle. At that moment a raven, which had silently settled upon a branch of the blasted tree above his head, solemnly snapped its beak and uttered its mind about the matter with an approving croak.

Pursuing his discovery of free gold with great zeal, which he probably credited to his conscience as a grave digger, Mr. Barney Bree had made an unusually deep sepulcher, and it was near sunset before Mr. Doman, laboring with the leisurely deliberation of one who has "a dead sure thing" and no fear of an adverse claimant's enforcement of a prior right, reached the coffin and uncovered it. When he had done so he was confronted by a difficulty for which he had made no pro-

vision; the coffin—a mere flat shell of not very
well-preserved redwood boards, apparently—
had no handles, and it filled the entire bottom
of the excavation. The best he could do without violating the decent sanctities of the situation was to make the excavation sufficiently
longer to enable him to stand at the head of
the casket and getting his powerful hands un-
derneath erect it upon its narrower end; and
this he proceeded to do. The approach of
night quickened his efforts. He had no
thought of abandoning his task at this stage to
resume it on the morrow under more advant-
ageous conditions. The feverish stimulation
of cupidity and the fascination of terror held
him to his dismal work with an iron authority.
He no longer idled, but wrought with a terrible zeal. His head uncovered, his outer garments discarded, his shirt opened at the neck
and thrown back from his breast, down which
ran sinuous rills of perspiration, this hardy
and impenitent gold-getter and grave-robber
toiled with a giant energy that almost digni-
fied the character of his horrible purpose; and
when the sun fringes had burned themselves
out along the crest line of the western hills,
and the full moon had climbed out of the
shadows that lay along the purple plain, he

had erected the coffin upon its foot, where it stood propped against the end of the open grave. Then, standing up to his neck in the earth at the opposite extreme of the excavation, as he looked at the coffin upon which the moonlight now fell with a full illumination he was thrilled with a sudden terror to observe upon it the startling apparition of a dark human head—the shadow of his own. For a moment this simple and natural circumstance unnerved him. The noise of his labored breathing frightened him, and he tried to still it, but his bursting lungs would not be denied. Then, laughing half-audibly and wholly without spirit, he began making movements of his head from side to side, in order to compel the apparition to repeat them. He found a comforting reassurance in asserting his command over his own shadow. He was temporizing, making, with unconscious prudence, a dilatory opposition to an impending catastrophe. He felt that invisible forces of evil were closing in upon him, and he parleyed for time with the Inevitable.

He now observed in succession several unusual circumstances. The surface of the coffin upon which his eyes were fastened was not flat; it presented two distinct ridges, one longitudinal and the other transverse. Where these intersected at the widest part there was a corroded metallic plate that reflected the moonlight with a dismal lustre. Along the outer edges of the coffin, at long intervals, were rust-eaten heads of nails. This frail product of the carpenter's art had been put into the grave the wrong side up!

Perhaps it was one of the humors of the camp—a practical manifestation of the facetious spirit that had found literary expression in the topsy-turvy obituary notice from the pen of Hurdy-Gurdy's great humorist. Perhaps it had some occult personal signification impenetrable to understandings uninstructed in local traditions. A more charitable hypothesis is that it was owing to a misadventure on the part of Mr. Barney Bree, who, making the interment unassisted (either by choice for the conservation of his golden secret, or through public apathy), had committed a blunder which he was afterward unable or unconcerned to rectify. However it had come about, poor Scarry had indubitably been put into the earth face downward.

When terror and absurdity make alliance, the effect is frightful. This strong-hearted and daring man, this hardy night worker among the dead, this defiant antagonist of darkness and desolation, succumbed to a ridiculous surprise. He was smitten with a thrilling chill—shivered, and shook his massive shoulders as if to throw off an icy hand. He no longer breathed, and the blood in his veins, unable to abate its impetus, surged hotly beneath his cold skin. Unleavened with oxygen, it mounted to his head and congested his brain. His physical functions had gone over to the enemy; his very heart was arrayed against him. He did not move; he could not have cried out. He needed but a coffin to be dead—as dead as the death that confronted him with only the length of an open grave and the thickness of a rotting plank between.

Then, one by one, his senses returned; the tide of terror that had overwhelmed his faculties began to recede. But with the return of his senses he became singularly unconscious of the object of his fear. He saw the moonlight gilding the coffin, but no longer the coffin that it gilded. Raising his eyes and turning his head, he noted, curiously and with surprise, the black branches of the dead tree, and tried to estimate the length of the weather-worn rope that dangled from its ghostly hand. The monotonous barking of distant coyotes affected

him as something he had heard years ago in a
dream. An owl flapped awkwardly above
him on noiseless wings, and he tried to fore-
cast the direction of its flight when it should
encounter the cliff that reared its illuminated
front a mile away. His hearing took account
of a gopher's stealthy tread in the shadow of
the cactus. He was intensely observant; his
senses were all alert; but he saw not the coffin.
As one can gaze at the sun until it looks black
and then vanishes, so his mind, having exhausted its capacities of dread, was no longer
conscious of the separate existence of anything
dreadful. The Assassin was cloaking the
sword.

It was during this lull in the battle that
he became sensible of a faint, sickening odor.
At first he thought it was that of a rattle-
snake, and involuntarily tried to look about his
feet. They were nearly invisible in the gloom
of the grave. A hoarse, gurgling sound, like
the death-rattle in a human throat, seemed to
come out of the sky, and a moment later a
great, black, angular shadow, like the same
sound made visible, dropped curving from the
topmost branch of the spectral tree, fluttered
for an instant before his face and sailed
fiercely away into the mist along the creek.

It was the raven. The incident recalled him to a sense of the situation, and again his eyes sought the upright coffin, now illuminated by the moon for half its length. He saw the gleam of the metallic plate and tried without moving to decipher the inscription. Then he fell to speculating upon what was behind it. His creative imagination presented him a vivid picture. The planks no longer seemed an obstacle to his vision and he saw the livid corpse of the dead woman, standing in grave-clothes, and staring vacantly at him, with lid-less, shrunken eyes. The lower jaw was fallen, the upper lip drawn away from the uncovered teeth. He could make out a mot-tled pattern on the hollow cheeks—the macu-lations of decay. By some mysterious process his mind reverted for the first time that day to the photograph of Mary Matthews. He contrasted its blonde beauty with the forbid-ding aspect of this dead face—the most be-loved object that he knew with the most hid-eous that he could conceive.

The Assassin now advanced and displaying the blade laid it against the victim's throat. That is to say, the man became at first dimly, then definitely, aware of an impressive coin-cidence—a relation—a parallel between the

face on the card and the name on the headboard. The one was disfigured, the other described a disfiguration. The thought took
hold of him and shook him. It transformed
the face that his imagination had created behind the coffin lid; the contrast became a resemblance; the resemblance grew to identity.
Remembering the many descriptions of
Scarry's personal appearance that he had
heard from the gossips of his camp-fire he
tried with imperfect success to recall the exact
nature of the disfiguration that had given the
woman her ugly name; and what was lacking
in his memory fancy supplied, stamping it
with the validity of conviction. In the maddening attempt to recall such scraps of the
woman's history as he had heard, the muscles
of his arms and hands were strained to a painful tension, as by an effort to lift a great
weight. His body writhed and twisted with
the exertion. The tendons of his neck stood
out as tense as whip-cords, and his breath
came in short, sharp gasps. The catastrophe
could not be much longer delayed, or the
agony of anticipation would leave nothing to
be done by the *coup de grâce* of verification.
The scarred face behind the lid would slay
him through the wood.

A movement of the coffin diverted his thought. It came forward to within a foot of his face, growing visibly larger as it approached. The rusted metallic plate, with an inscription illegible in the moonlight, looked him steadily in the eye. Determined not to shrink, he tried to brace his shoulders more firmly against the end of the excavation, and nearly fell backward in the attempt. There was nothing to support him; he had unconsciously moved upon his enemy, clutching the heavy knife that he had drawn from his belt. The coffin had not advanced and he smiled to think it could not retreat. Lifting his knife he struck the heavy hilt against the metal plate with all his power. There was a sharp, ringing percussion, and with a dull clatter the whole decayed coffin lid broke in pieces and came away, falling about his feet. The quick and the dead were face to face—the frenzied, shrieking man—the woman standing tranquil in her silences. She was a holy terror!

V

Some months later a party of men and women belonging to the highest social circles of San Francisco passed through Hurdy-Gurdy on their way to the Yosemite Valley by a new trail. They halted for dinner and during its preparation explored the desolate camp. One of the party had been at Hurdy-Gurdy in the days of its glory. He had, indeed, been one of its prominent citizens; and it used to be said that more money passed over his faro table in any one night than over those of all his competitors in a week; but being now a millionaire engaged in greater enterprises, he did not deem these early successes of sufficient importance to merit the distinction of remark. His invalid wife, a lady famous in San Francisco for the costly nature of her entertainments and her exacting rigor with regard to the social position and " antecedents" of those who attended them, accompanied the expedition. During a stroll among the shanties of the abandoned camp Mr. Porfer directed the attention of his wife and friends to a dead tree on a low hill beyond Injun Creek.

"As I told you," he said, " I passed through this camp in 1852, and was told that no fewer than five men had been hanged here by vigilantes at different times, and all on that tree. If I am not mistaken, a rope is dangling from it yet. Let us go over and see the place."

Mr. Porfer did not add that the rope in

question was perhaps the very one from whose fatal embrace his own neck had once had an escape so narrow that an hour's delay in taking himself out of that region would have spanned it.

Proceeding leisurely down the creek to a convenient crossing, the party came upon the cleanly picked skeleton of an animal which Mr. Porfer after due examination pronounced to be that of an ass. The distinguishing ears were gone, but much of the inedible head had been spared by the beasts and birds, and the stout bridle of horsehair was intact, as was the riata, of similar material, connecting it with a picket pin still firmly sunken in the earth. The wooden and metallic elements of a miner's kit lay near by. The customary remarks were made, cynical on the part of the men, sentimental and refined by the lady. A little later they stood by the tree in the cemetery and Mr. Porfer sufficiently unbent from his dignity to place himself beneath the rotten rope and confidently lay a coil of it about his neck, somewhat, it appeared, to his own satisfaction, but greatly to the horror of his wife, to whose sensibilities the performance gave a smart shock.

An exclamation from one of the party

gathered them all about an open grave, at the bottom of which they saw a confused mass of human bones and the broken remnants of a coffin. Coyotes and buzzards had performed the last sad rites for pretty much all else. Two skulls were visible and in order to investigate this somewhat unusual redundancy one of the younger men had the hardihood to spring into the grave and hand them up to another before Mrs. Porfer could indicate her marked disapproval of so shocking an act, which, nevertheless, she did with considerable feeling and in very choice words. Pursuing his search among the dismal débris at the bottom of the grave the young man next handed up a rusted coffin plate, with a rudely cut inscription, which with difficulty Mr. Porfer deciphered and read aloud with an earnest and not altogether unsuccessful attempt at the dramatic effect which he deemed befitting to the occasion and his rhetorical abilities:

MANUELITA MURPHY.
Born at the Mission San Pedro—Died in
Hurdy-Gurdy,
Aged 47.
Hell's full of such.

In deference to the piety of the reader and

the nerves of Mrs. Porfer's fastidious sister-
hood of both sexes let us not touch upon the
painful impression produced by this uncommon inscription, further than to say that the
elocutionary powers of Mr. Porfer had never
before met with so spontaneous and overwhelming recognition.

The next morsel that rewarded the ghoul
in the grave was a long tangle of black hair
defiled with clay: but this was such an anti-
climax that it received little attention. Suddenly, with a short exclamation and a gesture
of excitement, the young man unearthed a
fragment of grayish rock, and after a hurried
inspection handed it up to Mr. Porfer. As
the sunlight fell upon it it glittered with a
yellow luster—it was thickly studded with
gleaming points. Mr. Porfer snatched it, bent
his head over it a moment and threw it lightly
away with the simple remark:

"Iron pyrites—fool's gold."

The young man in the discovery shaft was
a trifle disconcerted, apparently.

Meanwhile, Mrs. Porfer, unable longer to
endure the disagreeable business, had walked
back to the tree and seated herself at its root.
While rearranging a tress of golden hair
which had slipped from its confinement she

was attracted by what appeared to be and really was the fragment of an old coat. Looking about to assure herself that so unladylike an act was not observed, she thrust her jeweled hand into the exposed breast pocket and drew out a mouldy pocket-book. Its contents were as follows:

One bundle of letters, postmarked " Elizabethtown, New Jersey."

One circle of blonde hair tied with a ribbon.

One photograph of a beautiful girl.

One ditto of same, singularly disfigured.

One name on back of photograph—" Jefferson Doman."

A few moments later a group of anxious gentlemen surrounded Mrs. Porfer as she sat motionless at the foot of the tree, her head dropped forward, her fingers clutching a crushed photograph. Her husband raised her head, exposing a face ghastly white, except the long, deforming cicatrice, familiar to all her friends, which no art could ever hide, and which now traversed the pallor of her countenance like a visible curse.

Mary Matthews Porfer had the bad luck to be dead.

THE SUITABLE SURROUNDINGS

THE NIGHT

ONE midsummer night a farmer's boy living about ten miles from the city of Cincinnati was following a bridle path through a dense and dark forest. He had lost himself while searching for some missing cows, and near midnight was a long way from home, in a part of the country with which he was unfamiliar. But he was a stout-hearted lad, and knowing his general direction from his home, he plunged into the forest without hesitation, guided by the stars. Coming into the bridle path, and observing that it ran in the right direction, he followed it.

The night was clear, but in the woods it was exceedingly dark. It was more by the sense of touch than by that of sight that the lad kept the path. He could not, indeed, very easily go astray; the undergrowth on both sides was so thick as to be almost impenetrable. He had gone into the forest a mile or more when he was surprised to see a feeble gleam of light shining through the foliage skirting the path on his left. The sight of it startled him and set his heart beating audibly.

"The old Breede house is somewhere about here," he said to himself. "This must be the other end of the path which we reach it by from our side. Ugh! what should a light be doing there?"

Nevertheless, he pushed on. A moment later he had emerged from the forest into a small, open space, mostly upgrown to brambles. There were remnants of a rotting fence. A few yards from the trail, in the middle of the "clearing," was the house from which the light came, through an unglazed window. The window had once contained glass, but that and its supporting frame had long ago yielded to missiles flung by hands of venturesome boys to attest alike their courage and their hostility to the supernatural; for the Breede house bore the evil reputation of being haunted. Possibly it was not, but even the hardiest sceptic could not deny that it was deserted—which in rural regions is much the same thing.

Looking at the mysterious dim light shining from the ruined window the boy remembered with apprehension that his own hand had assisted at the destruction. His penitence was of course poignant in proportion to its tardiness and inefficacy. He half expected to be set upon by all the unworldly and bodiless malevolences whom he had outraged by assisting to break alike their windows and their peace. Yet this stubborn lad, shaking in every limb, would not retreat. The blood in his veins was strong and rich with the iron of the frontiersman. He was but two removes from the generation that had subdued the Indian. He started to pass the house.

As he was going by he looked in at the blank window space and saw a strange and terrifying sight,—the figure of a man seated in the centre of the room, at a table upon which lay some loose sheets of paper. The elbows rested on the table, the hands supporting the head, which was uncovered. On each side the fingers were pushed into the hair. The face showed dead-yellow in the light of a single candle a little to one side. The flame illuminated that side of the face, the other was in deep shadow. The man's eyes were fixed upon the blank window space with a stare in which an older and cooler observer might have discerned something of apprehension, but which seemed to the lad altogether soul-less. He believed the man to be dead.

The situation was horrible, but not with out its fascination. The boy stopped to note it all. He was weak, faint and trembling; he could feel the blood forsaking his face. Nevertheless, he set his teeth and resolutely advanced to the house. He had no conscious intention—it was the mere courage of terror. He thrust his white face forward into the illuminated opening. At that instant a strange, harsh cry, a shriek, broke upon the silence of the night—the note of a screech-owl. The man sprang to his feet, overturning the table and extinguishing the candle. The boy took to his heels.

THE DAY BEFORE

" Good-morning, Colston. I am in luck, it seems. You have often said that my com-mendation of your literary work was mere civility, and here you find me absorbed—act-ually merged—in your latest story in the *Messenger*. Nothing less shocking than your touch upon my shoulder would have roused me to consciousness."

" The proof is stronger than you seem to know," replied the man addressed: " so keen is your eagerness to read my story that you are willing to renounce selfish considerations and forego all the pleasure that you could get from it."

"I don't understand you," said the other, folding the newspaper that he held and putting it into his pocket. "You writers are a queer lot, anyhow. Come, tell me what I have done or omitted in this matter. In what way does the pleasure that I get, or might get, from your work depend on me?"

"In many ways. Let me ask you how you would enjoy your breakfast if you took it in this street car. Suppose the phonograph so perfected as to be able to give you an entire opera, —singing, orchestration, and all; do you think you would get much pleasure out of it if you turned it on at your office during business hours? Do you really care for a serenade by Schubert when you hear it fiddled by an untimely Italian on a morning ferryboat? Are you always cocked and primed for enjoyment? Do you keep every mood on tap, ready to any demand? Let me remind you, sir, that the story which you have done me the honor to begin as a means of becoming oblivious to the discomfort of this car is a ghost story!"

"Well?"

"Well! Has the reader no duties corresponding to his privileges? You have paid five cents for that newspaper. It is yours. You have the right to read it when and where you will. Much of what is in it is neither helped nor harmed by time and place and mood; some of it actually requires to be read at once—while it is fizzing. But my story is not of that character. It is not 'the very latest advices' from Ghostland. You are not expected to keep yourself *au courant* with what is going on in the realm of spooks. The stuff will keep until you have leisure to put yourself into the frame of mind appropriate to the sentiment of the piece—which I respectfully submit that you cannot do in a street car, even if you are the only passenger. The solitude is not of the right sort. An author has rights which the reader is bound to respect."

"For specific example?"

"The right to the reader's undivided attention. To deny him this is immoral. To make him share your attention with the rattle of a street car, the moving panorama of the crowds on the sidewalks, and the buildings beyond—with any of the thousands of distractions which make our customary environment—is to treat him with gross injustice. By God, it is infamous!"

The speaker had risen to his feet and was steadying himself by one of the straps hanging from the roof of the car. The other man looked up at him in sudden astonishment, wondering how so trivial a grievance could seem to justify so strong language. He saw that his friend's face was uncommonly pale and that his eyes glowed like living coals.

"You know what I mean," continued the writer, impetuously crowding his words— "you know what I mean, Marsh. My stuff in this morning's *Messenger* is plainly subheaded 'A Ghost Story.' That is ample notice to all. Every honorable reader will understand it as prescribing by implication the conditions under which the work is to be read."

The man addressed as Marsh winced a trifle, then asked with a smile: "What conditions? You know that I am only a plain business man who cannot be supposed to understand such things. How, when, where should I read your ghost story?"

"In solitude—at night—by the light of a candle. There are certain emotions which a writer can easily enough excite—such as compassion or merriment. I can move you to tears or laughter under almost any circumstances. But for my ghost story to be effective you must be made to feel fear—at least a strong sense of the supernatural—and that is a difficult matter. I have a right to expect that if you read me at all you will give me a chance; that you will make yourself accessible to the emotion that I try to inspire."

The car had now arrived at its terminus and stopped. The trip just completed was its first for the day and the conversation of the two early passengers had not been interrupted. The streets were yet silent and desolate; the house tops were just touched by the rising sun. As they stepped from the car and walked away together Marsh narrowly eyed his companion, who was reported, like most men of uncommon literary ability, to be addicted to various destructive vices. That is the revenge which dull minds take upon bright ones in resentment of their superiority. Mr. Colston was known as a man of genius. There are honest souls who believe that genius is a mode of excess. It was known that Colston did not drink liquor, but many said that he ate opium. Something in his appearance that morning—a certain wildness of the eyes, an unusual pallor.

a thickness and rapidity of speech—were taken by Mr. Marsh to confirm the report. Nevertheless, he had not the self-denial to abandon a subject which he found interesting, however it might excite his friend.

"Do you mean to say," he began, "that if I take the trouble to observe your directions —place myself in the conditions that you demand: solitude, night and a tallow candle— you can with your ghostly work give me an uncomfortable sense of the supernatural, as you call it? Can you accelerate my pulse, make me start at sudden noises, send a nervous chill along my spine and cause my hair to rise?"

Colston turned suddenly and looked him squarely in the eyes as they walked. "You would not dare—you have not the courage," he said. He emphasized the words with a contemptuous gesture. "You are brave enough to read me in a street car, but—in a deserted house—alone—in the forest—at night! Bah! I have a manuscript in my pocket that would kill you."

Marsh was angry. He knew himself courageous, and the words stung him. "If you know such a place," he said, "take me there to-night and leave me your story and a

candle. Call for me when I've had time
enough to read it and I'll tell you the entire
plot and—kick you out of the place."

That is how it occurred that the farmer's
boy, looking in at an unglazed window of the
Breede house, saw a man sitting in the light
of a candle.

THE DAY AFTER

Late in the afternoon of the next day three
men and a boy approached the Breede house
from that point of the compass toward which
the boy had fled the preceding night. The
men were in high spirits; they talked very
loudly and laughed. They made facetious
and good-humored ironical remarks to the
boy about his adventure, which evidently they
did not believe in. The boy accepted their
raillery with seriousness, making no reply.
He had a sense of the fitness of things and
knew that one who professes to have seen a
dead man rise from his seat and blow out a
candle is not a credible witness.

Arriving at the house and finding the door
unlocked, the party of investigators entered
without ceremony. Leading out of the passage into which this door opened was another
on the right and one on the left. They entered the room on the left—the one which had

the blank front window. Here was the dead body of a man.

It lay partly on one side, with the forearm beneath it, the cheek on the floor. The eyes were wide open; the stare was not an agreeable thing to encounter. The lower jaw had fallen; a little pool of saliva had collected beneath the mouth. An overthrown table, a partly burned candle, a chair and some paper with writing on it were all else that the room contained. The men looked at the body, touching the face in turn. The boy gravely stood at the head, assuming a look of ownership. It was the proudest moment of his life. One of the men said to him, " You're a good 'un "—a remark which was received by the two others with nods of acquiescence. It was Scepticism apologizing to Truth. Then one of the men took from the floor the sheet of manuscript and stepped to the window, for already the evening shadows were glooming the forest. The song of the whip-poor-will was heard in the distance and a monstrous beetle sped by the window on roaring wings and thundered away out of hearing. The man read:

THE MANUSCRIPT

" Before committing the act which, rightly

or wrongly, I have resolved on and appearing before my Maker for judgment, I, James R. Colston, deem it my duty as a journalist to make a statement to the public. My name is, I believe, tolerably well known to the people as a writer of tragic tales, but the somberest imagination never conceived anything so tragic as my own life and history. Not in incident: my life has been destitute of adventure and action. But my mental career has been lurid with experiences such as kill and damn. I shall not recount them here—some of them are written and ready for publication elsewhere. The object of these lines is to explain to whomsoever may be interested that my death is voluntary—my own act. I shall die at twelve o'clock on the night of the 15th of July—a significant anniversary to me, for it was on that day, and at that hour, that my friend in time and eternity, Charles Breede, performed his vow to me by the same act which his fidelity to our pledge now entails upon me. He took his life in his little house in the Copeton woods. There was the customary verdict of ' temporary insanity.' Had I testified at that inquest—had I told all I knew, they would have called *me* mad!"

Here followed an evidently long passage

which the man reading read to himself only. The rest he read aloud.

"I have still a week of life in which to arrange my worldly affairs and prepare for the great change. It is enough, for I have but few affairs and it is now four years since death became an imperative obligation.

"I shall bear this writing on my body; the finder will please hand it to the coroner.

"JAMES R. COLSTON.

"P. S.—Willard Marsh, on this the fatal fifteenth day of July I hand you this manuscript, to be opened and read under the conditions agreed upon, and at the place which I designated. I forego my intention to keep it on my body to explain the manner of my death, which is not important. It will serve to explain the manner of yours. I am to call for you during the night to receive assurance that you have read the manuscript. You know me well enough to expect me. But, my friend, it *will be after twelve o'clock*. May God have mercy on our souls!

"J. R. C."

Before the man who was reading this manuscript had finished, the candle had been picked up and lighted. When the reader had done, he quietly thrust the paper against the flame and despite the protestations of the others held it until it was burnt to ashes. The man who did this, and who afterward placidly endured a severe reprimand from the coroner, was a son-in-law of the late Charles Breede. At the inquest nothing could elicit an intelligent account of what the paper had contained.

FROM "THE TIMES"

"Yesterday the Commissioners of Lunacy committed to the asylum Mr. James R. Colston, a writer of some local reputation, connected with the *Messenger*. It will be remembered that on the evening of the 15th inst. Mr. Colston was given into custody by one of his fellow-lodgers in the Baine House, who had observed him acting very suspiciously, baring his throat and whetting a razor—occasionally trying its edge by actually cutting through the skin of his arm, etc. On being handed over to the police, the unfortunate man made a desperate resistance, and has ever since been so violent that it has been necessary to keep him in a strait-jacket. Most of our esteemed contemporary's other writers are still at large."

THE BOARDED WINDOW

IN 1830, only a few miles away from what is now the great city of Cincinnati, lay an immense and almost unbroken forest. The whole region was sparsely settled by people of the frontier—restless souls who no sooner had hewn fairly habitable homes out of the wilderness and attained to that degree of prosperity which to-day we should call indigence than impelled by some mysterious impulse of their nature they abandoned all and pushed farther westward, to encounter new perils and privations in the effort to regain the meagre comforts which they had voluntarily renounced. Many of them had already forsaken that region for the remoter settlements, but among those remaining was one who had been of those first arriving. He lived alone in a house of logs surrounded on all sides by the great forest, of whose gloom and silence he seemed a part, for no one had ever known him to smile nor speak a needless word. His simple wants were supplied by the sale or barter of skins of wild animals in the river town, for not a thing did he grow upon the

land which, if needful, he might have claimed
by right of undisturbed possession. There
were evidences of "improvement"—a few
acres of ground immediately about the house
had once been cleared of its trees, the decayed
stumps of which were half concealed by the
new growth that had been suffered to repair
the ravage wrought by the ax. Apparently
the man's zeal for agriculture had burned
with a failing flame, expiring in penitential
ashes.

The little log house, with its chimney of
sticks, its roof of warping clapboards
weighted with traversing poles and its "chink-
ing" of clay, had a single door and, directly
opposite, a window. The latter, however,
was boarded up—nobody could remember a
time when it was not. And none knew why
it was so closed; certainly not because of the
occupant's dislike of light and air, for on those
rare occasions when a hunter had passed that
lonely spot the recluse had commonly been
seen sunning himself on his doorstep if heaven
had provided sunshine for his need. I fancy
there are few persons living to-day who ever
knew the secret of that window, but I am one,
as you shall see.

The man's name was said to be Murlock.

He was apparently seventy years old, actually about fifty.   Something besides years had had a hand in his aging.   His hair and long, full beard were white, his gray, lustreless eyes sunken, his face singularly seamed with wrinkles which appeared to belong to two intersecting systems.   In figure he was tall and spare, with a stoop of the shoulders—a burden bearer.   I never saw him; these particulars I learned from my grandfather, from whom also I got the man's story when I was a lad. He had known him when living near by in that early day.

One day Murlock was found in his cabin, dead.   It was not a time and place for coroners and newspapers, and I suppose it was agreed that he had died from natural causes or I should have been told, and should remember.   I know only that with what was probably a sense of the fitness of things the body was buried near the cabin, alongside the grave of his wife, who had preceded him by so many years that local tradition had retained hardly a hint of her existence.   That closes the final chapter of this true story—excepting, indeed, the circumstance that many years afterward, in company with an equally intrepid spirit, I penetrated to the place and ventured near enough to the ruined cabin to throw a stone against it, and ran away to avoid the ghost which every well-informed boy thereabout knew haunted the spot. But there is an earlier chapter—that supplied by my grandfather.

When Murlock built his cabin and began laying sturdily about with his ax to hew out a farm—the rifle, meanwhile, his means of support—he was young, strong and full of hope. In that eastern country whence he came he had married, as was the fashion, a young woman in all ways worthy of his honest devotion, who shared the dangers and privations of his lot with a willing spirit and light heart. There is no known record of her name; of her charms of mind and person tradition is silent and the doubter is at liberty to entertain his doubt; but God forbid that I should share it! Of their affection and happiness there is abundant assurance in every added day of the man's widowed life; for what but the magnetism of a blessed memory could have chained that venturesome spirit to a lot like that?

One day Murlock returned from gunning in a distant part of the forest to find his wife prostrate with fever, and delirious. There was no physician within miles, no neighbor; nor was she in a condition to be left, to summon help. So he set about the task of nursing her back to health, but at the end of the third day she fell into unconsciousness and so passed away, apparently, with never a gleam of returning reason.

From what we know of a nature like his we may venture to sketch in some of the details of the outline picture drawn by my grandfather. When convinced that she was dead, Murlock had sense enough to remember that the dead must be prepared for burial. In performance of this sacred duty he blundered now and again, did certain things incorrectly, and others which he did correctly were done over and over. His occasional failures to accomplish some simple and ordinary act filled him with astonishment, like that of a drunken man who wonders at the suspension of familiar natural laws. He was surprised, too, that he did not weep—surprised and a little ashamed; surely it is unkind not to weep for the dead. "To-morrow," he said aloud, "I shall have to make the coffin and dig the grave; and then I shall miss her, when she is no longer in sight; but now—she is dead, of course, but it is all right—it *must* be all right, somehow. Things cannot be so bad as they seem."

He stood over the body in the fading light, adjusting the hair and putting the finishing touches to the simple toilet, doing all mechanically, with soulless care. And still through his consciousness ran an undersense of conviction that all was right—that he should have her again as before, and everything explained. He had had no experience in grief; his capacity had not been enlarged by use. His heart could not contain it all, nor his imagination rightly conceive it. He did not know he was so hard struck; *that* knowledge would come later, and never go. Grief is an artist of powers as various as the instruments upon which he plays his dirges for the dead, evoking from some the sharpest, shrillest notes, from others the low, grave chords that throb recurrent like the slow beating of a distant drum. Some natures it startles; some it stupefies. To one it comes like the stroke of an arrow, stinging all the sensibilities to a keener life; to another as the blow of a bludgeon, which in crushing benumbs. We may conceive Murlock to have been that way affected, for (and here we are upon surer ground than that of conjecture) no sooner had

he finished his pious work than, sinking into
a chair by the side of the table upon which the
body lay, and noting how white the profile
showed in the deepening gloom, he laid his
arms upon the table's edge, and dropped his
face into them, tearless yet and unutterably
weary.   At that moment came in through the
open window a long, wailing sound like the
cry of a lost child in the far deeps of the dark-
ening wood! But the man did not move.
Again, and nearer than before, sounded that
unearthly cry upon his failing sense.   Perhaps it was a wild beast; perhaps it was a
dream.   For Murlock was asleep.

Some hours later, as it afterward appeared,
this unfaithful watcher awoke and lifting his
head from his arms intently listened—he knew
not why.   There in the black darkness by the
side of the dead, recalling all without a shock,
he strained his eyes to see—he knew not what.
His senses were all alert, his breath was suspended, his blood had stilled its tides as if to
assist the silence.   Who—what had waked
him, and where was it?

Suddenly the table shook beneath his arms,
and at the same moment he heard, or fancied
that he heard, a light, soft step—another—
sounds as of bare feet upon the floor!

He was terrified beyond the power to cry out or move. Perforce he waited—waited there in the darkness through seeming centuries of such dread as one may know, yet live to tell. He tried vainly to speak the dead woman's name, vainly to stretch forth his hand across the table to learn if she were there. His throat was powerless, his arms and hands were like lead. Then occurred something most frightful. Some heavy body seemed hurled against the table with an impetus that pushed it against his breast so sharply as nearly to overthrow him, and at the same instant he heard and felt the fall of something upon the floor with so violent a thump that the whole house was shaken by the impact. A scuffling ensued, and a confusion of sounds impossible to describe. Murlock had risen to his feet. Fear had by excess forfeited control of his faculties. He flung his hands upon the table. Nothing was there!

There is a point at which terror may turn to madness; and madness incites to action. With no definite intent, from no motive but the wayward impulse of a madman, Murlock sprang to the wall, with a little groping seized his loaded rifle, and without aim discharged it. By the flash which lit up the room with a vivid illumination, he saw an enormous panther dragging the dead woman toward the window, its teeth fixed in her throat! Then there were darkness blacker than before, and silence; and when he returned to consciousness the sun was high and the wood vocal with songs of birds.

The body lay near the window, where the beast had left it when frightened away by the flash and report of the rifle. The clothing was deranged, the long hair in disorder, the limbs lay anyhow. From the throat, dreadfully lacerated, had issued a pool of blood not yet entirely coagulated. The ribbon with which he had bound the wrists was broken; the hands were tightly clenched. Between the teeth was a fragment of the animal's ear.

A LADY FROM REDHORSE

CORONADO, JUNE 20.

I FIND myself more and more interested in him. It is not, I am sure, his—do you know any good noun corresponding to the adjective "handsome"? One does not like to say "beauty" when speaking of a man. He is beautiful enough, Heaven knows; I should not even care to trust you with him—faithfulest of all possible wives that you are—when he looks his best, as he always does. Nor do I think the fascination of his manner has much to do with it. You recollect that the charm of art inheres in that which is undefinable, and to you and me, my dear Irene, I fancy there is rather less of that in the branch of art under consideration than to girls in their first season. I fancy I know how my fine gentleman produces many of his effects and could perhaps give him a pointer on heightening them. Nevertheless, his manner is something truly delightful. I suppose what interests me chiefly is the man's brains. His conversation is the best I have ever heard and altogether unlike any one else's. He seems to know everything, as indeed he ought, for he has been everywhere, read everything, seen all there is to see—sometimes I think rather more than is good for him—and had acquaintance with the *queerest* people. And then his voice—Irene, when I hear it I actually feel as if I ought to have paid at the door, though of course it is my own door.

JULY 3.

I fear my remarks about Dr. Barritz must have been, being thoughtless, very silly, or you would not have written of him with such levity, not to say disrespect. Believe me, dearest, he has more dignity and seriousness (of the kind, I mean, which is not inconsistent with a manner sometimes playful and always charming) than any of the men that you and I ever met. And young Raynor—you knew Raynor at Monterey—tells me that the men all like him and that he is treated with something like deference everywhere. There is a mystery, too—something about his connection with the Blavatsky people in Northern India. Raynor either would not or could not tell me the particulars. I infer that Dr. Barritz is thought—don't you dare to laugh!—a magician. Could anything be finer than that?

An ordinary mystery is not, of course, so good as a scandal, but when it relates to dark and dreadful practices—to the exercise of unearthly powers—could anything be more piquant? It explains, too, the singular influence the man has upon me. It is the undefinable in his art—black art. Seriously, dear, I quite tremble when he looks me full in the eyes with those unfathomable orbs of his, which I have already vainly attempted to describe to you. How dreadful if he has the power to make one fall in love! Do you know if the Blavatsky crowd have that power —outside of Sepoy?

JULY 16.

The strangest thing! Last evening while Auntie was attending one of the hotel hops (I hate them) Dr. Barritz called. It was scandalously late—I actually believe that he had talked with Auntie in the ballroom and learned from her that I was alone. I had been all the evening contriving how to worm out of him the truth about his connection with the Thugs in Sepoy, and all of that black business, but the moment he fixed his eyes on me (for I admitted him, I'm ashamed to say) I was helpless. I trembled, I blushed, I—O

Irene, Irene, I love the man beyond expression and you know how it is yourself.

Fancy! I, an ugly duckling from Redhorse —daughter (they say) of old Calamity Jim— certainly his heiress, with no living relation but an absurd old aunt who spoils me a thousand and fifty ways—absolutely destitute of everything but a million dollars and a hope in Paris,—I daring to love a god like him! My dear, if I had you here I could tear your hair out with mortification.

. I am convinced that he is aware of my feeling, for he stayed but a few moments, said nothing but what another man might have said half as well, and pretending that he had an engagement went away. I learned to-day (a little bird told me—the bell-bird) that he went straight to bed. How does that strike you as evidence of exemplary habits?

JULY 17.

That little wretch, Raynor, called yesterday and his babble set me almost wild. He never runs down—that is to say, when he exterminates a score of reputations, more or less, he does not pause between one reputation and the next. (By the way, he inquired about you, and his manifestations of interest in you

had, I confess, a good deal of *vraisemblance*.)
Mr. Raynor observes no game laws; like
Death (which he would inflict if slander were
fatal) he has all seasons for his own.   But I
like him, for we knew each other at Redhorse
when we were young.   He was known in
those days as "Giggles," and I—O Irene, can
you ever forgive me?—I was called "Gunny."
God knows why; perhaps in allusion to the
material of my pinafores; perhaps because
the name is in alliteration with "Giggles,"
for Gig and I were inseparable playmates,
and the miners may have thought it a delicate
civility to recognize some kind of relationship
between us.

Later, we took in a third—another of Adversity's brood, who, like Garrick between
Tragedy and Comedy, had a chronic inability
to adjudicate the rival claims of Frost and
Famine.   Between him and misery there was
seldom anything more than a single suspender
and the hope of a meal which would at the
same time support life and make it insupportable.   He literally picked up a precarious living for himself and an aged mother by
"chloriding the dumps," that is to say, the
miners permitted him to search the heaps of
waste rock for such pieces of "pay ore" as

had been overlooked; and these he sacked up
and sold at the Syndicate Mill. He became
a member of our firm—" Gunny, Giggles, and
Dumps" thenceforth—through my favor; for
I could not then, nor can I now, be indifferent
to his courage and prowess in defending
against Giggles the immemorial right of his
sex to insult a strange and unprotected female
—myself. After old Jim struck it in the
Calamity and I began to wear shoes and go to
school, and in emulation Giggles took to
washing his face and became Jack Raynor, of
Wells, Fargo & Co., and old Mrs. Barts was
herself chlorided to her fathers, Dumps
drifted over to San Juan Smith and turned
stage driver, and was killed by road agents,
and so forth.

Why do I tell you all this, dear? Because
it is heavy on my heart. Because I walk the
Valley of Humility. Because I am subduing
myself to permanent consciousness of my un-
worthiness to unloose the latchet of Dr. Barritz's shoe. Because, oh dear, oh dear, there's
a cousin of Dumps at this hotel! I haven't
spoken to him. I never had much acquaintance with him,—but do you suppose he has
recognized me? Do, please give me in your
next your candid, sure-enough opinion about

it, and say you don't think so. Do you suppose He knows about me already, and that
that is why He left me last evening when He
saw that I blushed and trembled like a fool
under His eyes? You know I can't bribe *all*
the newspapers, and I can't go back on anybody who was civil to Gunny at Redhorse—
not if I'm pitched out of society into the sea.
So the skeleton sometimes rattles behind the
door. I never cared much before, as you
know, but now—*now* it is not the same. Jack
Raynor I am sure of—he will not tell Him.
He seems, indeed, to hold Him in such respect
as hardly to dare speak to Him at all, and I'm
a good deal that way myself. Dear, dear! I
wish I had something besides a million dollars! If Jack were three inches taller I'd
marry him alive and go back to Redhorse and
wear sackcloth again to the end of my miser-
able days.

JULY 25.

We had a perfectly splendid sunset last
evening and I must tell you all about it. I
ran away from Auntie and everybody and was
walking alone on the beach. I expect you to
believe, you infidel! that I had not looked out
of my window on the seaward side of the hotel
and seen Him walking alone on the beach. If

you are not lost to every feeling of womanly
delicacy you will accept my statement without
question.   I soon established myself under my
sunshade and had for some time been gazing
out dreamily over the sea, when he approached, walking close to the edge of the
water—it was ebb tide.   I assure you the wet
sand actually brightened about his feet!   As
he approached me he lifted his hat, saying,
"Miss Dement, may I sit with you?—or will
you walk with me?"

The possibility that neither might be agreeable seems not to have occurred to him.   Did
you ever know such assurance?   Assurance?
My dear, it was gall, downright *gall!*   Well,
I didn't find it wormwood, and replied, with
my untutored Redhorse heart in my throat, "I
—I shall be pleased to do *anything.*"   Could
words have been more stupid?   There are
depths of fatuity in me, friend o' my soul, that
are simply bottomless!

He extended his hand, smiling, and I delivered mine into it without a moment's hesitation, and when his fingers closed about it to
assist me to my feet the consciousness that it
trembled made me blush worse than the red
west.   I got up, however, and after a while,
observing that he had not let go my hand I

pulled on it a little, but unsuccessfully. He
simply held on, saying nothing, but looking
down into my face with some kind of smile—
I didn't know—how could I?—whether it was
affectionate, derisive, or what, for I did not
look at him. How beautiful he was!—with
the red fires of the sunset burning in the
depths of his eyes. Do you know, dear, if the
Thugs and Experts of the Blavatsky region
have any special kind of eyes? Ah, you
should have seen his superb attitude, the god-
like inclination of his head as he stood over
me after I had got upon my feet! It was a
noble picture, but I soon destroyed it, for I
began at once to sink again to the earth.
There was only one thing for him to do, and
he did it; he supported me with an arm about
my waist.

"Miss Dement, are you ill?" he said.

It was not an exclamation; there was
neither alarm nor solicitude in it. If he had
added: "I suppose that is about what I am
expected to say," he would hardly have expressed his sense of the situation more clearly.
His manner filled me with shame and indignation, for I was suffering acutely. I
wrenched my hand out of his, grasped the arm
supporting me and pushing myself free, fell

plump into the sand and sat helpless. My hat had fallen off in the struggle and my hair tumbled about my face and shoulders in the most mortifying way.

"Go away from me," I cried, half choking. "O *please* go away, you—you Thug! How dare you think *that* when my leg is asleep?"

I actually said those identical words! And then I broke down and sobbed. Irene, I *blubbered!*

His manner altered in an instant—I could see that much through my fingers and hair. He dropped on one knee beside me, parted the tangle of hair and said in the tenderest way: "My poor girl, God knows I have not intended to pain you. How should I?—I who love you—I who have loved you for—for years and years!"

He had pulled my wet hands away from my face and was covering them with kisses. My cheeks were like two coals, my whole face was flaming and, I think, steaming. What could I do? I hid it on his shoulder—there was no other place. And, O my dear friend, how my leg tingled and thrilled, and how I wanted to kick!

We sat so for a long time. He had released one of my hands to pass his arm about me again and I possessed myself of my handkerchief and was drying my eyes and my nose. I would not look up until that was done; he tried in vain to push me a little away and gaze into my face. Presently, when all was right, and it had grown a bit dark, I lifted my head, looked him straight in the eyes and smiled my best—my level best, dear.

"What do you mean," I said, "by 'years and years'?"

"Dearest," he replied, very gravely, very earnestly, "in the absence of the sunken cheeks, the hollow eyes, the lank hair, the slouching gait, the rags, dirt, and youth, can you not—will you not understand? Gunny, I'm Dumps!"

In a moment I was upon my feet and he upon his. I seized him by the lapels of his coat and peered into his handsome face in the deepening darkness. I was breathless with excitement.

"And you are not dead?" I asked, hardly knowing what I said.

"Only dead in love, dear. I recovered from the road agent's bullet, but this, I fear, is fatal."

"But about Jack—Mr. Raynor? Don't you know——"

"I am ashamed to say, darling, that it was through that unworthy person's suggestion that I came here from Vienna."

Irene, they have roped in your affectionate friend,

MARY JANE DEMENT.

P. S.—The worst of it is that there is no mystery; that was the invention of Jack Raynor, to arouse my curiosity. James is not a Thug. He solemnly assures me that in all his wanderings he has never set foot in Sepoy.

THE EYES OF THE PANTHER

I

ONE DOES NOT ALWAYS MARRY WHEN INSANE

A MAN and a woman—nature had done the grouping—sat on a rustic seat, in the late afternoon. The man was middle-aged, slender, swarthy, with the expression of a poet and the complexion of a pirate—a man at whom one would look again. The woman was young, blonde, graceful, with something in her figure and movements suggesting the word "lithe." She was habited in a gray gown with odd brown markings in the texture. She may have been beautiful; one could not readily say, for her eyes denied attention to all else. They were gray-green, long and narrow, with an expression defying analysis. One could only know that they were disquieting. Cleopatra may have had such eyes.

The man and the woman talked.

"Yes," said the woman, "I love you, God knows! But marry you, no. I cannot, will not."

"Irene, you have said that many times, yet always have denied me a reason. I've a right to know, to understand, to feel and prove my fortitude if I have it. Give me a reason."

"For loving you?"

The woman was smiling through her tears and her pallor. That did not stir any sense of humor in the man.

"No; there is no reason for that. A reason for not marrying me. I've a right to know. I must know. I will know!"

He had risen and was standing before her with clenched hands, on his face a frown—it might have been called a scowl. He looked as if he might attempt to learn by strangling her. She smiled no more—merely sat looking up into his face with a fixed, set regard that was utterly without emotion or sentiment. Yet it had something in it that tamed his resentment and made him shiver.

"You are determined to have my reason?" she asked in a tone that was entirely mechanical—a tone that might have been her look made audible.

"If you please—if I'm not asking too much."

Apparently this lord of creation was yield-

ing some part of his dominion over his co-
creature.

"Very well, you shall know: I am insane."

The man started, then looked incredulous
and was conscious that he ought to be amused.
But, again, the sense of humor failed him in
his need and despite his disbelief he was profoundly disturbed by that which he did not
believe. Between our convictions and our
feelings there is no good understanding.

"That is what the physicians would say,"
the woman continued—"if they knew. I
might myself prefer to call it a case of 'possession.' Sit down and hear what I have to
say."

The man silently resumed his seat beside
her on the rustic bench by the wayside. Over-
against them on the eastern side of the valley
the hills were already sunset-flushed and the
stillness all about was of that peculiar quality
that foretells the twilight. Something of
its mysterious and significant solemnity had
imparted itself to the man's mood. In the
spiritual, as in the material world, are signs
and presages of night. Rarely meeting her
look, and whenever he did so conscious of the
indefinable dread with which, despite their

feline beauty, her eyes always affected him, Jenner Brading listened in silence to the story told by Irene Marlowe. In deference to the reader's possible prejudice against the artless method of an unpractised historian the author ventures to substitute his own version for hers.

II

A ROOM MAY BE TOO NARROW FOR THREE, THOUGH ONE IS OUTSIDE

In a little log house containing a single room sparely and rudely furnished, crouching on the floor against one of the walls, was a woman, clasping to her breast a child. Outside, a dense unbroken forest extended for many miles in every direction. This was at night and the room was black dark: no human eye could have discerned the woman and the child. Yet they were observed, narrowly, vigilantly, with never even a momentary slackening of attention; and that is the pivotal fact upon which this narrative turns.

Charles Marlowe was of the class, now extinct in this country, of woodmen pioneers— men who found their most acceptable surroundings in sylvan solitudes that stretched along the eastern slope of the Mississippi Valley, from the Great Lakes to the Gulf of Mexico. For more than a hundred years these men pushed ever westward, generation after generation, with rifle and ax, reclaiming from Nature and her savage children here and there an isolated acreage for the plow, no sooner reclaimed than surrendered to their less venturesome but more thrifty successors. At last they burst through the edge of the forest into the open country and vanished as if they had fallen over a cliff. The woodman pioneer is no more; the pioneer of the plains— he whose easy task it was to subdue for occupancy two-thirds of the country in a single generation—is another and inferior creation. With Charles Marlowe in the wilderness, sharing the dangers, hardships and privations of that strange, unprofitable life, were his wife and child, to whom, in the manner of his class, in which the domestic virtues were a religion, he was passionately attached. The woman was still young enough to be comely, new enough to the awful isolation of her lot to be cheerful. By withholding the large capacity for happiness which the simple satisfactions of the forest life could not have filled, Heaven had dealt honorably with her. In her light household tasks, her child, her husband

and her few foolish books, she found abundant provision for her needs.

One morning in midsummer Marlowe took down his rifle from the wooden hooks on the wall and signified his intention of getting game.

"We've meat enough," said the wife; "please don't go out to-day. I dreamed last night, O, such a dreadful thing! I cannot recollect it, but I'm almost sure that it will come to pass if you go out."

It is painful to confess that Marlowe received this solemn statement with less of gravity than was due to the mysterious nature of the calamity foreshadowed. In truth, he laughed.

"Try to remember," he said. "Maybe you dreamed that Baby had lost the power of speech."

The conjecture was obviously suggested by the fact that Baby, clinging to the fringe of his hunting-coat with all her ten pudgy thumbs was at that moment uttering her sense of the situation in a series of exultant goo-goos inspired by sight of her father's raccoon-skin cap.

The woman yielded: lacking the gift of humor she could not hold out against his kindly badinage. So, with a kiss for the mother and a kiss for the child, he left the house and closed the door upon his happiness forever.

At nightfall he had not returned. The woman prepared supper and waited. Then she put Baby to bed and sang softly to her until she slept. By this time the fire on the hearth, at which she had cooked supper, had burned out and the room was lighted by a single candle. This she afterward placed in the open window as a sign and welcome to the hunter if he should approach from that side. She had thoughtfully closed and barred the door against such wild animals as might prefer it to an open window—of the habits of beasts of prey in entering a house uninvited she was not advised, though with true female prevision she may have considered the possibility of their entrance by way of the chimney. As the night wore on she became not less anxious, but more drowsy, and at last rested her arms upon the bed by the child and her head upon the arms. The candle in the window burned down to the socket, sputtered and flared a moment and went out unobserved; for the woman slept and dreamed.

In her dreams she sat beside the cradle of a

second child. The first one was dead. The father was dead. The home in the forest was lost and the dwelling in which she lived was unfamiliar. There were heavy oaken doors, always closed, and outside the windows, fastened into the thick stone walls, were iron bars, obviously (so she thought) a provision against Indians. All this she noted with an infinite self-pity, but without surprise—an emotion unknown in dreams. The child in the cradle was invisible under its coverlet which something impelled her to remove. She did so, disclosing the face of a wild animal! In the shock of this dreadful revelation the dreamer awoke, trembling in the darkness of her cabin in the wood.

As a sense of her actual surroundings came slowly back to her she felt for the child that was not a dream, and assured herself by its breathing that all was well with it; nor could she forbear to pass a hand lightly across its face. Then, moved by some impulse for which she probably could not have accounted, she rose and took the sleeping babe in her arms, holding it close against her breast. The head of the child's cot was against the wall to which the woman now turned her back as she stood. Lifting her eyes she saw two bright objects starring the darkness with a reddish-green glow. She took them to be two coals on the hearth, but with her returning sense of direction came the disquieting consciousness that they were not in that quarter of the room, moreover were too high, being nearly at the level of the eyes—of her own eyes. For these were the eyes of a panther.

The beast was at the open window directly opposite and not five paces away. Nothing but those terrible eyes was visible, but in the dreadful tumult of her feelings as the situation disclosed itself to her understanding she somehow knew that the animal was standing on its hinder feet, supporting itself with its paws on the window-ledge. That signified a malign interest—not the mere gratification of an indolent curiosity. The consciousness of the attitude was an added horror, accentuating the menace of those awful eyes, in whose steadfast fire her strength and courage were alike consumed. Under their silent questioning she shuddered and turned sick. Her knees failed her, and by degrees, instinctively striving to avoid a sudden movement that might bring the beast upon her, she sank to the floor, crouched against the wall and tried to shield the babe with her trembling body with-

out withdrawing her gaze from the luminous
orbs that were killing her. No thought of her
husband came to her in her agony—no hope
nor suggestion of rescue or escape. Her
capacity for thought and feeling had narrowed to the dimensions of a single emotion—
fear of the animal's spring, of the impact of its
body, the buffeting of its great arms, the feel
of its teeth in her throat, the mangling of her
babe. Motionless now and in absolute silence, she awaited her doom, the moments
growing to hours, to years, to ages; and still
those devilish eyes maintained their watch.

Returning to his cabin late at night with
a deer on his shoulders Charles Marlowe tried
the door. It did not yield. He knocked;
there was no answer. He laid down his deer
and went round to the window. As he turned
the angle of the building he fancied he heard
a sound as of stealthy footfalls and a rustling
in the undergrowth of the forest, but they
were too slight for certainty, even to his
practised ear. Approaching the window, and
to his surprise finding it open, he threw his
leg over the sill and entered. All was darkness and silence. He groped his way to the
fire-place, struck a match and lit a candle.

Then he looked about. Cowering on the floor against a wall was his wife, clasping his child. As he sprang toward her she rose and broke into laughter, long, loud, and mechanical, devoid of gladness and devoid of sense—the laughter that is not out of keeping with the clanking of a chain. Hardly knowing what he did he extended his arms. She laid the babe in them. It was dead—pressed to death in its mother's embrace.

III

THE THEORY OF THE DEFENSE

That is what occurred during a night in a forest, but not all of it did Irene Marlowe relate to Jenner Brading; not all of it was known to her. When she had concluded the sun was below the horizon and the long summer twilight had begun to deepen in the hollows of the land. For some moments Brading was silent, expecting the narrative to be carried forward to some definite connection with the conversation introducing it; but the narrator was as silent as he, her face averted, her hands clasping and unclasping themselves as they lay in her lap, with a singular suggestion of an activity independent of her will.

"It is a sad, a terrible story," said Bra-ding at last, "but I do not understand. You call Charles Marlowe father; that I know. That he is old before his time, broken by some great sorrow, I have seen, or thought I saw. But, pardon me, you said that you—that you——"

"That I am insane," said the girl, without a movement of head or body.

"But, Irene, you say—please, dear, do not look away from me—you say that the child was dead, not demented."

"Yes, that one—I am the second. I was born three months after that night, my mother being mercifully permitted to lay down her life in giving me mine."

Brading was again silent; he was a trifle dazed and could not at once think of the right thing to say. Her face was still turned away. In his embarrassment he reached impulsively toward the hands that lay closing and unclos-ing in her lap, but something—he could not have said what—restrained him. He then re-membered, vaguely, that he had never alto-gether cared to take her hand.

"Is it likely," she resumed, "that a person born under such circumstances is like others— is what you call sane?"

Brading did not reply; he was preoccupied with a new thought that was taking shape in his mind—what a scientist would have called an hypothesis; a detective, a theory. It might throw an added light, albeit a lurid one, upon such doubt of her sanity as her own assertion had not dispelled.

The country was still new and, outside the villages, sparsely populated. The professional hunter was still a familiar figure, and among his trophies were heads and pelts of the larger kinds of game. Tales variously credible of nocturnal meetings with savage animals in lonely roads were sometimes current, passed through the customary stages of growth and decay, and were forgotten. A recent addition to these popular apocrypha, originating, apparently, by spontaneous generation in several households, was of a panther which had frightened some of their members by looking in at windows by night. The yarn had caused its little ripple of excitement—had even attained to the distinction of a place in the local newspaper; but Brading had given it no attention. Its likeness to the story to which he had just listened now impressed him as perhaps more than accidental. Was it not possible that the one story had suggested the other—that finding congenial conditions in a morbid mind and a fertile fancy, it had grown to the tragic tale that he had heard?

Brading recalled certain circumstances of the girl's history and disposition, of which, with love's incuriosity, he had hitherto been heedless—such as her solitary life with her father, at whose house no one, apparently, was an acceptable visitor and her strange fear of the night, by which those who knew her best accounted for her never being seen after dark. Surely in such a mind imagination once kindled might burn with a lawless flame, penetrating and enveloping the entire structure. That she was mad, though the conviction gave him the acutest pain, he could no longer doubt; she had only mistaken an effect of her mental disorder for its cause, bringing into imaginary relation with her own personality the vagaries of the local myth-makers. With some vague intention of testing his new "theory," and no very definite notion of how to set about it he said, gravely, but with hesitation:

"Irene, dear, tell me—I beg you will not take offence, but tell me——"

"I have told you," she interrupted, speaking with a passionate earnestness that he had not known her to show—" I have already told you that we cannot marry; is anything else worth saying?"

Before he could stop her she had sprung from her seat and without another word or look was gliding away among the trees toward her father's house. Brading had risen to detain her; he stood watching her in silence until she had vanished in the gloom. Suddenly he started as if he had been shot; his face took on an expression of amazement and alarm: in one of the black shadows into which she had disappeared he had caught a quick, brief glimpse of shining eyes! For an instant he was dazed and irresolute; then he dashed into the wood after her, shouting: "Irene, Irene, look out! The panther! The panther!"

In a moment he had passed through the fringe of forest into open ground and saw the girl's gray skirt vanishing into her father's door. No panther was visible.

IV

AN APPEAL TO THE CONSCIENCE OF GOD

Jenner Brading, attorney-at-law, lived in a cottage at the edge of the town. Directly behind the dwelling was the forest. Being a bachelor, and therefore, by the Draconian moral code of the time and place denied the services of the only species of domestic servant known thereabout, the "hired girl," he boarded at the village hotel, where also was his office. The woodside cottage was merely a lodging maintained—at no great cost, to be sure—as an evidence of prosperity and respectability. It would hardly do for one to whom the local newspaper had pointed with pride as "the foremost jurist of his time" to be "homeless," albeit he may sometimes have suspected that the words "home" and "house" were not strictly synonymous. Indeed, his consciousness of the disparity and his will to harmonize it were matters of logical inference, for it was generally reported that soon after the cottage was built its owner had made a futile venture in the direction of marriage—had, in truth, gone so far as to be rejected by the beautiful but eccentric daughter of Old Man Marlowe, the recluse. This was publicly believed because he had told it himself and she had not—a reversal of the usual order of things which could hardly fail to carry conviction.

Brading's bedroom was at the rear of the house, with a single window facing the forest.

One night he was awakened by a noise at that
window; he could hardly have said what it
was like. With a little thrill of the nerves he
sat up in bed and laid hold of the revolver
which, with a forethought most commendable in one addicted to the habit of sleeping
on the ground floor with an open window, he
had put under his pillow. The room was in
absolute darkness, but being unterrified he
knew where to direct his eyes, and there he
held them, awaiting in silence what further
might occur. He could now dimly discern
the aperture—a square of lighter black.
Presently there appeared at its lower edge two
gleaming eyes that burned with a malignant
lustre inexpressibly terrible! Brading's heart
gave a great jump, then seemed to stand still.
A chill passed along his spine and through his
hair; he felt the blood forsake his cheeks. He
could not have cried out—not to save his life;
but being a man of courage he would not, to
save his life, have done so if he had been able.
Some trepidation his coward body might feel,
but his spirit was of sterner stuff. Slowly the
shining eyes rose with a steady motion that
seemed an approach, and slowly rose Brading's right hand, holding the pistol. He
fired!

Blinded by the flash and stunned by the report, Brading nevertheless heard, or fancied that he heard, the wild, high scream of the panther, so human in sound, so devilish in suggestion. Leaping from the bed he hastily clothed himself and, pistol in hand, sprang from the door, meeting two or three men who came running up from the road. A brief explanation was followed by a cautious search of the house. The grass was wet with dew; beneath the window it had been trodden and partly leveled for a wide space, from which a devious trail; visible in the light of a lantern, led away into the bushes. One of the men stumbled and fell upon his hands, which as he rose and rubbed them together were slippery. On examination they were seen to be red with blood.

An encounter, unarmed, with a wounded panther was not agreeable to their taste; all but Brading turned back. He, with lantern and pistol, pushed courageously forward into the wood. Passing through a difficult undergrowth he came into a small opening, and there his courage had its reward, for there he found the body of his victim. But it was no panther. What it was is told, even to this day, upon a weather-worn headstone in the village churchyard, and for many years was attested daily at the graveside by the bent figure and sorrow-seamed face of Old Man Marlowe, to whose soul, and to the soul of his strange, unhappy child, peace. Peace and reparation.

In the Midst of Life

By *Ambrose Bierce*

More and more the fame of Ambrose Bierce grows, not so much from his fantastic life and mysterious death, but from his haunting and unforgettable tales. His art is candidly inhuman, yet the clarity and perfection of his style and his dramatic fervor give these "terror tales" a secure place among the classic short stories of literature. The first two stories in this volume —"A Horseman in the Sky" and "An Occurrence at Owl Creek Bridge"—are generally considered Bierce's best.

✶ ✶ ✶ ✶

THE MODERN LIBRARY puts into your home the greatest book treasures of the past and present